# SKI
## the French way

PETER STUYVESANT TRAVEL
PRESENTS

# SKI
## the French way

YVES GAUDEZ

THE OFFICIAL TECHNIQUE
OF THE ECOLE DU SKI FRANÇAIS

PELHAM BOOKS

Ski the French Way was conceived, edited and designed for Peter Stuyvesant Travel Ltd. by James Wotton Limited, 7 Stafford Mansions, Albert Bridge Road, London SW11, and Graham Davis Associates and Nicholas Bevan, 10 Amwell Street, London EC1

First published in Great Britain by

Pelham Books Ltd.
44 Bedford Square
London WC1B 3DP
1984

© Peter Stuyvesant Travel Ltd. 1984
All Rights Reserved. No part of this publication may be reproduced, stored in a retrieval system, or transmitted in any form or by any means, electronic, mechanical, photocopying or otherwise, without the prior written permission of the Copyright owner

Gaudez, Yves
   Ski the French Way
   1. Skis and skiing – France – Handbooks,
   manuals, etc.
I Title
   796.93'0944   GV 854.8.F7

ISBN 0 7207 1602 0
Typeset by Text Filmsetters, Orpington, UK.
Printed and bound in the Netherlands by
Royal Smeets Offset, BV Weert.

Peter Stuyvesant Travel wish to express their thanks and appreciation to the Ecole du Ski Français for their kind help, invaluable advice and technical contribution in the preparation of this book.

A special thanks is due to Bernard Chevallier, president of the ESF, Renaud Artru, administrative director, Roger Mure-Ravaud, technical director alpine skiing and Jean Secrentant, technical director cross-country skiing.

We are also most grateful to Alain Girier, professor of Skiing and Alpinism at the Ecole Nationale.

Finally, a special word of thanks to André Broche, director, and all the instructors of the ESF Belle Plagne for their unhesitating help and willingness to demonstrate the technical aspects of skiing which were so vividly captured by Kjell Langset the photographer.

# CONTENTS

| | | | |
|---|---|---|---|
| 6 | Introduction | 78 | The basic parallel turn |
| 8 | Before You Go | 80 | The basic wedel |
| 10 | 8000 Years of skiing | 82 | Advanced skiers: Class 3 |
| 12 | Physical preparation | 84 | Simple jumps |
| 13 | The anatomy of a skier | 86 | Skiing moguls |
| 14 | General exercises | 88 | The evasion turn |
| 15 | Exercising on the slopes | 90 | The GT turn |
| 16 | Traditional alpine resorts | 92 | The performance turn |
| 18 | Modern alpine resorts | 94 | GT and performance wedeling |
| 20 | The choice of travel | 96 | Powder skiing |
| 22 | The skiing regions | 98 | Slalom racing |
| 24 | Facilities for children | 100 | Competition skiing |
| 26 | Finding your level | 102 | Reducing sources of braking |
| 28 | Choosing skis | 104 | Skid turn: Avalement |
| 30 | Making sure the boots fit | 105 | Carved turn with sideways step |
| 32 | The importance of bindings | 106 | Slalom skiing |
| 34 | Clothing and accessories | 108 | Giant slalom |
| 36 | Ski teaching in France | 110 | Downhill techniques |
| 38 | Who are the instructors? | 112 | Super giant and parallel slalom |
| 42 | Your first time on skis | 114 | ESF Slalom test |
| 44 | Length of ski and the skier | 116 | Le Grand Ski |
| 46 | How to move on level ground | 118 | Free skiing in trees |
| 48 | Falling down and getting up | 120 | Crust and ice |
| 50 | Side step and herringbone | 122 | Moguls |
| 52 | Initial balancing | 124 | Ultimate off-piste |
| 54 | Step turns | 126 | Fringe skiing |
| 56 | The snow plough | 128 | Freestyle skiing |
| 58 | The design of ski lifts | 130 | Summer skiing |
| 60 | Improved beginners: Class 1 | 132 | Cross country |
| 62 | Introducing turns | 134 | Skis, boots and accessories |
| 64 | Kick turns | 136 | On the flat and uphill |
| 66 | Traversing and change of slope | 138 | The double pole push |
| 68 | Side slipping | 140 | Stepping turns |
| 70 | Side slipping diagonal and linked | 142 | At the resort |
| 72 | The elementary turn | 144 | A selection of alpine resorts |
| 74 | Intermediate skiers: Class 2 | 154 | A skiing glossary |
| 76 | Side slipping diagonal | 158 | Index |

# INTRODUCTION

With every new winter sports season, the French mountains seem to 'grow': new resorts appear, new skiing areas open to the public, and services constantly improve. The Ecole du Ski Français keeps pace with this progress, developing and refining its teaching methods, and increasing its presence in the resorts. Our Association of Instructors is now 9,400 strong.

The ESF has been teaching beginners, intermediate and advanced skiers for more than 40 years, and during that time it has learned that lessons should be both instructive *and* fun. Also, thanks to the ever-increasing number of English-speaking instructors, skiers from countries other than France have been able to appreciate the benefits of ESF tuition.

So, when Peter Stuyvesant Travel suggested a joint project with the ESF for a book which would not only set out the official French teaching method but also enable many more skiers to derive greater satisfaction and enjoyment from their sport, we did not need to think twice.

Peter Stuyvesant Travel has built up a flourishing winter holiday business and publishes excellent instructional books and videos. It was therefore a logical step for the ESF and PST to collaborate in the production of this new book and its companion video: *Ski the French Way*.

A French skiing holiday is a blend of many things: the magic of the mountains, the warmth of our unique brand of hospitality and, above all, the exhilaration and fulfilment of learning to ski well. *Ski the French Way* is about all these and more. I am sure that it will help you to make the most of your next holiday.

Bon ski!

*Bernard Chevallier*
President of the Ecole du Ski Français

# BEFORE YOU GO

In this section we look at and discuss all you need to know, to plan, and then to set off on your skiing trip. For the experienced skier it forms a useful *aide mémoire* whilst for the beginner it introduces all the pre-ski elements he needs to be aware of before starting out.

# 8000 YEARS OF SKIING

8,000 years of skiing? Some historians will view this figure with scepticism but one can at least say, without fear of contradiction, that man has been using skis for several thousand years. Evidence of this exists in stone carvings, manuscripts and, above all, archaeological finds. The oldest of the latter is the 'Hoting ski', unearthed in 1921 in a Swedish marsh – from which it takes its name – and proving that skis were used in this region some 4,500 years ago. Subsequently, other objects were found in Sweden, as well as Norway and Finland, all dating back three or four thousand years. The most significant of many stone carvings showing skiers, believed by some to date from the fifth millennium BC, was discovered on a small Norwegian island in 1932. Moving on through history, Chinese literature dating from several centuries BC includes skiing references, the most interesting being a mention of 'Turks riding wooden horses' – a fairly graphic description of men on skis.

Northern European literature of more recent date, between AD 800 and 1300, contains many allusions to skiing, although fact is often laced with a large measure of fiction. The first momentous skiing exploit, however, according to Arnold Lunn in his *History of Skiing*, occurred in 1520 when the use of skis played a surprisingly vital role in the formation of the Kingdom of Sweden. It seems that, at that time, many Swedish loyalists were languishing in Danish prisons, one of their number being Gustav Eriksson Vasa, the Swedes' leader, who had been captured by King Christian II two years earlier. Vasa managed to escape and returned to his home town of Mora, where he tried to raise a revolt against the Danes. Faced with a marked lack of enthusiasm on the part of his compatriots, Vasa decided to leave Sweden, put on his skis, and set off alone for Salen and the border, some 87 km away. Not long after he had started out on his journey, the Swedes had a change of heart and sent their best skiers after their leader. The posse overtook Vasa, who willingly returned to Mora and masterminded the eviction of the Danes. By the following year, Vasa had been crowned king and the Kingdom of Sweden had been established. To commemorate this epic historical ski journey an annual cross-country race, first staged in 1922, is held: the world-famous Vasaloppet, with up to 12,000 competitors covering the 87 km from Salen to Mora.

Although skis had been in use for civilian and military transport for some time, it was not until the 17th century, in Lapland, that the concept of com-

*Left:* Even the earliest skiers appreciated the 'ups' and 'downs' associated with learning to ski, as this print shows.

*Below left:* Some of the first exponents of the Telemark turn. Holding hands was one of the more flamboyant ways of executing the turn.

*Right:* The fashion conscious skier at the turn of the century. Note the long, hand carved tips to the skis and the heavy wooden poles.

petitive skiing appeared. The next major development came in 1860, when, according to Arnold Lunn, a Norwegian called Nordheim jumped the impressive distance of 30.5 m, having made the all-important discovery that it is much easier and less painful to land on a slope than on a flat surface.

It was at about this time that America produced its own skiing phenomenon: one John A. Thompson, born Jon Thorsteinson, and nicknamed 'Snowshoe' Thompson, for reasons which will become apparent. Norwegian by birth, Thompson was responsible for transporting the mail from Placeville, California, to Carson City in Nevada: 150 snowbound km to cover with a backpack of letters weighing some 50 kg! Snowshoe's solution was to fashion himself a pair of skis 3 m long by 10 cm wide, with which he could cover the distance in less than three days. Few people recognized the magnitude of Thompson's achievement, and he died a poor and solitary man.

Skiing began to gain in popularity towards the end of the 19th century, when the Norwegian explorer Fridtjof Nansen crossed Greenland on skis in 42 days. He wrote a book about the 1888 expedition – the first to provide any technical information for would-be skiers. Before long, the first ski clubs sprang up: Switzerland in 1893; Italy and France in 1897; the USA in 1900; and Britain in 1903. The new century and the so-called 'Belles Dames de Megève' saw added interest in skiing and the first signs of rifts between its devotees. The Scandinavian countries veered towards cross-country skiing and ski-jumping, while the downhill sport proved most popular in the Alps and Britain. The final seal of approval for this new leisure activity came in 1924, when skiing was featured in the Olympic Games at Chamonix. The first ski-tow appeared in 1932, courtesy of Alex Foster of Quebec, while the first ski-lift was installed at Davos, Switzerland, three years later.

Skiing technique evolved as the sport became more popular. The telemark turn, introduced by the Norwegian Sondre Nordheim, fell out of favour (although it was fairly recently revived in western America, where it has several thousand new adherents); Austria's Arlberg school then led the world, until a new rival came on the scene in about 1935, in the form of Emile Allais' French technique.

The real boom, however, started in 1960 and soon, instead of a few thousand, the number of keen skiers throughout the world could be numbered in millions. Skis themselves – once mere wooden planks – evolved into technological thoroughbreds, while peaceful mountain villages were transformed into bustling, purpose-built resorts. It is this modern sport which we would like to help you to enjoy.

# PHYSICAL PREPARATION

Skiing brings into play all parts of your body as this photograph shows. Some areas have to withstand greater strain and stress than others. Therefore, in addition to keeping yourself generally fit (you can check your fitness level with the Ruffier test), pay special attention during training to the specific areas pinpointed in the illustration on the right.

Whether you are a recreational skier or a seasoned competitor, and whatever the style of skiing you enjoy – be it Alpine, cross-country, freestyle, etc – you need to be in good psychological and physical shape. As far as the mental approach is concerned, the mountains in winter are a very different kettle of fish from a summertime beach holiday: the environment, weather and atmospheric conditions are completely different. It is a much more relaxing proposition to sunbathe on the sand, lulled by the sound of the sea, than it is to finish a ski run in a snowstorm at minus 5 or 6°C! So your reflexes and mental stamina have to be up to scratch, but you also need to be fairly fit physically, for skiing calls for a great deal more than just sliding along over the snow with your hands in your pockets. Your lower body has to give with the bumps, you have to bend and stretch hundreds of times as you weave your way down the mountain, and cope with the strain of almost continual vibration coming up through your legs. And this is not all: a skier has to use cumbersome equipment, learn how to fall and get up again without making a meal of it, and develop the ability to anticipate and to co-ordinate his movements. To ski well, therefore, you need to be supple, with fast reactions – brute strength is not enough.

The fitter and better prepared you are, the more you will enjoy your skiing, and the following programme of mini work-outs, designed with the recreational skier in mind, should get you in shape. The most important point is that you should not leave starting your training until the week before you go, as this will do more harm than good. The ideal is to begin your preparation, however gently, several months before your winter holiday; the best time would be as soon as you return from your summer break. Jogging or cycling for two or three hours a week, combined with a few exercises, will ensure that you enjoy your skiing to the full.

No matter whether you are a recreational or a competition skier, you will use the same muscles. Although you need not train so intensively before your one week a year on the slopes, you still need strength, suppleness and good reflexes.

# THE ANATOMY OF A SKIER

Skiing calls for a high general level of fitness, although a recreational skier need not train as intensively as a Grand Prix competitor. Nevertheless, whether you are a once-a-year skier or a race-tuned professional, you use the same muscles and joints when you ski, and they need exercising before you head for the snow. These exercises are aimed not only at strengthening the appropriate muscles and joints, but also at making them more supple, which is vital if your body is to respond to variations in terrain and snow. If you watch a skier in action, it will be obvious which parts of the body are used most: arms, shoulders, hips, thighs, knees and ankles.

It is very important that any exercise you undertake is correctly planned beforehand. The strength of the skier is principally around the joints – knees and ankles – so do take very good care with your exercise regime. Avoid punishing techniques which jar the legs, concentrate on building up the muscular strength using, for instance, weight training machinery. These days most good gyms in most major towns have safe, good equipment – don't hesitate to use it. Take it carefully at first using repetitious sets of exercises and gradually build up your strength to the required level.

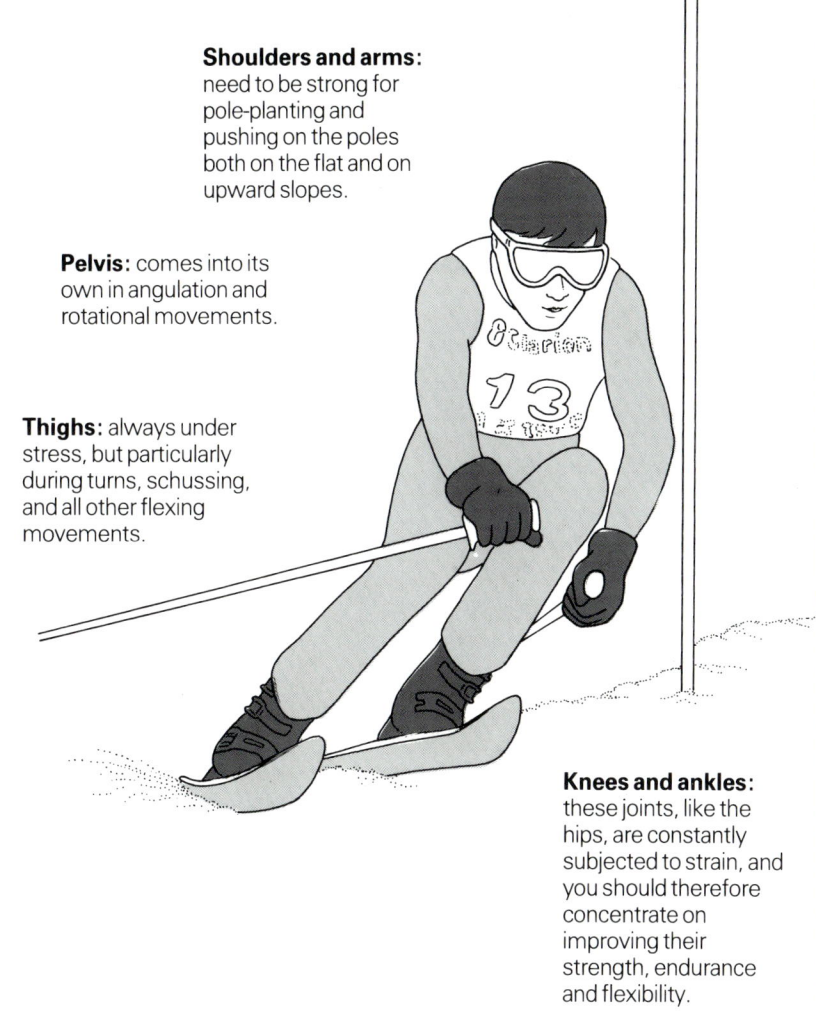

**Shoulders and arms:** need to be strong for pole-planting and pushing on the poles both on the flat and on upward slopes.

**Pelvis:** comes into its own in angulation and rotational movements.

**Thighs:** always under stress, but particularly during turns, schussing, and all other flexing movements.

**Knees and ankles:** these joints, like the hips, are constantly subjected to strain, and you should therefore concentrate on improving their strength, endurance and flexibility.

# THE RUFFIER TEST

The Ruffier test is a good way of telling whether you are fit. Start by taking your pulse at rest, then do 30 knee-bends in 45 seconds. Check your pulse rate again for 15 seconds.

...Repeat one minute later. Add together the three pulse rates and divide by ten. If the result is less than 5, you are in good shape; between 5 and 10, you need to train.

# GENERAL EXERCISES

As far as a skier is concerned, what does physical fitness mean? It means being able to ski for several days in succession without tiring. This means, in turn, that your whole body – heart, lungs and digestive system – must be in tip-top condition. It means having stamina. It means being able to hold a flexed position, to absorb bumps, etc, and this requires strength. It also means being able to increase your work rate without endangering your health. It means endurance. These few exercises will meet all the above requirements.

These simple exercises are the basis for all-over fitness, and will improve your balance, suppleness and co-ordination. Increase your work rate gradually; begin with ten minutes a day, taking care not to strain yourself, and your fitness will steadily increase without causing you any physical problems. The exercises we suggest are very basic, and you can always supplement them with a sport like tennis, football, rugby, cycling, skating, etc. And remember... don't take the lift when you can climb the stairs!

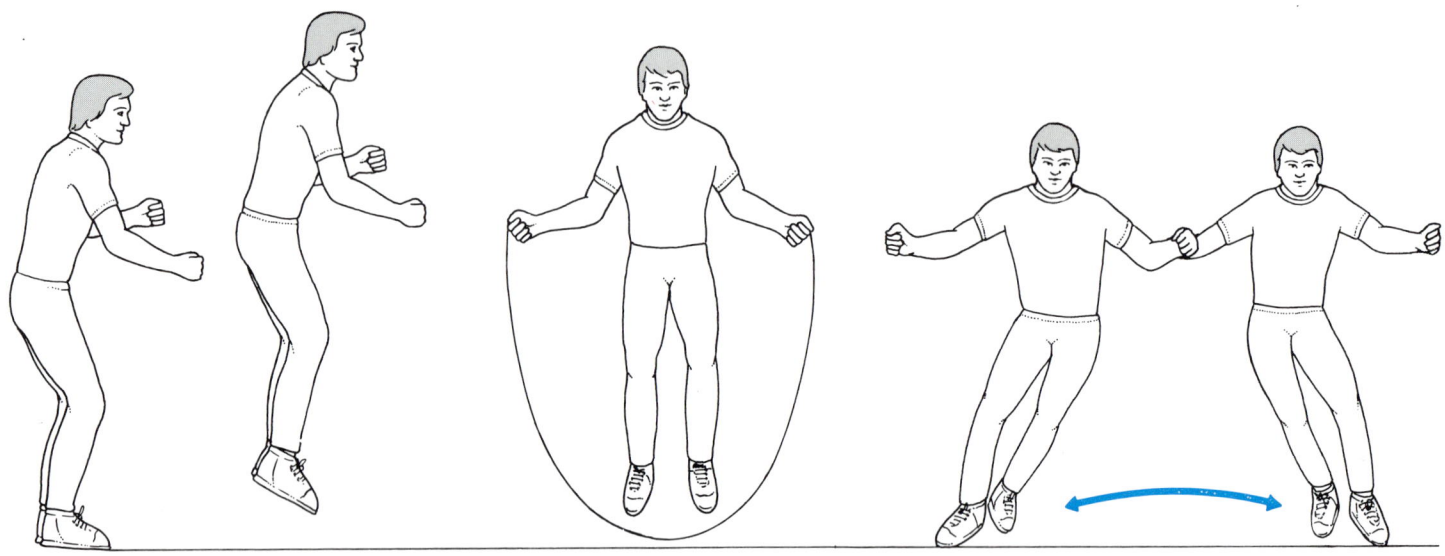

**For suppleness – rhythmical jumps.** Starting in a slightly flexed position, do 50 to 100 gentle, vertical jumps; as your fitness improves, repeat. If you have enough room, perform the jumps with a skipping rope. This is ideal for exercising the calves, thighs and lower back.

**For arms, shoulders and stomach – a few series of press-ups.** This well-known but nonetheless effective exercise gives excellent results. While you are about it, you can add in a few more stretching and bending floor exercises.

**For your hips – rocking jumps.** Starting with your knees slightly flexed, jump from your left leg on to your right leg and vice versa. This is an excellent hip-strengthener, and it will help you with angulation.

**For abdominal muscles – sit-ups.** Lie on your back with your arms spread and, if necessary, wedge your feet under a chair or sofa. Raise your upper body, starting with your head, then your shoulders, and finally your lower back. Repeat 20 to 30 times, and build up repetitions of the sequence, with a few minutes' rest in between.

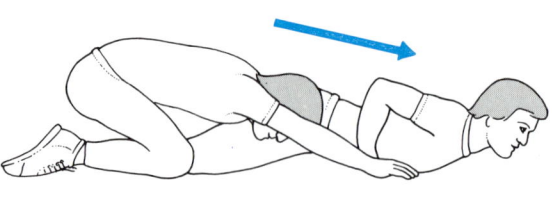
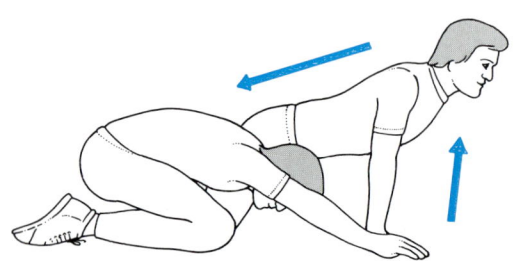
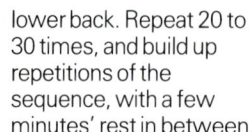
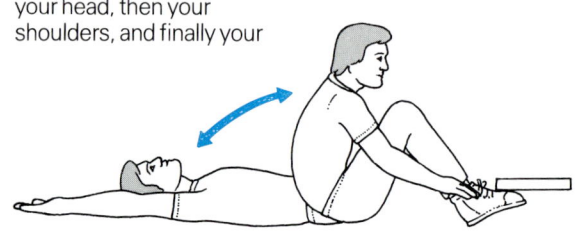

# EXERCISING ON THE SLOPES

Assuming that you have arrived at your resort in good physical shape, you still should not go straight into a schuss from the top of the piste without taking a couple of minutes to warm up. If you have ever seen world-class racers before a slalom or downhill you will have noticed that they spend ten or 15 minutes warming up before they are called to the start. Do as they do, and do not worry about any funny looks you might get – you may be sparing yourself a nasty muscle strain.

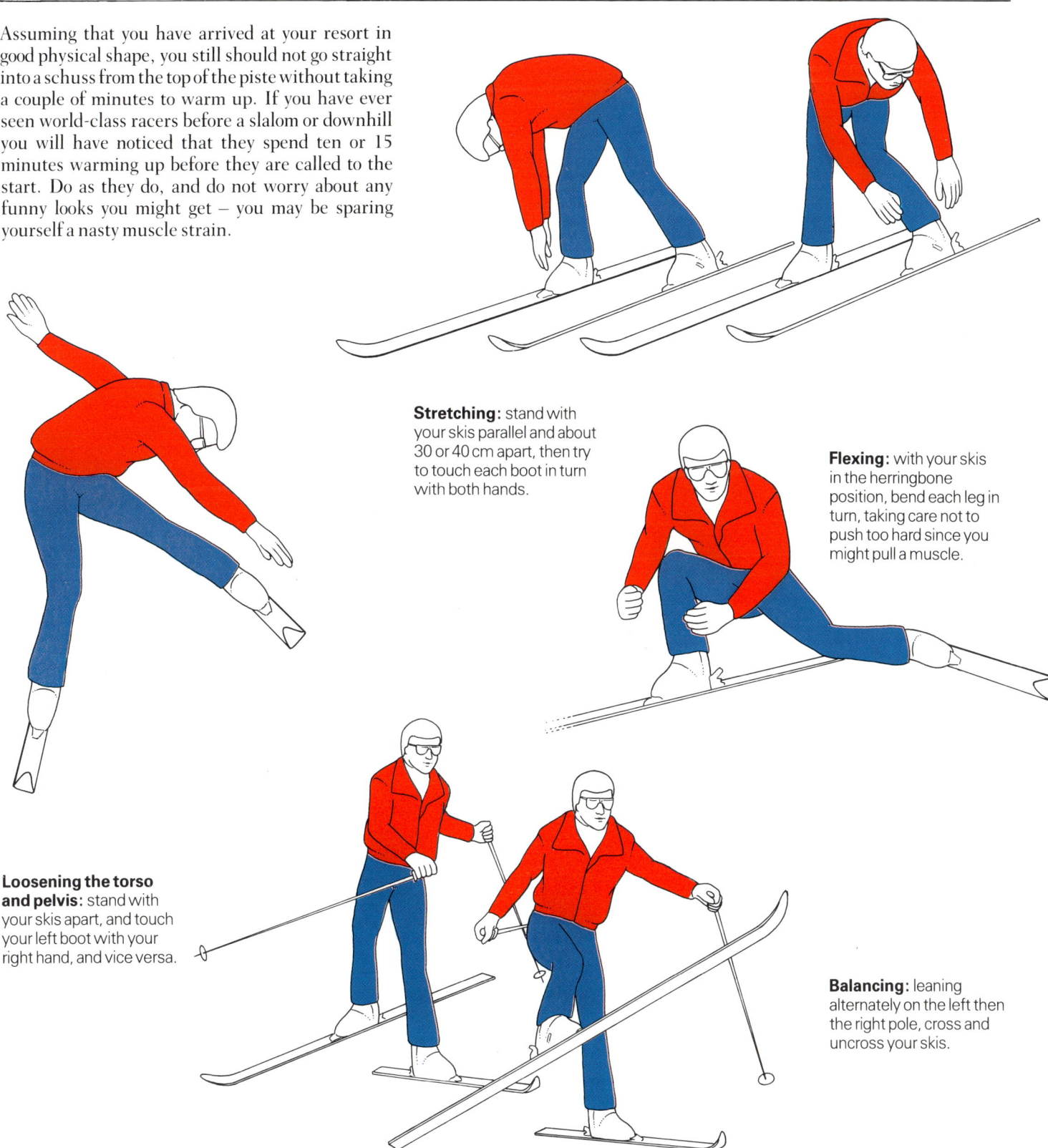

**Stretching:** stand with your skis parallel and about 30 or 40 cm apart, then try to touch each boot in turn with both hands.

**Flexing:** with your skis in the herringbone position, bend each leg in turn, taking care not to push too hard since you might pull a muscle.

**Loosening the torso and pelvis:** stand with your skis apart, and touch your left boot with your right hand, and vice versa.

**Balancing:** leaning alternately on the left then the right pole, cross and uncross your skis.

# TRADITIONAL ALPINE RESORTS

Lapp or Mongol hunters may well have invented skis thousands of years ago, but skiing did not take off as a recreational and competitive sport until the beginning of this century, and the first world championships – in Chamonix – were not held until 1924. Also, before the Second World War, the original skiing 'speed merchants' congregated in spa resorts situated in the Alpine foothills (St Gervais-les-Bains or Villard de Lans in France, St Moritz in Switzerland, etc), or in the larger resorts with an established summer tourist trade (Chamonix, Megève, Val d'Isère). The transformation of these spa and mountain villages into ski resorts was a very slow process. Forty years later, the distinguishing features of these old-established resorts are frequently long journeys on foot or by bus between ski-lifts, or even between the resort and its pistes; but on the plus side they have undeniable charm with their quaint chalets, proper village life – due to a permanent resident population – and rural atmosphere. Megève, in France, is perhaps the most attractive of these resorts. As long ago as 1920, fashionable ladies from Paris held house-parties there, but today the village has expanded to provide not only sunshine and ski-slopes, but also a sports complex which would not disgrace a city.

It was after the Second World War that skiing really took off as a participator sport, and existing resorts soon found that they could not accommodate the annual influx. This led to the emergence of a new generation of resorts which were more functional, but which still blended into the landscape: each small landowner built his own guest-house or ski-lift, with no central resort planning. Products of this individual enterprise were Alpe d'Huez, Les Deux Alpes and Méribel, a favourite haunt of the British, as St Moritz had been some 30 years earlier. These second-generation resorts were somewhat primitive at the outset, but the worst planning blunders have since been corrected, and for the last decade they have enjoyed a reputation for being mountain villages which blend old-fashioned charm with modern skiing facilities.

Many of the very early traditional resorts were found within the valleys, therefore relatively low and thus often short of snow. As a consequence there was often a long journey to reach the better slopes – a mixture of walking and endless ski lifts.

*Left:* Megève once renowned as a mountain retreat of fashionable Parisian ladies, Megève is one of France's original ski resorts. It is now a modern sporting complex, with pistes for skiers of all levels, but providing the added bonus of a real village atmosphere.

*Far left:* A rather bleak day in a traditional resort where the snow has turned to slush. A point to remember when organising your holiday.

*Above:* Méribel situated in the heart of the 'Trois Vallées', Méribel has one of the largest skiing areas in the world (400 km of pistes and 160 ski-lifts) and has become a favourite with the British. Happily it has retained its traditional village charm, while developing into a large, bustling resort.

# MODERN ALPINE RESORTS

*Above:* Belle Plagne is the most recent of the high-altitude stations which make up the La Plagne complex. Belle Plagne was built in the style of an Alpine village, but 2,050 m above sea-level. Architecturally, it is a very attractive resort, with spacious wood-faced chalets situated right on the ski slopes. There is direct access by gondola to the Bellecôte glacier.

The 'white gold-rush' started in earnest in 1960, and lasted until about 1975. It was during this 15-year period that the third generation of French ski resorts appeared, with whole towns being given over to skiing. These ski stations are located at altitudes of between 1,800 and 2,200 m and you put on your skis as you leave your apartment, since travelling by car, or even walking, are virtually banned.

Many people have the mistaken impression that, because these resorts are inhabited for only part of the year (six months in winter and, in some cases, three months in summer), the region lacks genuine character. How wrong they are. This is paradise for skiers and, for the real enthusiast, there's no place to beat it. Everything is designed with skiing in mind, whether at La Plagne, with its 25,000 beds divided among six high-altitude ski stations and four village resorts, 185 km of pistes and 86 ski-lifts, or Valmorel – the most recent French resort – with 6,500 beds, 27 ski-lifts and 62 pistes laid out, or again Tignes, which boasts 23,000 beds, 54 ski-lifts, 60 pistes, and summer skiing (as does La Plagne). The pistes benefit from 24-hour maintenance and most finish in the resort centre; there is a wealth of ski-equipment shops; emergency services are continually on standby; and, most importantly, there are ESF ski schools in each resort (with children's classes, and kindergartens for the little ones). 'Ski Evolutif' is the method used to teach first-time skiers at La Plagne and neighbouring Les Arcs, amongst others.

At La Plagne, too, all the resorts are interconnected, but each is self-contained, with its own shops, restaurants, bars, and lifts. For the more adventurous skier, the La Plagne lift pass can be used at Les Arcs, as well. Pistes in all these resorts are designed to offer great diversity, and you can ski, literally, from your own front door!

*Below left:* Club Peter Stuyvesant members relaxing at Belle Plagne.

*Below right:* Valmorel is one of the fourth-generation ski resorts, Valmorel was opened in the early 1980s; it combines traditional Alpine village layout – the buildings are grouped around a village square – with modern facilities designed exclusively with skiing in mind.

# THE CHOICE OF TRAVEL

France has about 50 classified ski resorts, 80 more affiliated to the Association des Maires des Stations Françaises de Sports d'Hiver (Association of French Winter Sports Resorts' Mayors) and nearly 200 other ski centres. But what do these different descriptions imply? Well, first the classified resorts. They have to measure up to certain standards, the most important of which are:

*Altitude*: a minimum of 800 m in the Alps, Jura and Vosges, 1,000 m in the Massif Central and Corsica, and 1,200 m in the Pyrenees. These figures take account of the area's latitude and sunshine quota.

*Access*: there must be a regular shuttle service between a railway station and the resort.

*Accommodation*: at least 1,500 beds must be available for tourists; 50% self-catering and 20% in good hotels.

*Advice*: every resort must have a permanent tourist office.

*Organization*: medical services must be available on site, with at least two ambulances, as well as emergency services on the pistes. Other requirements are: a piste with a drop of at least 500 m; a children's play area; an avalanche map; and a ski school with a minimum of six instructors.

These guidelines, which have been in existence for more than ten years, guarantee a certain standard of amenities, reached by many of the non-classified resorts also, especially the great majority of those affiliated to the Association des Maires des Stations Françaises de Sports d'Hiver.

'Ski centres', on the other hand, have no set standards, and the term can be used to describe anything from just one basic hotel plus drag-lift to a complete mountain village with a dozen or more lifts. In these cases it is best to check out the centre *before* you go.

You can see that there is a vast choice of French ski resorts. Other important factors to be borne in mind are the differences between ski areas caused by their geological nature, latitude, exposure and climate. For example, in the Vosges the snow line is 500 m lower than it is in the Alps; in the northern Alps there is often more powder snow than elsewhere, but also less sunshine; in the Dauphiné and southern Alps there may be just as much snow as in the northern Alps, but the sunnier climate leads to much more variable snow conditions. The same goes for the equally sunny Pyrenees. As for Corsica, which is blessed with an abundance of snow from February to April, more often than not you will be skiing on ice, and the rugged terrain on this Mediterranean island makes it unsuitable for all but the most expert ski mountaineer.

Before deciding which French resort to visit, it is worth contacting the Association des Maires des Stations Françaises, 61 boulevard Haussmann, F-75008 Paris (Tel: [010 33] 1-742-23-32) for detailed information.

# THE SKIING REGIONS

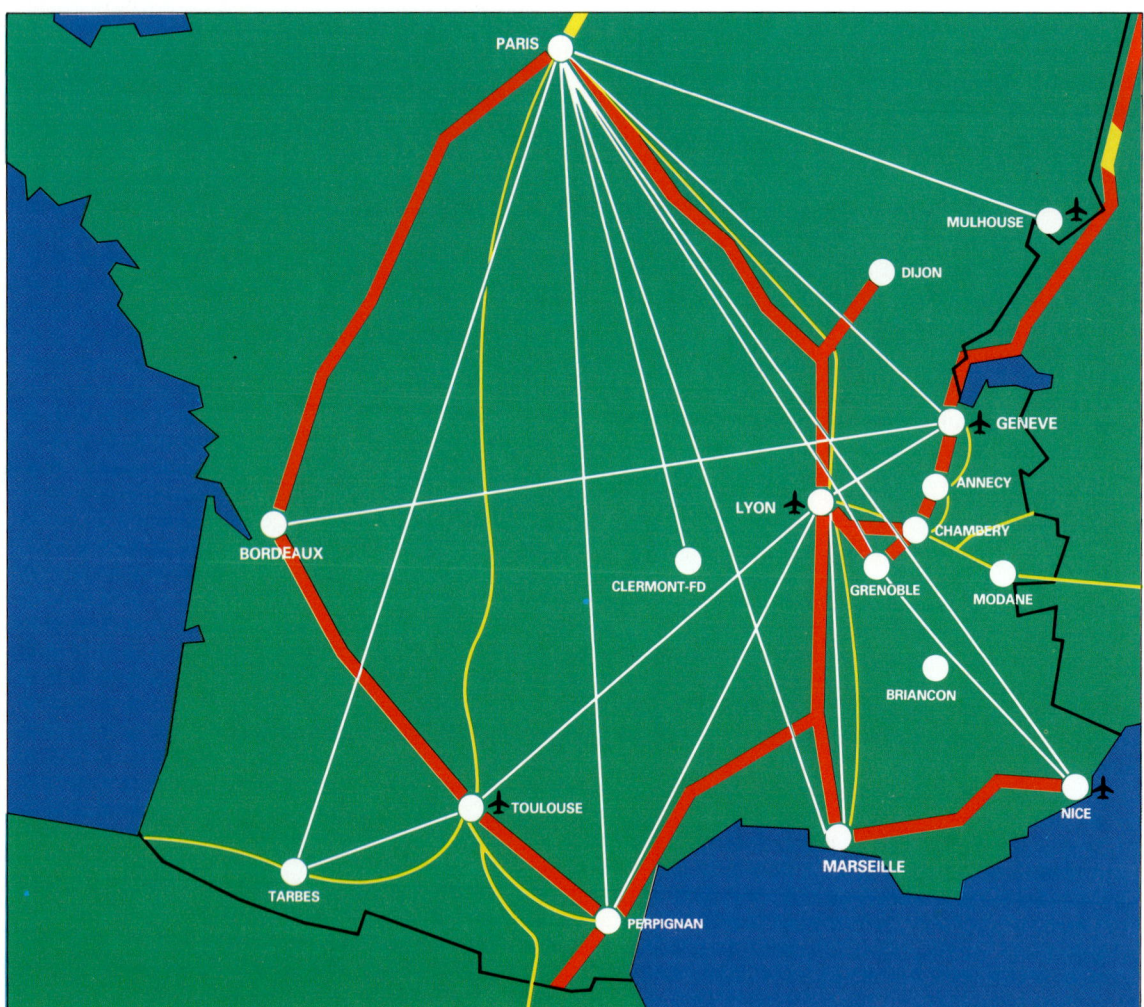

*Left:* the airports and autoroutes serving the main ski areas. By car it's a tiring drive. By train, you can leave Paris in the evening and be skiing the next morning, but you have to carry your luggage. Air travel is fastest, but ski resorts tend to be a long way from airports. As for coach travel, you are faced with a long and wearing trip. A good travel company, however, will look after your needs and make the journey as trouble-free as possible.

When planning your skiing holiday from Britain do consider carefully the various options open for travelling to your destination. Most people tend to go by aeroplane as this generally appears to create the least problems, is cheap and gets you to your resort quickly. Also, of course, most package companies plan around charter flights which fly from all the major airports in Britain.

However it is well worth considering other modes of transport. The aeroplane can have drawbacks. You will be restricted on the amount of luggage you can take as well as being confined to your resort. Remember that you have to arrange your own transport in order to reach and leave the airport. If you drive, parking can be costly.

If you live in the south of England, within easy reach of the channel ports, it is well worthwhile investigating the cost of driving down to the Alps or the Pyrenees. During the winter, ferry tarifs are reduced, the roads less congested, and the trip down interesting and informative.

Lastly you can travel by rail or coach. By coach down the autoroutes is a very direct method of getting to the resort as once you board you will not have to make any other arrangements – it's door to door. Rail is not really recommended, from Britain, as it will entail a number of changes. However, trains from Paris will take you to within about 30 km of most resorts and buses usually provide a shuttle service between the railway station and the centre.

The main French airports are Mulhouse for the Vosges; Geneva or Lyons for the Northern Alps and the Massif Central; Lyons for the Dauphine; Turin, in Italy for the Hautes Alpes; Nice for the southern Alps; Toulouse or Barcelona for the Pyrenees.

**The Jura:** a region of deep valleys, plenty of snow, and crisp, dry air. It is a paradise for cross-country skiers, but Alpine skiers will also find pistes to suit them, particularly at Les Rousses and Métabief.

**The Vosges:** a low mountain range with good snow cover. Instead of 'ski-factories', you will find authentic villages suitable for both cross-country and Alpine skiers. The slopes are short and steep – ideal for slalom.

**The northern Alps:** 15 of the 20 principal resorts are located in this French mecca for Alpine skiers. You can ski at altitudes between 800 and 4,000 m, the pistes (suitable for all abilities) are excellent, and the snow conditions first class. The only drawback is that sunshine cannot always be guaranteed.

**The Massif Central:** Alpine and cross-country skiing co-exist happily here. The altitude is fairly low, but there is plenty of snow, kept in condition by the constant, but not unpleasant, cold. As with the Jura and Vosges, traditional mountain villages predominate.

**The Hautes Alpes:** these are very similar to the northern Alps, but have the benefit of more sunshine at the expense of occasionally inferior-quality snow. It is an ideal region for ski-mountaineering (the La Meije valleys) and summer skiing (Sarenne and Jandri glaciers).

**The Pyrenees:** this mountain range is often unfavourably compared with the Alps; unjustly so, since the pistes are good with an adequate snow cover. The sun does tend to turn the powder into hard-packed snow, but the snow-making machines make short work of that problem.

**The Vercors** An easily accessible region, only a few kilometres from Grenoble, with one of France's first ski resorts – Villard de Lans – at its heart. Although the mountains are not the highest in the country, the snow cover is perfectly adequate throughout the season.

**The southern Alps:** this is the place for that winter tan! Despite the strong sun, there is usually plenty of good-quality snow and, in any case, the warm Mediterranean hospitality, certain tan and enjoyable skiing make an unbeatable trio.

# FACILITIES FOR CHILDREN

Two questions are repeatedly asked by parents anxious about the coming winter holidays: 'How old should our child be before we take him to a ski resort?' and 'At what age can children start skiing?' Any doctor can answer the first question: there is no reason for not taking a baby, however young, on a winter sports holiday, although you should choose a low-altitude resort, making changes in altitude gradually, and make sure that your infant is well protected from the weather. As for the second question, any ESF instructor will tell you that there is no age limit for learning to ski, provided that the child wants to learn and is happy being in the snow. Some will be ready at two years of age, others at seven, but never force a child to put on skis if he does not want to, as this will put him off for life.

Children should see skiing as an exciting new game. Most ESFs and French resorts have realized this: witness the fact that they have created many new children's areas – separate resorts in all but name, where budding skiers have their own pistes, ski-lifts, games rooms, and even their own restaurants. More importantly, young children are given the appropriate modern instruction and care in an ideal environment, with the emphasis on teaching by example rather than by instruction, and with a structured system to cater for different ages and levels. The first of these 'villages' for children was opened at Orcières-Merlette in France, more than 20 years ago. Nowadays, every resort has special children's facilities, so that parents can ski off on their own in the knowledge that their offspring are in safe hands, and progressing at their own pace.

One point to remember is that you should make sure that your children are properly kitted out before leaving them in the 'village': sunglasses or goggles that they cannot lose, warm and waterproof gloves, clothes that will keep them well covered all the time and – top of the priority list – good ski boots. Children are affected by cold more than adults, and their feet are just as vulnerable. They will be taught the same techniques – provided they are appropriate – as those learned by adults.

*Left:* Children will always find the time to enjoy themselves especially in such an inviting landscape as snow.

*Above:* Teaching children to ski is always very rewarding as the instructor knows he is giving them knowledge and skills that will last a lifetime.

*Right:* children's 1 *etoile* (1 star) level, equivalent to an adult's Class 1, leading to the elementary turn.

*Left:* children's 2 *etoile* level, equivalent to an adult's class 2, leading to the first parallel turn.

*Bottom left:* children's 3 *etoile* level, equivalent to an adult's Class 3, and leading to parallel turns and an introduction to slalom.

## COMPETITION SKIING

In no time at all, and often much sooner than adults, children are trying their hands at competitive skiing: slalom; parallel slalom; bumps; speed; jumping; etc. From this point onwards, youngsters and their parents will be taking the same tests. Future World Champions have to start training at an early age, as it takes many years to reach the top.

*Below:* Parallel slalom is a good way for children to see if they can ski better than their friends.

# FINDING YOUR LEVEL

If you are about to have your first taste of skiing, there is no need to worry yourself silly with visions of floundering about helplessly in the snow. Once you have checked in to your hotel, pop down to the Ecole du Ski Français office to book some lessons in the beginners' class (better still, book your lessons in advance, by post, by writing to the director of the resort's ski school, particularly if you are going during the school holidays). It is vital to have an instructor when you first start skiing; you *can* try to teach yourself, but it will take ten times longer, and you are bound to learn bad habits.

However, if you already have some experience (be it in France or elsewhere), you will need to find your own level in the scale of classes on offer. You can do this by referring to the table of international standards provided below, so, before booking lessons, consult the table and decide whether Class 1, 2, 3 or, if you are more advanced, the competition and 'grand touring' class is the one for you.

As well as these international classifications, the ESF also provides performance tests for those who want to gauge their competition ability. In Alpine skiing, a competent instructor takes the first run down the slalom, giant slalom or downhill course, and his time is used as a yardstick for those taking the test. Skiers going for gold in the slalom, for example, have to complete the course within a margin of five per cent of the instructor's time, while those competing for the bronze have up to 50 per cent longer than the instructor's time allowed them by the judges.

Snowflake

1st star

2nd star

3rd star

1st International degree

2nd International degree

3rd International degree

Bronze Rocket
Silver Rocket
Vermeil Rocket
Golden Rocket

Kid
Bronze chamois
Silver chamois
Vermeil chamois
Golden chamois

Dart
Bronze Arrow
Silver Arrow
Vermeil Arrow
Golden Arrow

| Ski-class | Adults | Children |
|---|---|---|
|  Beginners | Study of the gliding wedge and introduction to the wedge turn<br>• checking the balance, first gliding motions<br>• walking on flat terrain<br>• initiation to ski-lift use<br>• recommended short skis | • to put the skis on, to walk to check one's balance while sliding, to work toward a good basic position, the climbing steps<br>• the gliding wedge<br>• initiation to the wedge turn |
|  1 | Studying and improving the basic turn<br>• the straight runs<br>• slippings<br>• rudiments of the stem christie<br>• recommended intermediate ski length | • to slide, to stop, to turn<br>• the basic turn<br>• the traverse<br>• rudiments of slipping |
|  2 | Study for the basic parallel turn<br>• first shortswings<br>• improvement of the straight runs and slippings<br>• recommended intermediate ski length | • the first skidded turns<br>• straight run 2nd degree<br>• initiation to the basic parallel turn |
|  3 | Improvement of the parallel turns<br>• skiing all kinds of slopes<br>• skiing slopes, bumpy slopes<br>• skiing all kinds of snow (frozen, deep)<br>• initiation to slalom<br>• recommended traditional and technical skis | • initiation to the slalom<br>• the shortswings<br>• perfecting the slippings<br>• the basic parallel turn<br>• straight run 3rd degree |
|  Competition | Preparation for racing<br>• slalom, giant slalom, downhill race, jumping<br>• improvement of the already acquired techniques<br>• special type of skis recommended | • speed and efficiency in the movements, naturalness<br>• skiing in all kinds of snow and terrain<br>• slalom, giant slalom, downhill, race, jumping<br>• training for competitions in slalom, giant slalom, downhill, jumping |
| | • off the trail skiing<br>• ski-tour, overnight ski excursions, corridors<br>• special type of skis indispensable | |

# CHOOSING SKIS

It is not that long – 30 years – since skis were carved from a piece of wood, with the edges simply screwed on. During the last three decades, these 'wooden planks', have changed more than in all the previous 8,000-odd years of skiing history, and have become real Formula 1s of the slopes. This transformation began back in the 1950s, when some Americans tried a metal/wood combination. Ten years later, Europe made its contribution – plastic. The most radical advance was seen at the 1966 Portillo world championships: all trace of wood had vanished (although it was to reappear later in the 'core'), as had haphazard trial-and-error development. There were now laboratories specializing in glass fibre (later, carbon fibre – or 'Kevlar' – came on the scene), experimenting with metal and, occasionally, retaining a wooden core. Some introduced the box design, while others were playing with layered, or 'sandwich' construction, methods. But, whatever the case, manufacturers were suddenly obsessed with torsion, vibration, flexibility, profile, thickness, camber, weight, length, width: the day of the modern ski had dawned. Today, skis come in one of four main groups: competition, 'grand sport', sports and compacts, and specialist skis (mogul, ballet, mountaineering, évolutif, jumping and flying kilometre, not forgetting junior skis).

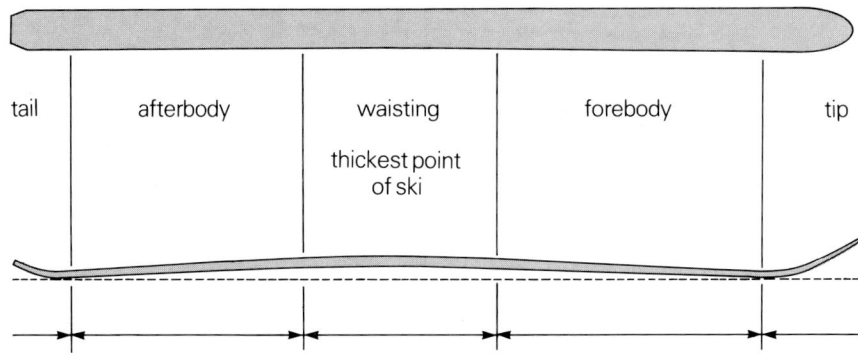

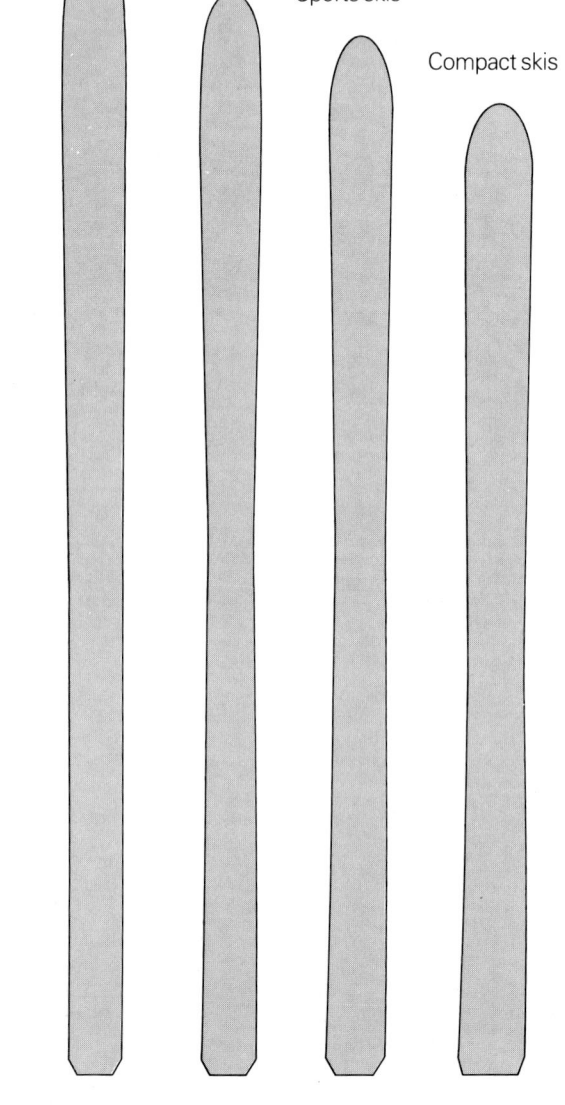

*Below:* To find the right length of ski for you, simply place a ruler so that it links your weight (left-hand column) with your height (right-hand column). Read off the ski length where this line crosses through the appropriate ski type. These are recommended lengths for the average-ability skier. More advanced skiers should choose the next length up.

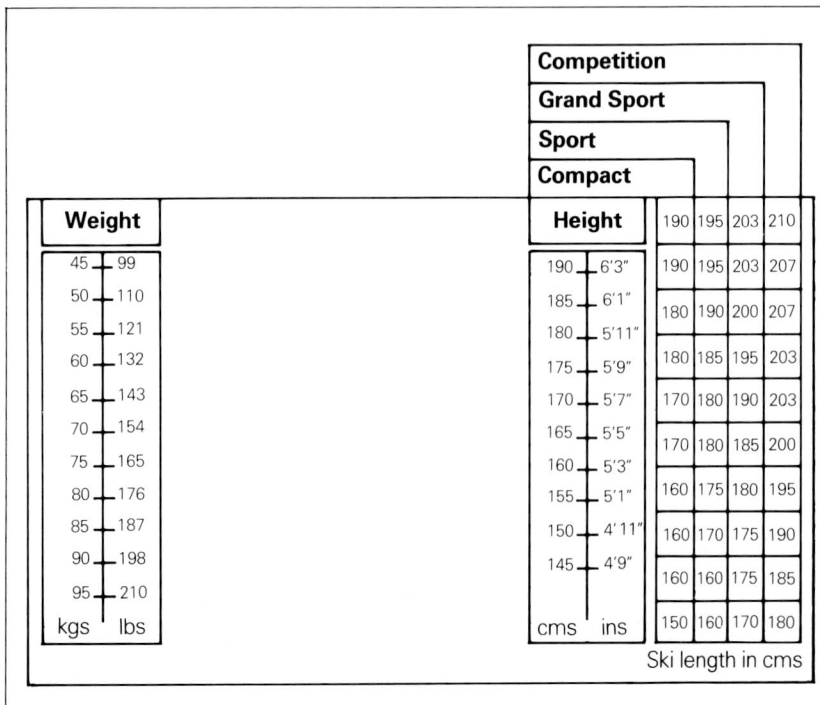

## LOOKING AFTER YOUR SKIS

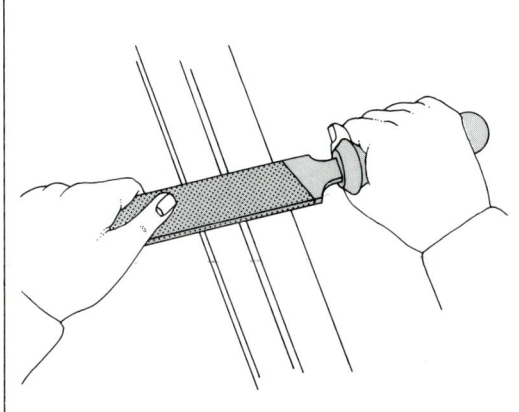

Modern skis are much more robust than those of 20 years ago, but they still need routine maintenance and care. First, if you transport them on the roof-rack of your car, always wash them when you reach your destination, because the salt spread on winter roads will rust the edges and bindings and will damage the running surfaces. Occasionally, the edges will need sharpening, especially if you are going to ski on icy snow. You can do it yourself with a very fine file, but it is safer to have it done at a specialist shop. This will only cost a few francs, and the running surfaces will be expertly waxed into the bargain.

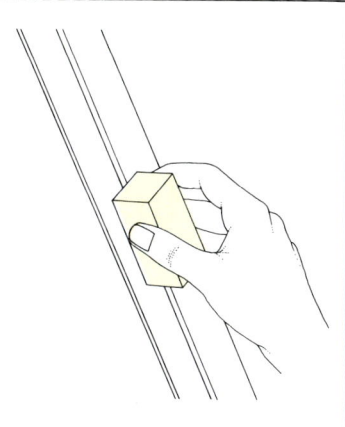

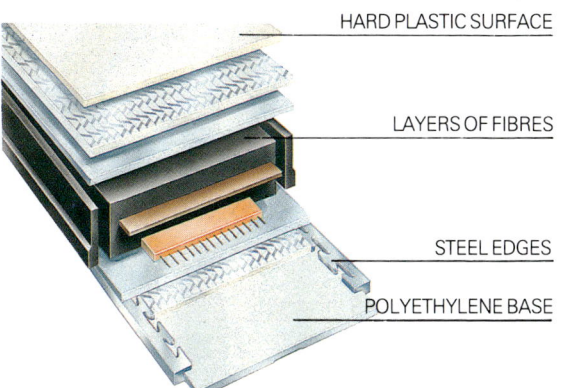

*Three ski types*
**Rossignol Stardust:** a Grand Sport ski, made of carbon, glass and 'Kevlar' fibres.

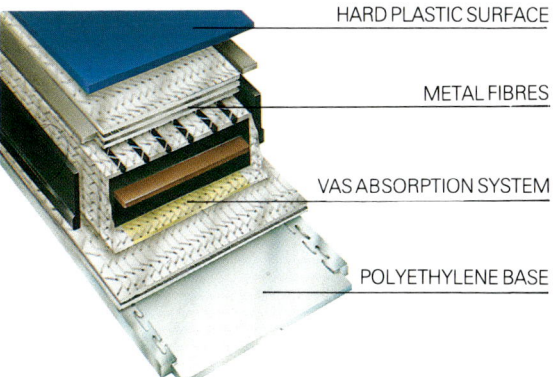

**Rossignol Starline:** a Grand Sport ski; metal fibre with Zicral, glass fibre and VAS (anti-vibration) system.

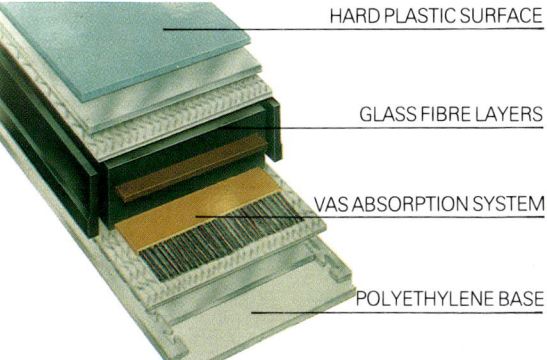

**Rossignol First:** a powder snow ski; glass fibre/Zicral sandwich with VAS absorber.

## COMPACT

COMPACT skis revolutionized ski teaching when they were first introduced ten years ago. Although they were easy to turn on soft or powder snow, their one major drawback was that they did not grip on ice, and they are becoming much less popular.

## SPORTS

SPORTS skis have largely replaced compacts, as they retain the good features while eliminating most of the faults – they grip well on hard snow and have better stability at moderate speeds. They are designed for beginners, intermediates, and the less aggressive advanced skier.

## PERFORMANCE

PERFORMANCE (or Grand Sport) skis come somewhere between sports skis (ease of use in all snow conditions) and competition skis (good grip, stability and performance). They are intended for advanced and expert skiers who are looking for versatility from their skis, even to the point where they can double for competition skiing.

## COMPETITION

COMPETITION skis, as their name indicates, are designed for competition use. Some are specifically for special or giant slalom, others for downhills, the flying kilometre, etc. Nevertheless, some modern competition models can be used by good skiers in all snow conditions.

# MAKING SURE THE BOOTS FIT

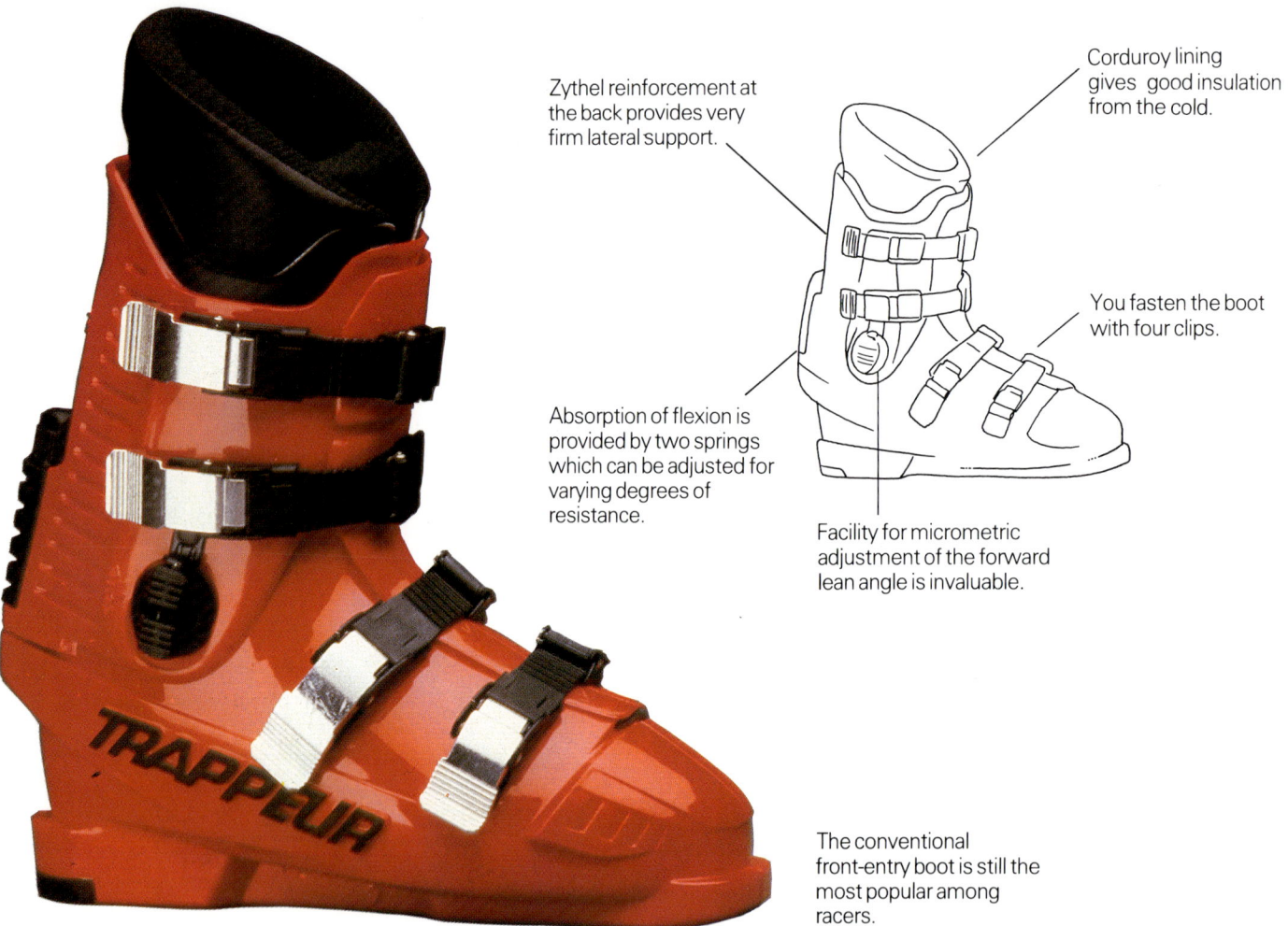

Zythel reinforcement at the back provides very firm lateral support.

Corduroy lining gives good insulation from the cold.

You fasten the boot with four clips.

Absorption of flexion is provided by two springs which can be adjusted for varying degrees of resistance.

Facility for micrometric adjustment of the forward lean angle is invaluable.

The conventional front-entry boot is still the most popular among racers.

If there is one particularly important item of ski equipment, it must be boots You can make progress on a mediocre pair of skis in a week's skiing, but one day wearing the wrong boots will probably put an end to your winter sports holiday – ruined by sore, aching feet – or at the very least you will have no hope of improving your technique. The days of leather boots which made skiing a sport for masochists are, thankfully, long gone. Nowadays, the manufacturers have succeeded in reconciling the irreconcilable by providing both comfort *and* precision.

The first plastic boots (made by Lange) were used at the 1968 Olympic Games in Grenoble. They had been imported from America, and four years later any manufacturer who had either not managed, or not wanted, to change to plastic had disappeared from the market. However, the early days were not easy, as plastic outer shells posed a real problem: if the boot responded with precision, then it was very uncomfortable; if it was comfortable, then it resembled a slipper and made precision skiing impossible. Today, all the major Italian, French and Austrian manufacturers have, fortunately, managed to combine these two important factors.

You should therefore have no problem in finding boots to suit your feet. However, this does not mean that any boot will do, so try several different models before you decide. It is not lack of choice that will pose a problem: one of the main options is whether to go for the more traditional front-opening boots, or for the modern rear-entry style which are easier to put on. If you are a beginner, you do not need competition boots, but it is still worth investing in a good-quality pair – you will not regret the extra expense.

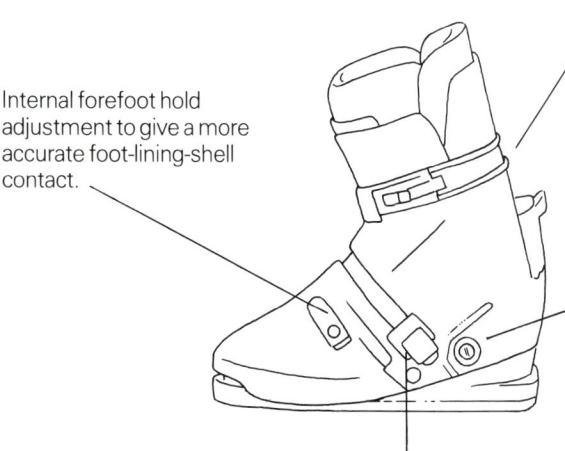

Internal forefoot hold adjustment to give a more accurate foot-lining-shell contact.

Side flex adjustments at the top of the boot. Choice of three positions to give good ski contact with the snow.

Heel hold-down through internal adjustment. This facility gives optimum results for steering the skis.

Micrometrically adjustable clip for the lower leg to ensure a snug fit.

Certain qualities are needed in a modern rear-entry boot if it is to be both efficient and comfortable.

Rear-entry boots are the latest thing on the fashionable slopes. They are a recent introduction and, when provided with superior internal adjustment systems, they give a higher standard of comfort and precision. Some, unfortunately, lack support at the back. However, there is no doubt that these are the boots of the future.

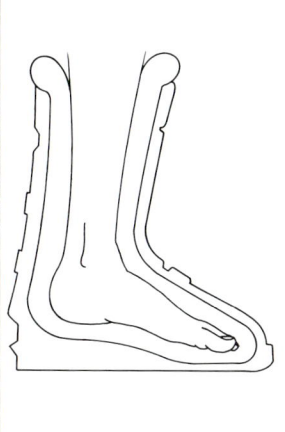

Ten aspects which affect comfort:

**1.** A high, supple leg.

2. No uncomfortable joins or edges at the tops.

**3.** An accurately moulded ankle section.

**4.** The top of the foot should not be constricted.

**5.** Toes should always be comfortable, not squashed.

**6.** The sole should give arch support.

**7.** There should be no discomfort around the ankle.

**8.** The spoiler must not chafe or hurt.

**9.** The boots should be leakproof in all kinds of snow.

**10.** There should be an adequate number of clips.

Eight aspects which affect precision:

**1.** The forward lean angle should suit your foot.

**2.** Angle of flare at the sides should follow your lower-leg profile

**3.** Your heel should be held down firmly: this is vital.

**4.** Allowance for flexing at the front of the boot is indispensable.

**5.** Rear support is also indispensable during flexing.

**6.** The front part of your foot must have good side support for steering your skis.

**7.** Firm support on the inside of the boot tops is needed during edging manoeuvres.

**8.** A poor fit round the front of your foot can affect heel support.

# THE IMPORTANCE OF BINDINGS

Safety bindings started out as simple devices for keeping boot and ski attached, but, like everything else in Alpine skiing, they have developed into very sophisticated pieces of equipment which are virtually 100 per cent safe. Why, then, do skiers still end up with broken bones? Well, to begin with, human error is responsible for almost all skiing accidents, and a fall from a stationary position, when the muscles are relaxed, is more dangerous than a tumble at speed. Second, however good a binding may be, it cannot prevent a skier colliding with an animate – or inanimate – object! And, last but by no means least, more than 60 per cent of bindings are not adjusted according to the manufacturers' instructions. This is sheer stupidity, since nothing could be easier than to find someone qualified to help you – and one turn of a screwdriver could save you from ending up ignominiously on a stretcher. Remember, too, that children's legs are just as fragile as adults', so make sure that their bindings are properly adjusted as well as your own.

There are several types of bindings on the market, but 90 per cent of them consist of a toe-piece, heel-piece and ski-stopper (the other 10 per cent are plate bindings). All of them are multi-directional (but not omni-directional, since few will release in a fall straight backwards) and most are elastic (to stay put during 'false alarms'); some have pivots, some sensors; some open diagonally . . . and so on. All this sophisticated technology is capable of coping with 99.9 per cent of falls.

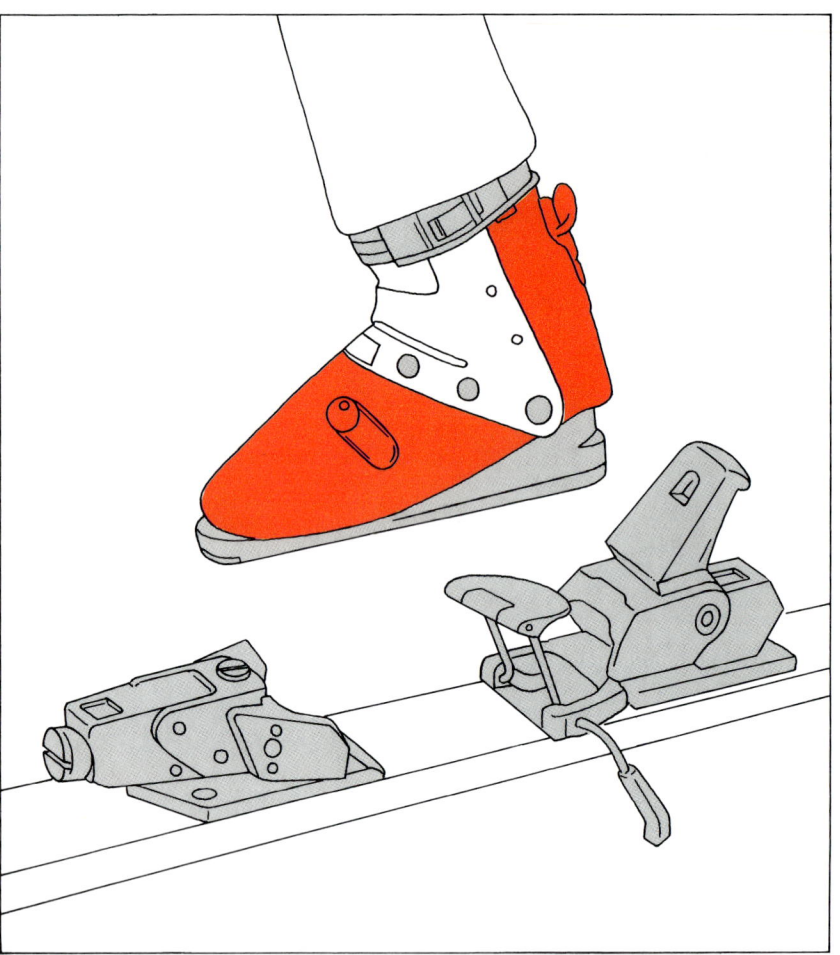

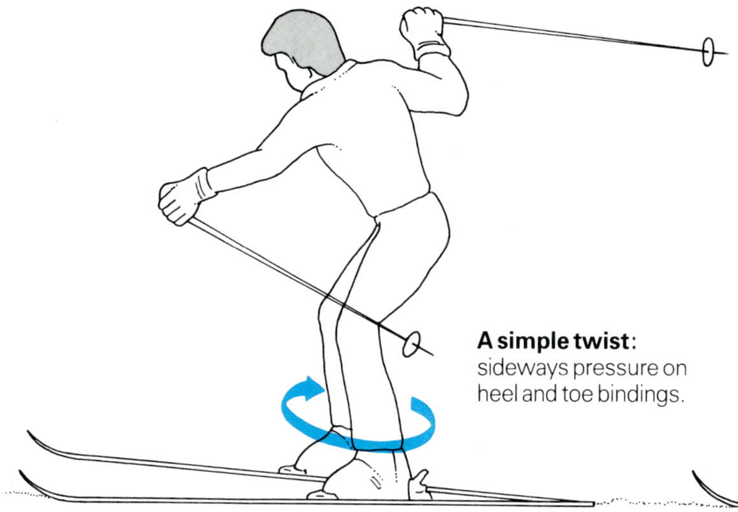

**A simple twist:** sideways pressure on heel and toe bindings.

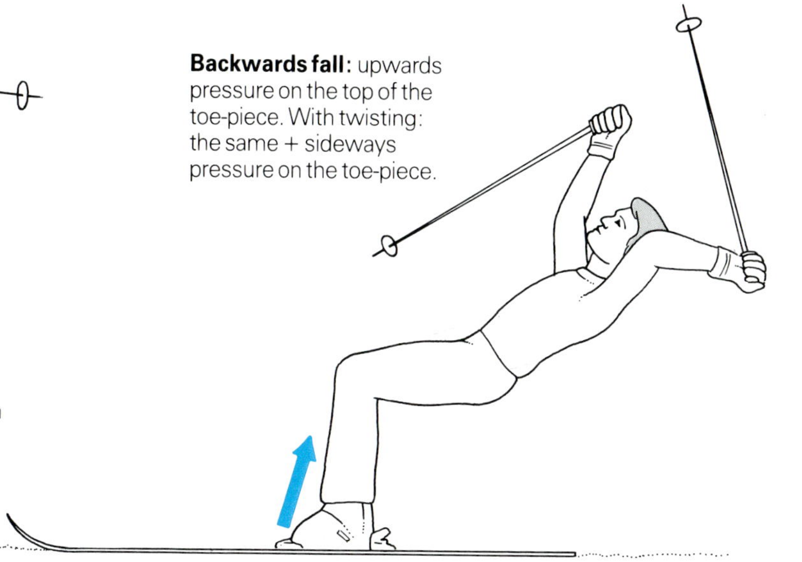

**Backwards fall:** upwards pressure on the top of the toe-piece. With twisting: the same + sideways pressure on the toe-piece.

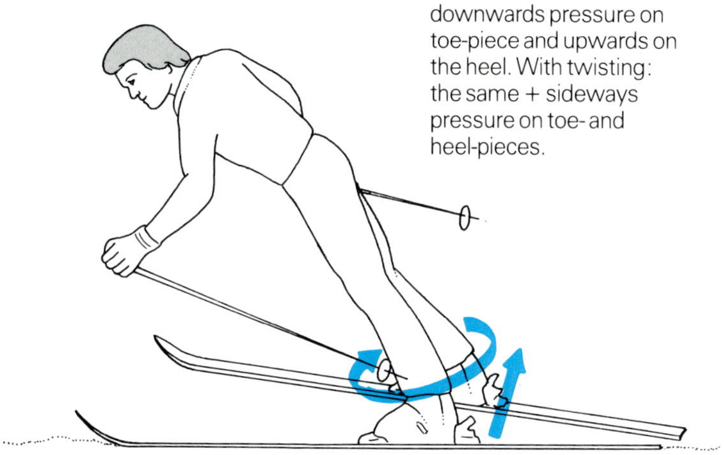

**Forwards fall:** downwards pressure on toe-piece and upwards on the heel. With twisting: the same + sideways pressure on toe- and heel-pieces.

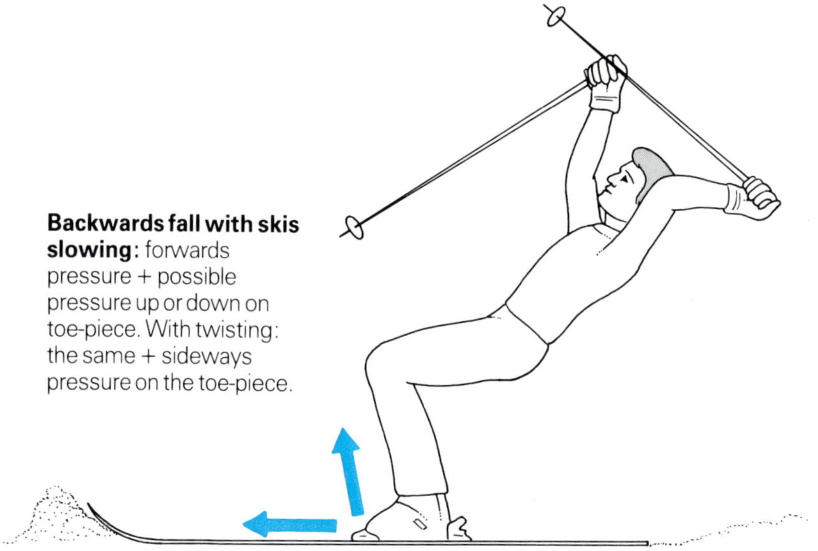

**Backwards fall with skis slowing:** forwards pressure + possible pressure up or down on toe-piece. With twisting: the same + sideways pressure on the toe-piece.

A recent innovation in ski design and safety is the ski-brake. This is a spring-loaded device which comes into action should the ski be separated, on the piste, from the skier. The brake bites into the snow and stops the ski sliding out of reach. It is then relatively simple to find the errant ski and continue on your way.

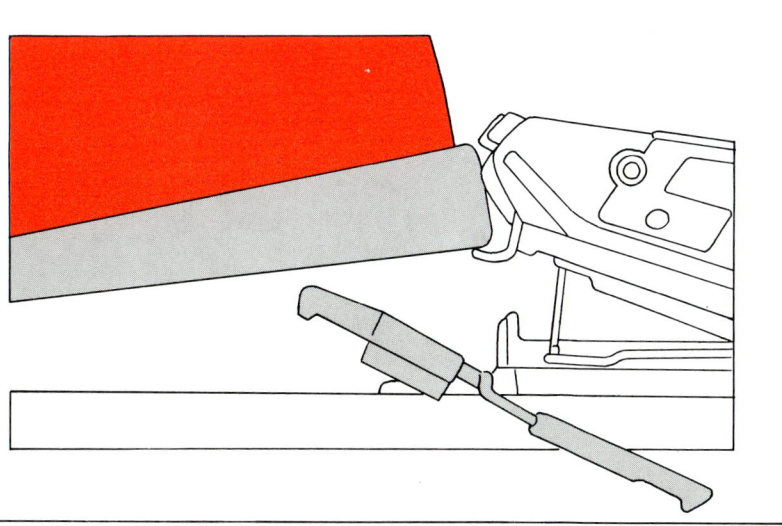

*Above:* This sequence of illustrations demonstrates the ways in which bindings react to the different directional pressures which are imposed in falling. There is no such thing as a straight forward fall, but most can be classified under one of the illustrated headings.

# CLOTHING AND ACCESSORIES

Skis, boots and bindings are three indispensable parts of a skier's equipment, but other items are needed as well. The main ones are given below, although the list is not exhaustive.

CLOTHING: either salopettes/trousers and an anorak, or a one-piece suit. The material should be non-slip, the trouser bottoms should fit snugly around the leg of the boot and, of course, warmth and comfort are of the essence.

POLES: should have moulded handles or straps, but in either case must be well balanced. They need to be slightly longer than average for powder snow skiing.

GLOVES: should be made of supple, waterproof leather. Never dry them on a radiator.

HATS OR CAPS: choose as fashionable a style as you like but remember that a ski hat should keep your ears warm and should not fly off when you start to pick up speed.

SUNGLASSES OR GOGGLES: the latter are useful in powder or when it snows. The essential for either is that the lenses really protect your eyes, otherwise you risk getting snow-blindness. Goggles are preferable in poor visibility (yellow lens for mist, brown for sunshine) and for children (it is harder to lose goggles!).

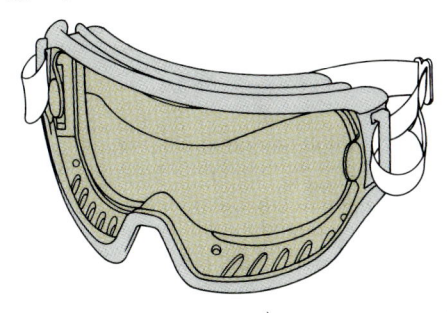

*Right:* One advantage of goggles is that you can slide them up your arm if you want to change to sunglasses or take them off for sunbathing – weather permitting!

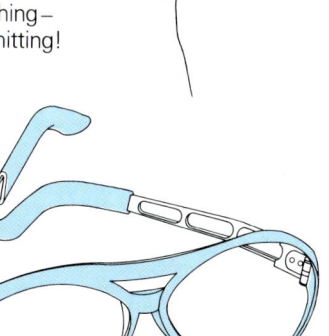

*Above:* Sunglasses should be of good quality, with lenses which completely screen out the ultraviolet rays. They should also fit snugly on your nose, as nothing is more annoying than having to keep pushing them back in place.

A one-piece, lined, waterproof ski suit for warmth and comfort. Poles should have good handles, straps and balance.
Gloves and mittens must be waterproof, and not too tight.
Headgear must fit well to keep you warm.
Après-ski boots, of whatever style, should be waterproof, and have non-slip soles.
A bag may be useful for carrying spare clothing or a packed lunch . . .

35

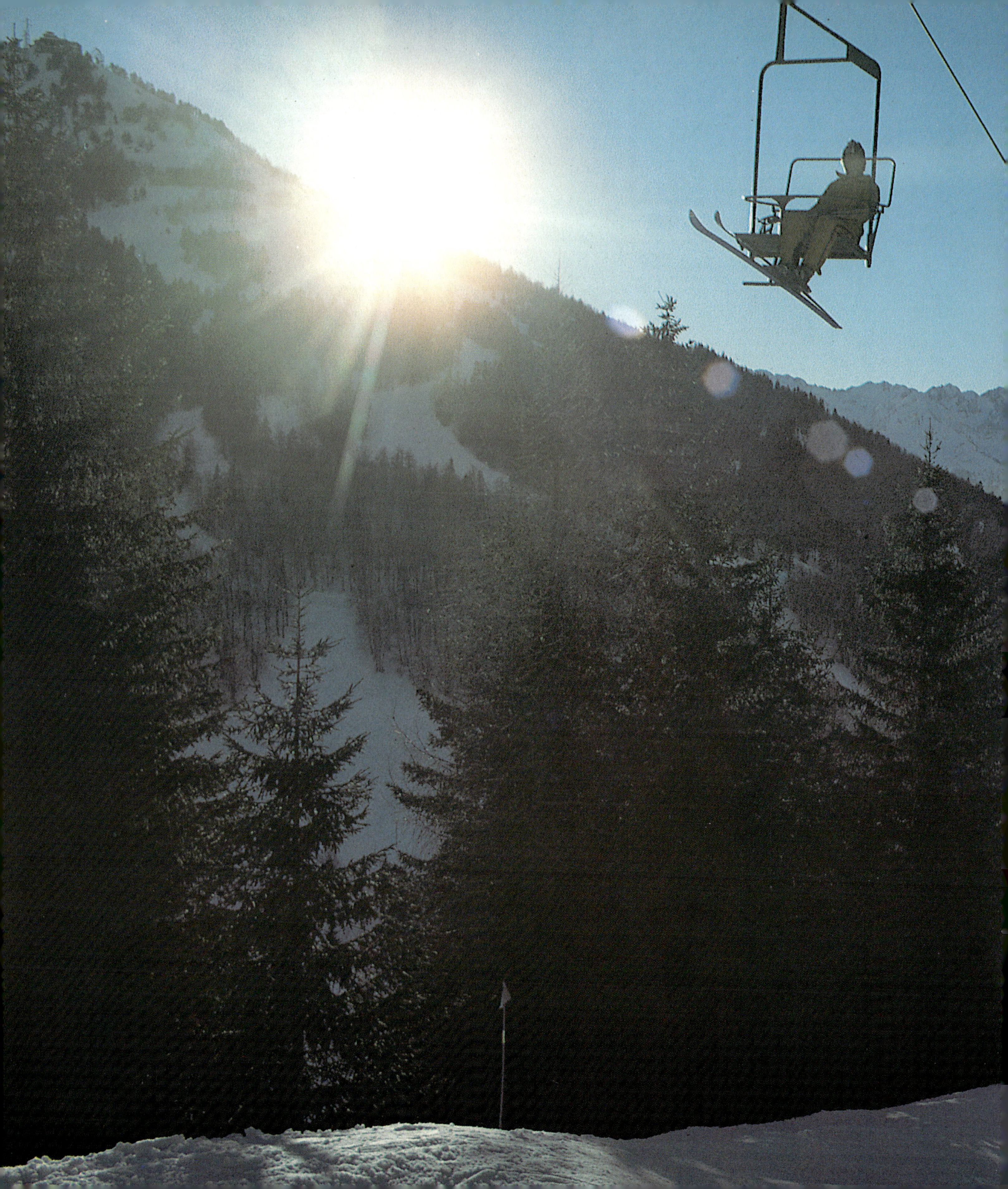

# SKI TEACHING IN FRANCE

This section looks at exactly what happens once you have arrived at your resort. It deals in detail with the teaching elements of each class and progresses beyond that to the excitement and the thrills you feel in off-piste activities.

# WHO ARE THE INSTRUCTORS?

**EVERY RESORT HAS ITS ESF**
In each French ski resort, all the instructors with a State Diploma in the area are grouped together under the central administration of an ESF. The aim of this voluntary arrangement is to provide a more efficient service. The director, instructors and secretaries are on hand at the ESF reception centre to give advice and to take bookings. The ESF functions in all 207 French resorts, sometimes with several branch offices within a single resort. Nationwide, there are some 9,400 instructors operating under the aegis of the ESF.

*Above:* The headquarters of the ESF in Grenoble. This is where the organisation and administration of the ski instructors is controlled.

*Left:* You can identify an ESF instructor by this badge. A symbol received after successfully completing the three years of training to become qualified to teach.

## ESF ORGANIZATION

To ensure that reception and instruction are properly co-ordinated, there is only one ESF in each resort. The director is an instructor who has been elected to serve a fixed term by the other instructors; the workload and tuition fees are distributed fairly evenly. Over the years since the creation of the first ESFs in 1945, shared training, mutual support and friendly rivalry between the instructors have been shown to produce a high level of competence.

The administrative tasks carried out by the ESF office staff consist of making bookings and confirmations, timetabling, accounts, issuing test results and providing information.

Once a school reaches a certain size, a technical director is elected to help the director with the on-piste organization of lessons and tests, and to supervise the quality of the instruction.

## MADE-TO-MEASURE COURSES

The range of ESF pupils covers a broad spectrum of motivation, ages, levels of fitness and financial means. The ESF therefore needs to offer an equally wide range of services, and instructors can teach you how to ski and to perfect your technique, or simply provide encouragement and guidance to make the most of the ski area. Whatever your level in Alpine or cross-country skiing, whether you are on your own or with friends, you can join group lessons (often structured as a course), have private tuition, or even book an instructor for the whole day. Whichever you choose, you would be well advised to book in advance at the ESF office.

## GROUP LESSONS

Groups consist of about ten skiers of similar age, motivation and ability. Courses are planned over a week, during which the instructor follows a set teaching plan, forming part of the overall progressive tuition scheme. Each group lesson lasts between two and three hours.

It makes sense to take a week's course of lessons if you want to achieve steady progress, and this can be done by going to the ESF office and buying a morning (six morning lessons), afternoon (six afternoon lessons) or daily (12 lessons) 'weekly card'.

Most ESFs cater for pupils whose stay is of a less conventional duration and a single ticket can be bought if you wish to attend only one lesson.

Pupils meet their instructor at a designated signboard and lessons always start promptly. On Mondays, when most group courses begin, the instructors put their pupils through their paces to make sure that they are all at the same level, and to avoid too much changing during the week.

*Above and below:* A group of ski instructors at one selected resort and, below, getting the feel of the snow.

## PRIVATE LESSONS

Skiers can have the instructor of their choice by booking him at the ski-school office. If the lesson is going to last just one or two hours, it is classed as a private lesson; if the instructor is booked for one or more days, this is full-time private instruction. If you do not know any of the instructors, or if the one you want is unavailable, the ESF will offer you someone suitable.

In both private lessons and full-time tuition, either an individual or a group of friends can book an instructor. Private lessons consist of tuition in technique – a detailed explanation of the various movements and correction of faults – while full-time instruction is usually more of a guided tour of the ski area, sometimes travelling from one resort to another. In both cases, the number of pupils is limited to four.

## GROUPS, PARTIES, RACES

If a larger group needs one or more instructors, the leader can ask the ESF director, who will deal with their request, bearing in mind the group's needs and the availability of instructors.

This is standard practice for day outings, organized parties of children or adults, or for arranging races for sports clubs which may need extra equipment and a specialist instructor.

## ESF TESTS

These tests are used for measuring pupils' progress and for gauging their ability so that they can be put in the right class. Both in Alpine and cross-country skiing there are two categories: marked class tests, the results of which show what technical level a skier has reached in the official syllabus of ski tuition; and timed performance tests, which provide a comparison between individual skiers and the fastest instructors, who set the base times on which medal awards are calculated.

These tests are held regularly every week. In all cases, a good showing in the tests is a stimulus to improvement, a way of checking your own ability and a reward for the hard work.

The Syndicat National des Moniteurs du Ski Français makes sure that the tests are set at the same standard in all ESFs. There is also an international scheme for grading pupils within the International Association of Ski Instructors.

## SKI INSTRUCTORS ARE PROFESSIONALS

Today there are more than 9,000 instructors working with the Ecole du Ski Français. You may wonder what sort of people they are, how they learned their job, and what kind of training they have had.

Well, ski instructors are put through very demanding training programmes. Anyone 17 years of

*Left:* A group of beginners taking instruction from their ESF teacher.

*Above:* The advanced or competent skier will go with an instructor to a higher altitude and engage in off-piste skiing.

*Right:* There is room too for the children. Here a child is learning to jump.

age or over, with a minimum of the silver chamois ski medal, the ability to speak at least one foreign language, and education up to fourth-form level, can take the entrance test. The would-be instructors begin their training with a technical examination, which they must pass before they can go on to take a regional introductory course. This course consists of 45 days in a ski school, combining a mixture of compulsory general and more specific courses, together with a technical and theoretical training common to all who intend to work in the field of mountain sports. After this varied basic training, the candidate can apply to the Ecole Nationale de Ski et d'Alpinisme at Chamonix for a place on their six-week course.

42

**BEGINNERS**

# YOUR FIRST TIME ON SKIS

There you are, kitted out from head to toe and all ready to make your dream come true. At last the time has come to put on your skis; they may not be as long as racing skis, but still... Words like 'anticipation', 'counter-rotation', 'carving' and the idea of 'swallowing the bumps' might as well be Chinese at this stage, but your instructor will see you through those first anxious moments and give you confidence. To begin with you will probably feel like a fish out of water in this new environment of cold, snowy weather at an unaccustomed altitude; your skis will seem too long, your boots stiff and like lead weights, and your balance will desert you – one minute you will be convinced you are about to topple forwards, and the next that you are about to land on your bottom. As for keeping a sideways balance, the least said the better! However, over the next two or three days, you will learn to feel at home on the snow. This is the aim of the beginners' class. You will learn to move on the snow; first on the flat, then on gentle slopes.

**BEGINNERS**

# LENGTH OF SKI AND THE SKIER

There are certain factors to take into account when choosing the length of your skis. These include your ability level, of course, but also what kind of skiing you are going to do, your physical fitness, temperament (aggressive or passive), etc. If you are a novice your best course is to choose compact skis of your own height, or even a little shorter. In this case, you would be well advised to hire rather than buy, since you will only need them for a week or two until you have finished Class 1. If you do decide to buy, you can use compact skis later on for powder snow skiing. Once you have graduated to elementary technique (Class 2), you can change to 'sports' skis, some 10 to 15 cm longer than your height, depending on your weight and temperament. You can stay with these skis right up to competition level although, once you reach Class 3, it might be better to use 'Grand Sports', or even competition (giant slalom-type) skis, which are between 15 and 25 cm longer than your height. With 'Grand Sports' you will be comfortable both on the pistes and on trickier surfaces, while competition skis will give better results on ice and hard-packed snow, and slightly reduced efficiency in poor snow or powder. Competition skis, as the name implies, are intended for competition skiing; in other words, for aggressive skiers.

Grand Sports skis, on the other hand, are for high-altitude touring and recreational skiing. In both cases, these skis will last you for many years.

The principal French manufacturers classify their skis into four groups: Competition, Grand Tourisme, Tourisme and Compact. These skis are designed for different conditions or uses, but they can all play a part in the ESF teaching programme.

**Competition**
Used for competition and ice skiing – competition class: + 20 to 30 cm.

**Grand Tourisme**
Used in all snow conditions and terrains – competition class and Class 3: + 20 cm.

**Tourisme**
Used on-piste – Classes 1 and 2: + 10 cm.

**Compacts**
Used for beginners and Class 1, good for powder snow: skier's height.

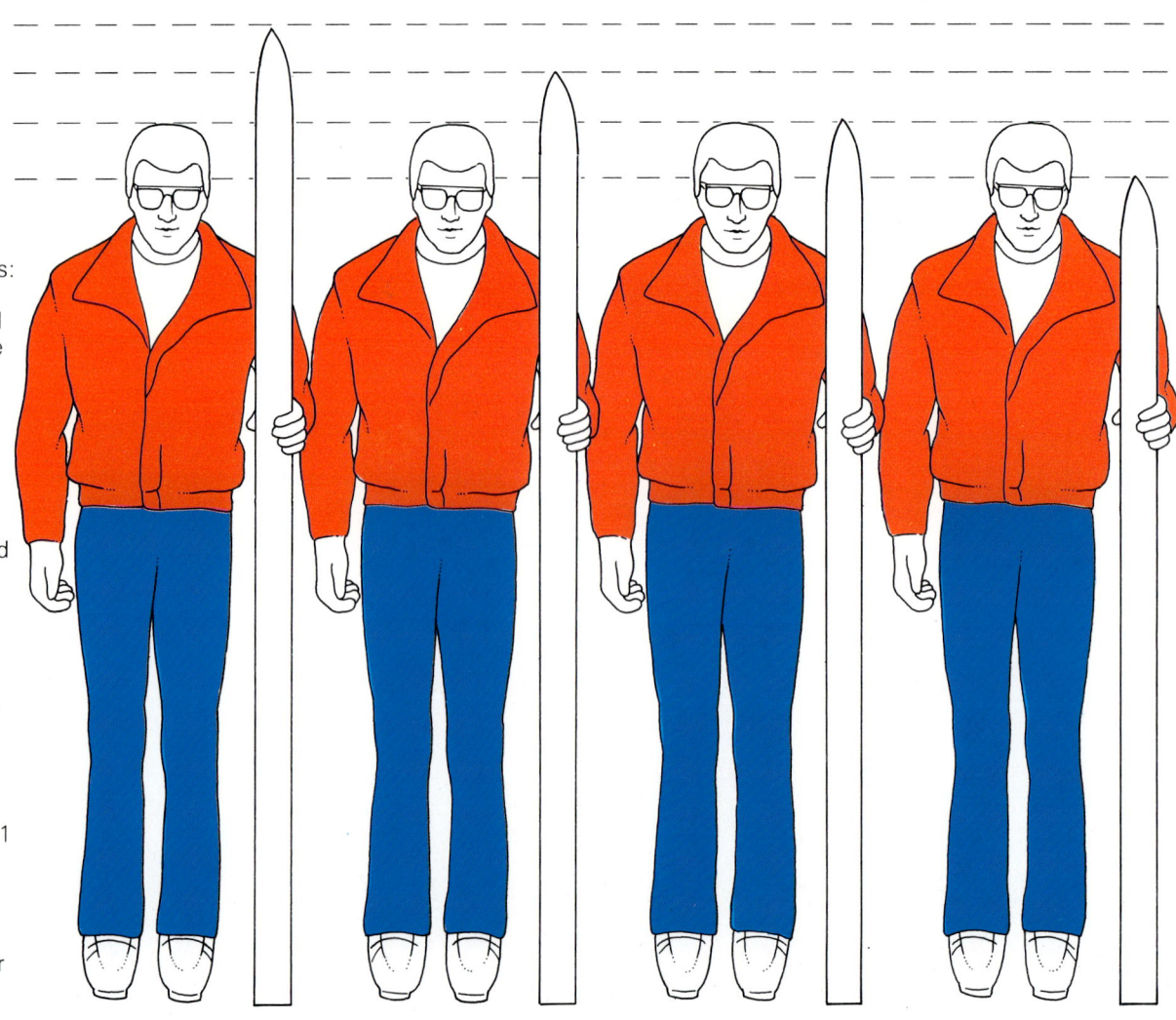

**Ski Évolutif**
Ten years or so ago, calculating the correct ski length was a straightforward affair. You simply stood your skis upright next to you, stretched up your arm and, if your fingertips were level with the ski tip, then your skis were the right length. This system meant that even beginners wore skis which were between 30 and 35 cm longer than their height, and the result was that they found learning to ski very hard work indeed. This is why 'ski évolutif' was devised. Novices started out with 1-metre skis then, as they progressed, moved on to longer skis. A more recent development was the introduction of compact skis (equal to the skier's height). They are very easy to handle on the piste although in some resorts, beginners can still choose to start on 1.3 m skis.

**BEGINNERS**

# HOW TO MOVE ON LEVEL GROUND

Boots on, heart beating sixteen to the dozen, you have just met your instructor and fellow beginners and, on foot, with your skis in one hand and your poles in the other, you set off for your first training area. It will be so gentle a slope as to be virtually level, and close to the resort. Now you have to learn how to move and walk again on a completely alien surface; and skis are not going to make your life any easier to begin with!

The first important lesson is, of course, how to put on your skis. You will already have tried them on in the shop, but then you were in the warm, with somebody to show you how the bindings work, and how to place your boot. Suddenly, in the snow, things are different: the cold makes you all fingers and thumbs, especially with those dratted thick leather gloves, and the altitude will make you slightly breathless. Take your time. Set the bindings, then lay your skis parallel on a flat piece of snow (later you will lay them at right-angles to the slope, otherwise you might have to scramble down the mountain to retrieve them). Put first one foot, then the other (toe against the front) in the bindings, making sure before you do so that no snow is stuck to the soles of your boots. Then simply push your heels down into the back parts of the bindings.

Now you will begin to experience all kinds of new sensations. Those long 'planks' under your feet are surprisingly heavy and cumbersome, with a disconcerting tendency to slide in the wrong direction. There is no need to panic; your instructor will soon teach you how to show your skis who is master.

Your first lesson, with a pole in each hand (remember to put the straps on properly), will be how to walk on the flat by sliding your skis forward one at a time. This is a simple movement to learn – the alternating step – in which the right ski goes forward at the same time as the left pole, then you follow with a simultaneous movement of the left ski and right pole. Another basic technique learnt at this stage is the pole-push: a simultaneous push on both poles to make you slide forwards with both skis together. Whether by 'walking' or the pole-push, you will soon reach the limit of your training area. How do you turn round? This will be the third movement in your first day's teaching programme: the step turn, executed first on the flat, then on a slight slope. To begin with, turning left on the flat: lift the left ski tip and move it round a little to the left, then bring your right ski alongside. If you repeat this movement enough times, you will end up facing the way you wish to travel. The movement on a gentle slope is the same, except that you have to place your poles behind you and lean on them to avoid sliding backwards. After you have mastered this technique – very much the beginner – you then develop the kick turn.

*Right:* Cleaning the soles of your boots. Before putting on your skis, make sure that there is no snow on the soles of your boots. If there is, scrape it off with the point of your pole.

*Right:* Putting on your skis. Do not forget to raise the heel of the binding. Place your skis on the snow, either one at a time or simultaneously, but never pointing downhill.

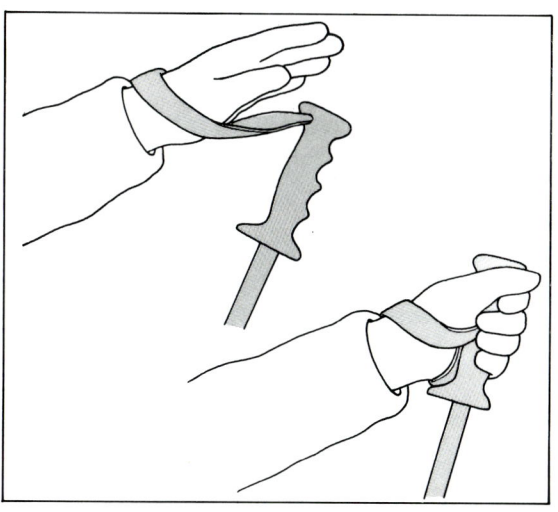

*Left:* Taking hold of the poles. Your poles should be held securely, which is why the straps are so important. First adjust the strap length, then put your hand through the loop from below and close your fingers around the top of the strap and the pole grip.

*Above:* Step turn on the flat. On level ground you can practise this movement without poles. To turn left, lift the tip of your left ski, move it round then bring the right ski alongside. Repeat as necessary.

*Below:* The alternating step (walking). This is the usual step for level ground. Move the right ski and left pole forward together, then the left ski and right pole.

**BEGINNERS**

# FALLING DOWN AND GETTING UP

Falling down is, hopefully, a fringe activity, but you still need to learn how to do it painlessly and, above all, how to get up again without wasting energy.

As soon as a fall seems inevitable, bend your legs as quickly as you can (you will not have so far to fall) and try to keep your knees together. Whatever happens, do your best to fall sideways (preferably the uphill side if you are on a slope) and slightly backwards. This will ensure that you do the minimum of damage to yourself and that the bindings release easily. Falling forwards is a nasty experience on hard-packed snow, but on powder you should come out of it in one piece, and your companions can enjoy a good laugh at your expense!

Once down, you need to learn the best way of getting back on your feet. This is simple on level ground: just bring your skis parallel, get your legs underneath your upper body, and use your poles to help you stand up. On a slope, however, the manoeuvre is slightly more complicated. First, untangle your skis and place them parallel, at right angles to the fall-line and downhill of your body. Dig the ski edges well into the snow and lever yourself upright with your poles. If the slope is very steep (or if you have parted company with your poles), push yourself up with an arm. Never try to get up unless your skis are lying across the fall line, or you will end up back on your bottom.

Whatever you do after falling, take your time in doing it. Do not panic. If you fall and tumble or skid just relax until you stop. Then orientate yourself to the slope, have a look around and get up.

*Left:* On level ground: getting up is as easy as pie. Just place your skis parallel and bend your legs slightly. Then, using your poles, sit up, and with one more push you are on your feet. Poor ski positioning is the cause of much wasted energy.

*Below:* On a slope: the procedure is roughly the same, except that the skis must be not only parallel, but also placed straight across the fall line, otherwise you will end up in the snow again.

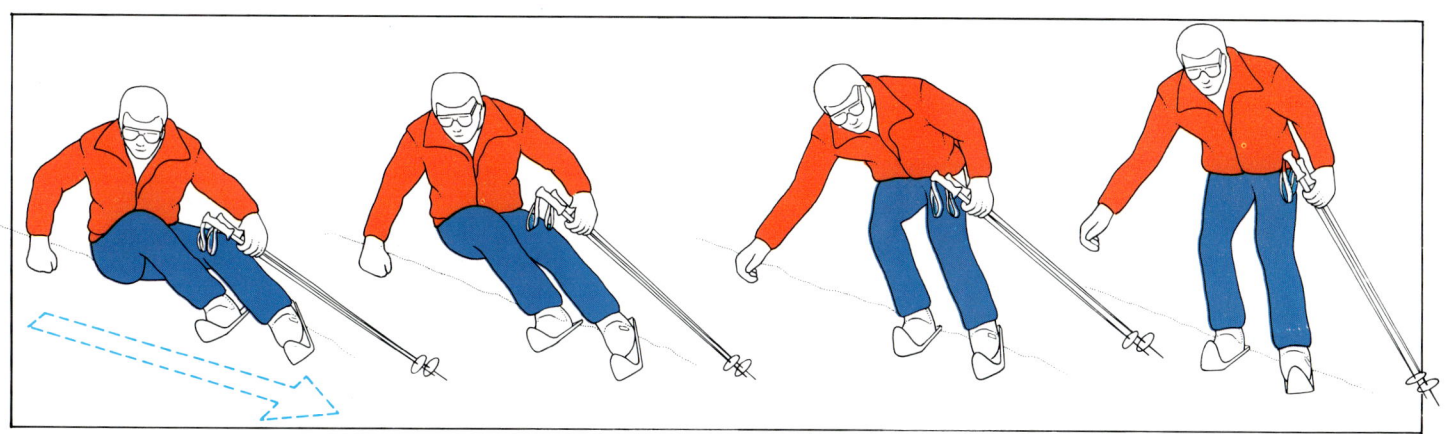

49

## BEGINNERS

# SIDE STEP AND HERRINGBONE

Level ground is fine to start with, but you will soon want to try out the slopes, and he who comes down must first go up. Ski-lifts come later, but in the meantime there are three different techniques you can use for going uphill. Once you have learned them, you can use them as necessary, according to how fit you are, where you want to get to, and the steepness of the slope.

SIDE-STEPPING: useful for steep slopes. Aim for the steepest line, keeping your skis at right angles to the fall line to avoid sliding back down. Plant your poles level with your bindings, with the uphill one slightly further away from your skis. Then, leaning on both poles, step sideways and upwards with each ski alternately.

DIAGONAL SIDE-STEPPING: this is a little less tiring, but also less effective. You use the same basic movement, but moving your skis forward as well as uphill. Here, too, you can move your poles as you move the uphill ski, then bring the downhill ski alongside, just as in normal side-stepping.

HERRINGBONE ideal for gentler slopes. Face uphill and, keeping your ski-tips apart, progress up the slope by lifting and putting down your skis on either side of the fall line, pressing on your inside edges all the time. Push down on the tops of your poles with the palms of your hands. Your arms have to work very hard in the herringbone movement and you may tire quickly. Also, the steeper the slope, the wider the angle between your skis should be. Avoid damaging the running surfaces of your skis by lifting your skis and putting them down again far enough apart to make sure that the tails do not knock together. You will soon discover that this technique is less exhausting if you rock slightly from side to side with each step.

None of these techniques are meant to take you very far but they must be mastered. They are needed especially after a fall or in times of emergency when you may need to reach safety quickly.

*Right:* Side-stepping is used for steep slopes. Advanced skiers also use this technique for climbing slopes without having to take off their skis. Lean on both poles as you move alternate skis.

*Left and right:* The herringbone step is for gentler slopes. Take alternate steps, facing the steepest line of the slope, tips pointing outwards on either side of the fall line, and keeping pressure on the inside edges. Remember to lean on your poles to avoid sliding back down.

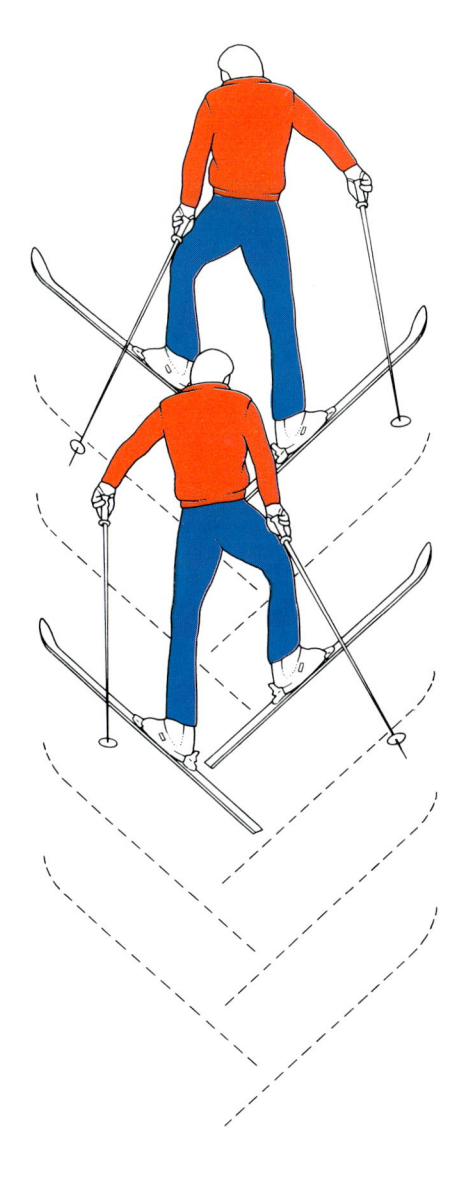

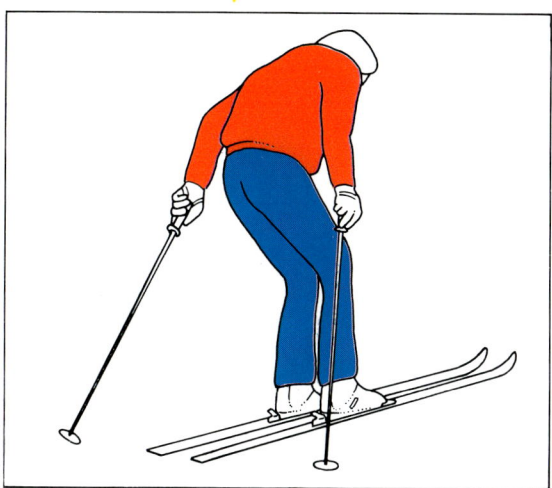

*Left:* Ending a side-step climb. When you reach the end of your side-step climb, execute a step turn on a gently sloping part of the hill until you are in the right position.

**BEGINNERS**

# INITIAL BALANCING

Straight running is when, according to the official definition, 'the direction of movement is the same as the axis of the skis, the latter being maintained parallel'. This can be either straight down the fall line, or at an angle to it. You will be working on straight running throughout your skiing tuition, starting with gentle slopes, then over changing gradients, accelerating over bumps and, finally, high-speed schussing. Before anything so ambitious, you have to learn the correct stance for straight running on a gentle slope, since your balance depends on your stance. Once you have mastered this basic position, all the variants called for by changes in terrain, slope, speed, etc, will come naturally.

To start with, choose a fairly gentle, even slope, beginning and ending on level ground, and ski down the fall line, keeping your skis parallel and 10 to 20 cm apart. Your weight should be spread equally over both feet; your ankles, knees and hips should be slightly flexed; your upper body should lean forward slightly; your arms should be held apart in front of you, the elbows bent and hands holding the poles in a relaxed position. Do not alter your stance during your first few runs – this will help you to overcome any initial tendency to stiffness. This basic position can, of course, be modified – in soft snow the skis should be closer together, on ice further apart (and on their inside edges).

Other important points are: do not look down at your ski tips but rather, as when driving a car, look well ahead and try to relax as much as possible. To help you relax, try the following few basic movements as you ski down the slope: turn your head, first to one side, then the other; stretch your arms out then pull them back into your body, while at the same time shifting your weight from one ski to the other, or bending down as though you are picking something up from the ground.

When you are traversing, this stance alters again because of the different ski positioning. Although the distance between the skis remains effectively the same, you have to create a gap by advancing the uphill ski by about 10 cm compared with the downhill ski. Your upper body will then tend to lean slightly away from the slope, automatically exerting more pressure on the downhill ski.

Now that you have learned a good basic stance, you must concentrate on finding a balanced position in all circumstances.

The basic position: your balance depends on this. It lies somewhere between the leaning backwards or too far forwards which you will experience during your early lessons.

The correct stance:
1. Never look down at your skis (they are not going anywhere without you!), but look ahead at least 20 m. This ensures that you will be aware of, and anticipate, changes in terrain.

2. Shoulders should face down the slope during schussing down the fall line, and slightly downhill during traversing.

3. Your upper body should lean forwards slightly.

4. Hold your arms loosely open, elbows bent and wrists relaxed.

5. Ankles, knees and hips should be always slightly flexed.

6. Hold your poles firmly, but not with clenched fists. Pole points should be planted, when necessary, about 20 cm outside your skis.

7. Skis should always be parallel, and the distance between them will vary, according to snow conditions, between 10 and 20 cm.

## BEGINNERS

# STEP TURNS

You probably still feel a little awkward on skis, but the following exercise will enable you to feel more in control: the star turn. Practise it first on the flat, then on a gentle slope. A star turn is achieved through a series of angled movements of your skis, either with or without poles. You can pivot around either the tips or the tails of your skis.

On the flat, this is a relatively problem-free exercise. To turn left, for example, you lift the tip of the left ski and move it to the left, keeping the ski tail on the snow. Then bring the right ski round alongside the left one. Carry on repeating this movement until you are facing the way you want. Things become somewhat trickier on a slight slope, as you will have to use your poles. Stick them in behind you and lean on the tops of the handles to stop yourself sliding backwards. If you are facing uphill you will obviously have to pivot around your tails. If you are at the top of the hill and want to turn to ski down (at the top of a ski-lift, for example), you will use a star turn, but with the tips as a pivoting point. Assuming you have side-stepped up a gentle slope and want to ski back down, then a star turn round your tips is the one to choose. Twist your upper body away from the slope, plant your poles down near your ski tips, and execute a star turn round your tips. Once you are pointing downhill, simply stop leaning on your poles. If you are on short skis and are fit enough, you can always try doing this 90° turn with a small jump.

After mastering the step turn the same movement can now be applied in other circumstances. If you find you are sliding on a gentle slope exactly the same procedure can be used to turn – while on the move. But only one or two steps can be taken. Therefore it is not so much a turn as an effective way of changing direction. For example you may find it necessary to change direction slightly in order to maintain your momentum by keeping in the fall line.

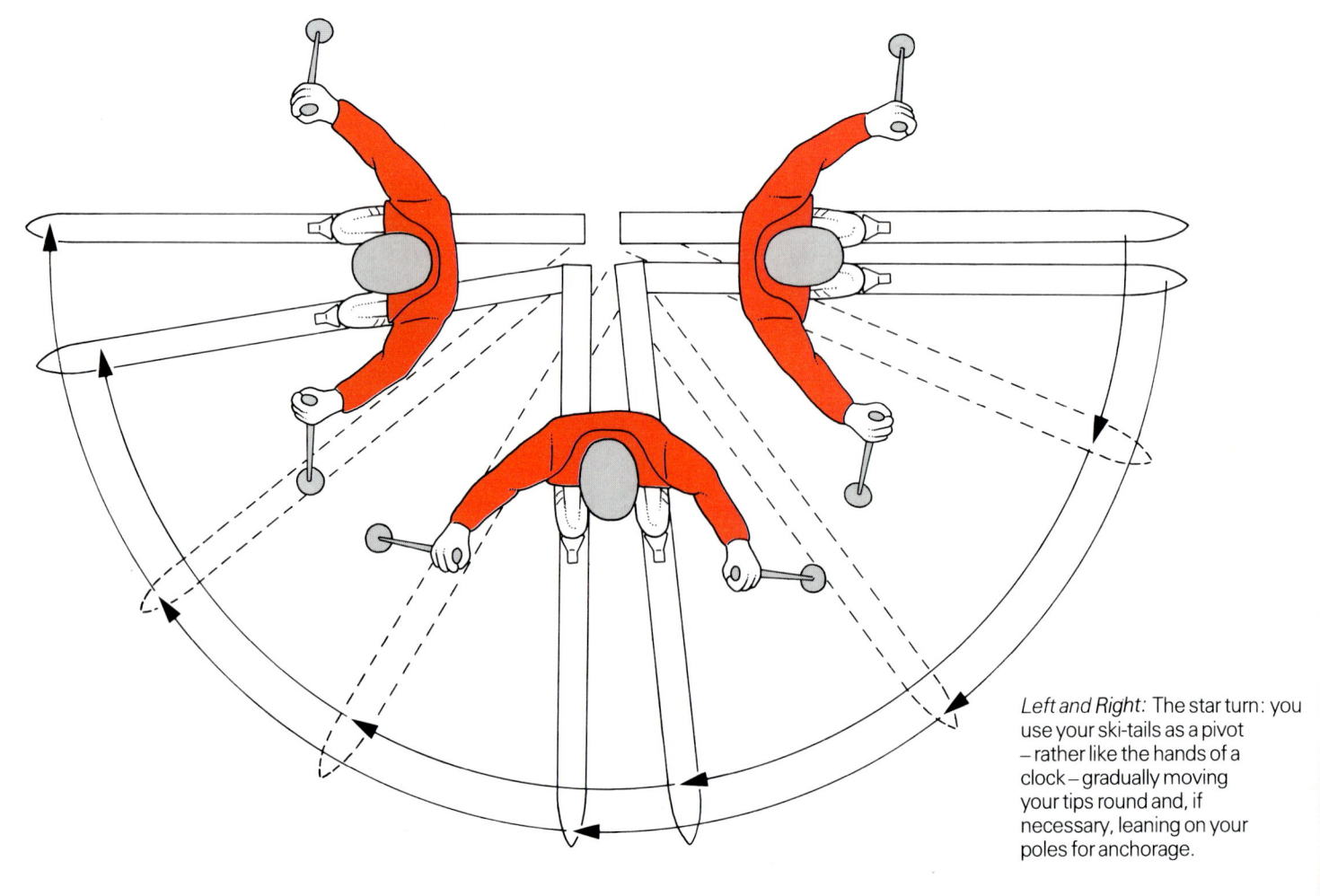

*Left and Right:* The star turn: you use your ski-tails as a pivot – rather like the hands of a clock – gradually moving your tips round and, if necessary, leaning on your poles for anchorage.

*Left and Right:* To turn to face down the slope: use your tips as a pivot and your poles for support

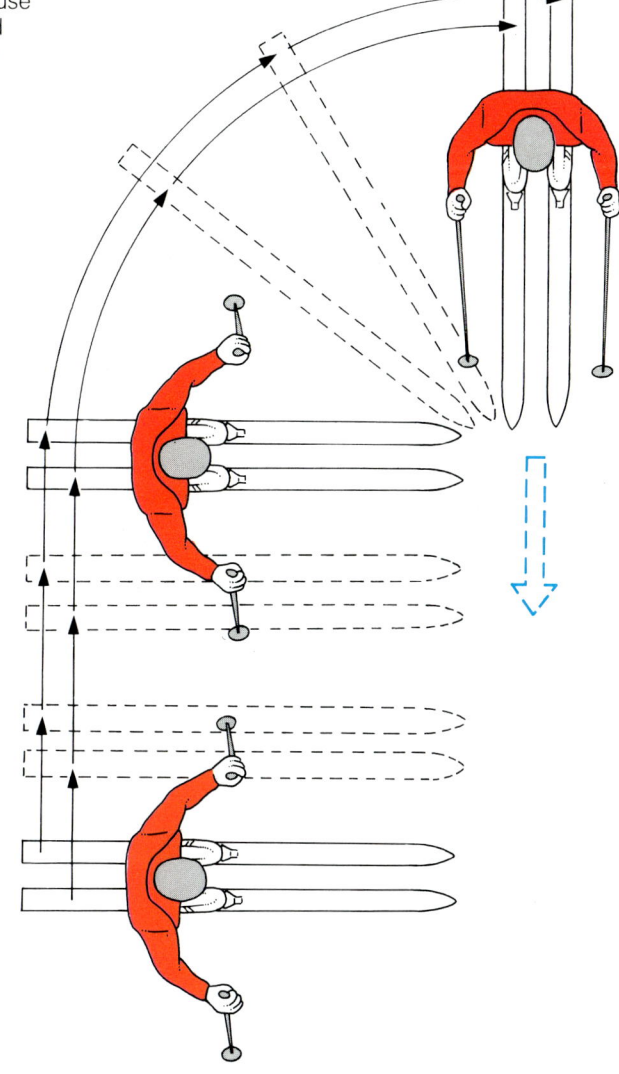

*Left:* this is what happens if you do not keep the ski-tail pressed down on the snow – you lose your pivoting point.

55

**BEGINNERS**

# THE SNOW PLOUGH

The snowplough is one of your most important early lessons since it can be used both as a brake and in your first turns. Starting from a straight-running position down the slope, ski-tips level, separate your skis by about 30 to 40 cm, keep your weight evenly over both skis, then press outwards with your heels and turn your ankles inwards. The tails of your skis will automatically open as you do this. For the best results, your hips, knees and ankles should be flexed, and your knees turning slightly inwards. Make sure you do not let your ski-tips cross. For your first attempts choose a gentle slope which levels off at the bottom and is covered with well-packed snow.

At the first opportunity, learn the snowplough turn, as it leads naturally into the elementary turn. Traverse the slope in a snowplough position, then steadily increase the pressure on the uphill ski as you pivot it in the direction of the turn. The uphill ski starts off almost flat and gradually moves on to its inside edge while, simultaneously, the weight is transferred from the edge of the downhill ski. Keep your body centred between the skis throughout the move. As soon as the outside ski has crossed the fall line, put more weight on it and maintain the pivoting, at the same time keeping the inside ski as flat as possible.

Once you have mastered the snowplough turn you will be ready for the ski-lift, Class 1 and the elementary turn. This latter is a complete turn downhill, starting with a snowplough or a stem (a stem is a manoeuvre in which one ski is placed at an angle to the other one which stays parallel to the direction of movement). A stem turn can be uphill or downhill: an uphill stem is a gliding movement while traversing, in which the tail of the uphill ski is opened; a downhill stem is a braking manoeuvre in a traverse, in which the tail of the downhill ski is opened.

Snowplough and stem movements are often instinctively used by beginners in defensive situations, and, while the snowplough is only briefly introduced in ESF classes, it is a useful way of controlling your speed or direction at this stage. Where instruction takes place on short skis, the convergence may hardly be noticed.

*Left:* This photograph of a skier on short skis demonstrates the fundamental technique of the snowplough to get the skis onto their inside edges is more important than having them appear to converge.

*Above:* The snowplough: this is the first way of controlling your speed. Used on gentle slopes, it is only a brief stage in your learning programme, as is the snowplough turn which evolves from it. You are advised not to stray from the fall line in this turn.

*Left and below:* This sequence demonstrates how the snowplough can be used to stop on gentle slopes. This is the technique used by beginners during their early days on the piste.

# THE DESIGN OF SKI LIFTS

Climbing slopes by pole-pushing is all very well to begin with, or if you are ski-touring on skins, but except in those two cases there is a better method. A ski-lift can take you up one or two thousand metres within a few minutes so that you can really enjoy your descent, and not be exhausted before you start. You should therefore learn how to use the lifts at the earliest opportunity. There are several types current in France: ski-tows, where your skis stay on the ground and you are pulled along by a bar or cable; chairlifts (2-, 3- or 4-seaters) in which you keep your skis on but are carried through the air at a maximum distance from the ground of 20 m; and finally télé-cabines and cablecars, which are cabins slung from cables with a maximum load of between four and 150 people carrying their skis. While even a beginner can cope with a cablecar, ski-tows and chairlifts do take a little getting used to.

Two of the simplest and most popular ski-tows are the T-bar and the button lift. The T-bar is designed to drag two skiers sitting adjacent to each other up the hill whereas the button lift is for a single skier. The technique necessary to master each of these designs is similar. As you stay upright in both instances it is important to stay relaxed and let the tow do the work.

*Below:* The procedure for getting on a chairlift. Place your skis parallel on the line which shows where you should stand when your turn has come for sitting on the chairlift. As the seat comes up behind you, steady it with a hand to prevent it giving you a nasty knock on the calves, sit down promptly, then immediately pull down the safety bar, which usually has a ski rest attached to it. When it comes to getting off, remember to lift the bar just before you reach the summit, and to lift your ski-tips so that they do not catch on the platform edge.

*Above:* Télécabines require you to place your skis in the rack outside, and take your poles inside.

*Above:* Ski-tows should not present any problems. When it is your turn, stand with your skis parallel in the tracks, keeping your legs straight but not rigid, and hold your poles in the offside hand. Take the bar in the other hand, keeping your elbow bent to take the jerk as the lift moves off. Then just relax and let yourself be towed along; but do not sit down on the bar. At the top of the lift, pull on the cable to make it easier to move away from the bar. A step turn will take you clear of the ramp – do not dawdle at this stage, or you might collide with the skier coming up behind. Always remember to move quickly away from the summit once you have left the lift so the skiers behind you also have easy access.

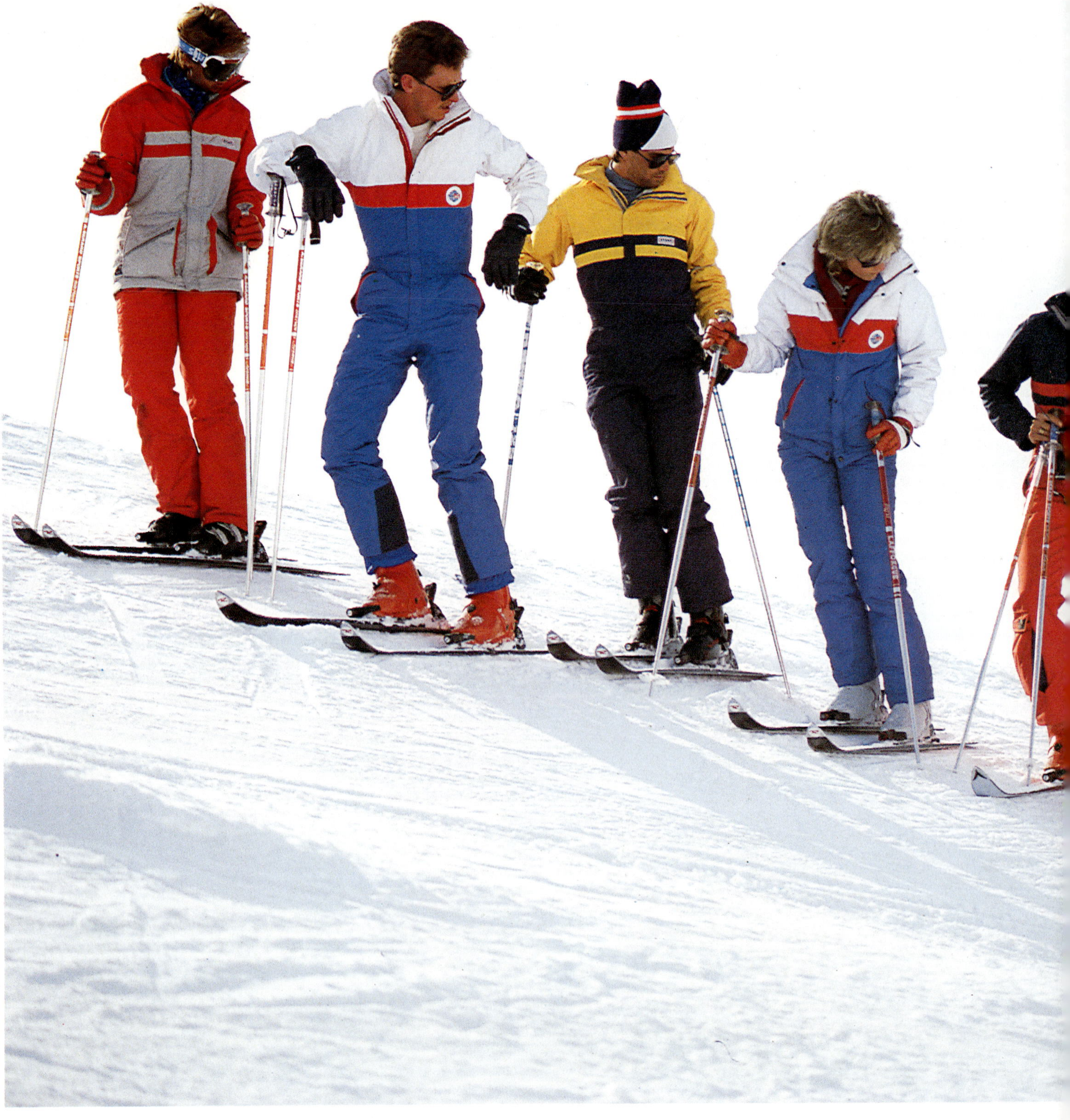

# CLASS 1

# IMPROVED BEGINNERS

In the beginners' class you will have become familiar with the equipment and, more importantly, with the surface on which you are moving – snow. Class 1 (using the same length skis) is where emphasis will be placed on improving your balance with a view to executing your first elementary turns.

BALANCE AND SLIDING. The worst thing about snow is that it is slippery, as you will have discovered to your cost. Luckily, the instructor is there to show you how to control this sliding, and how to keep your balance.

SNOWPLOUGH TURNS. Another problem with snow is that it is not really smooth. You have to learn how to twist and turn to avoid those disconcerting dips and bumps.

SIDE-SLIPPING. Sliding across the slope is nothing like straight running. You will feel as though your skis are taking you down into the valley, but, however unpleasant those first side-slips, they will soon prove their worth.

CHANGING DIRECTION. Skiing across the piste is all very well, but you will have to turn round unless you want to end up in the trees or ravines. Learning the elementary turn will save you this indignity.

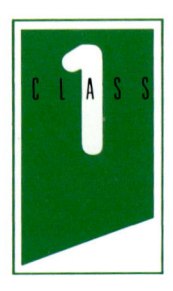

# INTRODUCING TURNS

Thanks to advances in skiing tuition, equipment and conditions (short skis, better running surfaces, rigid boots, well-prepared pistes and refined training methods), you will soon be practising your first turns. Class 1 turns begin with skidded turns based on the snowplough and the stem combined with different types of side-slipping. These lead gradually to the elementary turn. From Class 2 onwards you will learn and perfect parallel turns, which employ unweighting, pivoting and steering techniques. We shall discuss these when we come to them. In the meantime, below is a diagram summarizing the different forces you will come across as you progress, and any techniques they have in common.

When travelling in a curve the directional force is tending to push the body towards the outside of the curve and away from the direction of the turn. Therefore this must be counteracted by the correct positioning of the body. This enables you to keep the skis on the right line. Common faults in learning to master turning techniques include too much weight being applied to the inside ski with the consequence that the ski slides out from beneath you resulting in a fall. Again, the same effect occurs if the skis are kept too flat.

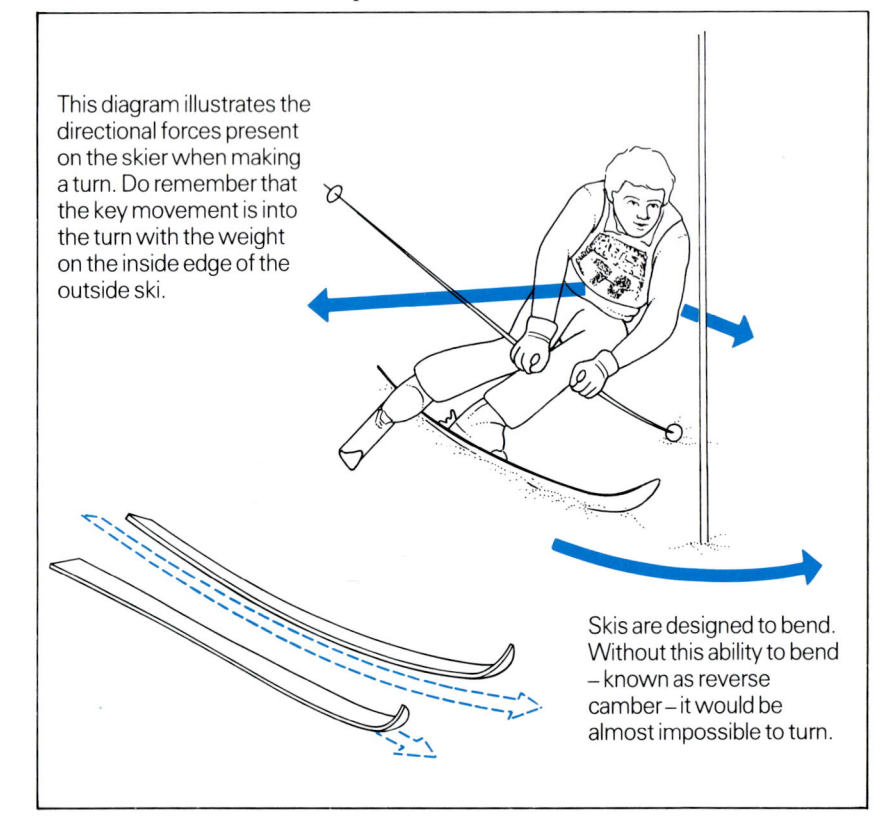

This diagram illustrates the directional forces present on the skier when making a turn. Do remember that the key movement is into the turn with the weight on the inside edge of the outside ski.

Skis are designed to bend. Without this ability to bend – known as reverse camber – it would be almost impossible to turn.

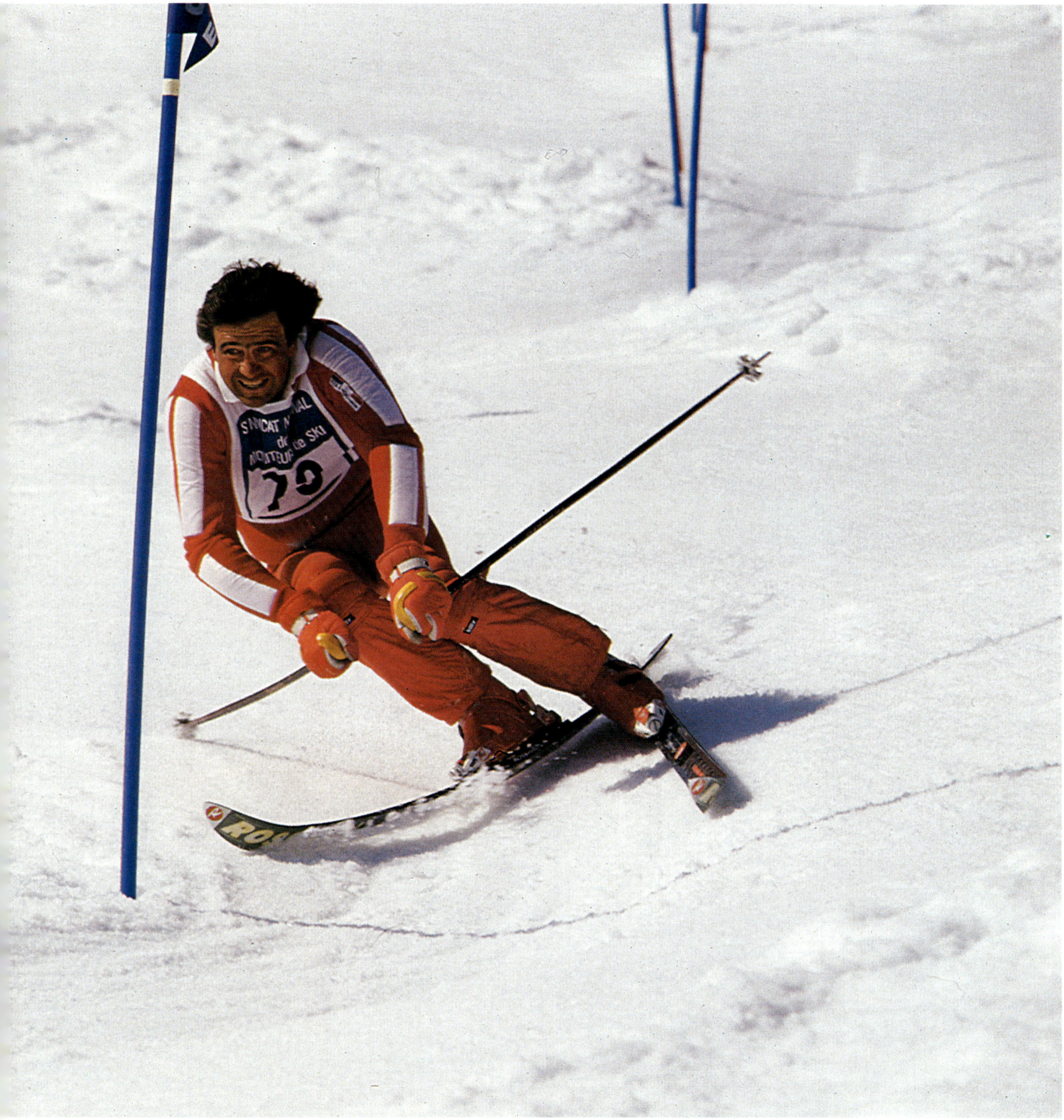
SKI
70

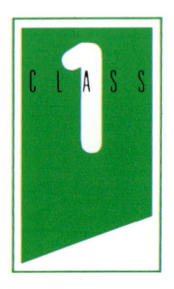

## KICK TURNS

Kick turns are very useful for intermediate skiers who have just graduated to steeper pistes, and also for more advanced skiers who need to turn in a tricky position, such as a gully. A kick turn is a 180° turn, either left or right. Practise both versions on the flat before trying a kick turn on the slopes.

RIGHT TURN: start in the normal parallel-ski position, then pivot your body slightly to the right while lifting your poles. Plant them behind you on the right between your boot and ski-tail – both poles should be at least 50 cm distant, especially from the left ski. Leaning on your poles, lift your right leg forwards and upwards, then place the tail of the ski next to the tip of the left ski. Then swing the right ski round, turning your body to the right so that you are parallel with, but facing in the opposite direction to, the left ski. Bend your knees, rest your weight on your right ski and pole, and bring the left ski round alongside the right ski, together with the left pole.

LEFT TURN: you start the same way, but this time first swing the heel of the right ski behind that of the left ski.

TURNING ON A SLOPE: the manoeuvre is the same as on the flat, but needs more care if you are not going to end up on your backside. Throughout the kick turn you will have to keep the uphill edges pressed into the snow at right angles to the fall line. Three final pieces of advice: on gentle slopes, turn towards the slope; on steep slopes, away from the hill; and in powder, make a small platform to give you more stability. You will also find it easier to practise with short skis.

*Right:* This illustration highlights the importance of correct body position when attempting to turn on a slope. The body must face into the turn with the knees slightly bent. The skis are kept parallel and the poles are held well apart. Leaning on the ski pole will allow you to bring the opposite ski around to complete the turn.

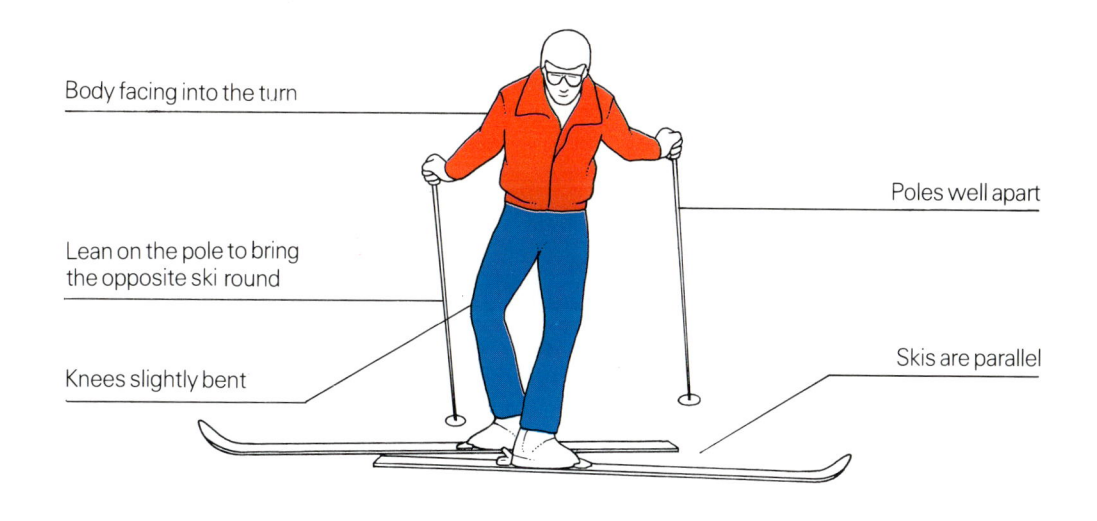

Body facing into the turn

Poles well apart

Lean on the pole to bring the opposite ski round

Knees slightly bent

Skis are parallel

To turn to the right, start in a normal position with both poles at least 50 cm from the left ski. Twist your body...

...and raise the right ski, placing the right tail next to the left ski-tip...

...and carry on round until the two skis are back to front, but parallel.

Once you have reached this position, bend your knees slightly...

...then transfer your weight on to the right-hand pole and ski.

Lift the left ski, keeping the tip raised...

...bring it round (together with the left-hand pole) and put it down parallel to the right ski

65

## CLASS 1

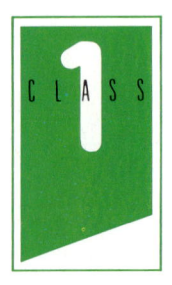

# TRAVERSING AND A CHANGE OF SLOPE

Traversing means travelling along the axis of parallel skis at an angle to the fall line. Unlike straight running down the fall line, the traversing technique requires that the tip of the uphill ski should be 10 cm in front of the downhill tip. Distance between the parallel skis should be between 10 and 20 cm. Most of your weight will automatically be on the downhill ski, and your body will lean slightly away from the slope. Of course, the technique should be adjusted to take account of varying slopes, snow conditions, speeds, etc. So, if you are on good snow (well packed, with a thin layer of powder on a smooth base), the uphill ski need only be a few centimetres in front, whereas, if the snow is heavy going, the gap may be as much as 20 to 30 cm. Similarly, on soft snow and a gentle slope, your body will be more or less vertical. Angulation (where your torso and legs form an angle at the hips, seen from the front) is necessary only as the snow gets harder and the slope steeper.

As preparation for this technique, do the same exercises as for straight running down the fall line, but, as you glide, try to lift the uphill ski. This will gradually force you to put all your weight on the downhill ski. As you progress, you will be practising on harder, deeper, more difficult snow, and you will get used to sudden accelerations, changes in the gradient, unexpected changes of speed caused by different snow conditions, and, above all, you will learn to exploit changes in the terrain for accelerating, braking and absorbing bumps at increasingly fast speeds. This search for a balanced position during the traverse will lead you to the different elements in aerodynamic positions which increase speed (by reducing wind resistance), and also the best position for taking bumps at speed (a Class 3 technique). But first you must learn to cope with changes in the slope angle.

Do not look down at your skis

Stay relaxed...

...with your upper body facing slightly downhill.

Keep your skis parallel...

...with the uphill ski 10 cm in front.

Put your weight on the downhill ski.

Tips: train on progressively steeper slopes, avoiding putting your weight on the uphill ski (try lifting it slightly), and practise rotating your hips.

## CHANGING GRADIENTS

Mountain slopes are not even; the gradient changes all the time, not just because of the terrain, but also because of bumps on the piste and varying snow depths. You must therefore learn how to cope with these variations in the slope, and how to use them to accelerate, brake and absorb bumps. Doing this will certainly add to your fun.

Begin by practising at a moderate speed on a gentle slope. Start in the standard position, with your weight evenly distributed over both skis. Then, as the slope changes, flex down slightly to absorb it, and then return to your basic position. Next, repeat the movement, but travelling faster, and on a more marked gradient change. If you are skiing from an average slope on to a steep slope, your skis will accelerate and you will tend to lean backwards, thus losing your balance. So, as the slope changes, lean forwards as well as flexing down so that you can keep a balanced position. However, if the change is in the opposite direction – from a steep to a more gentle slope – your skis will brake slightly and you will feel yourself toppling forward. To compensate, lean backwards as you flex down. If you are faced with high bumps, you will have to learn how to 'swallow' them and, if the bumps are close together, your legs will have to act as shock-absorbers... but more of that later.

*Above left:* The basic position where your weight is equally distributed over both feet.

*Above:* If the gradient increases, you will have to lean forward and flex down slightly to keep a perfect balance through the acceleration.

*Above right:* If the gradient lessens, you will have to lean back and up-extend slightly (stand straighter) to cope with the braking effect.

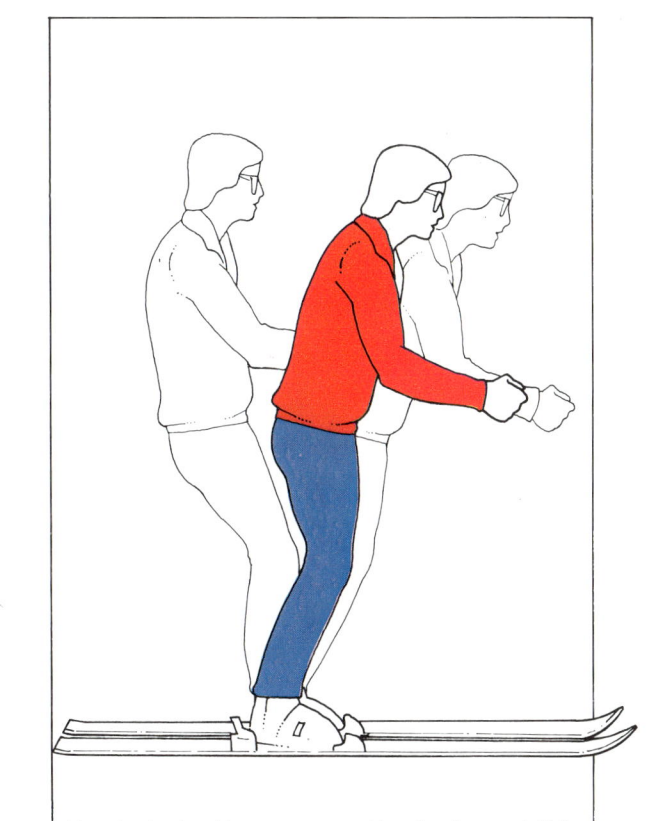

Your body should compensate for the acceleration and braking forces caused by changes in the slope; flexing down and leaning forwards if the gradient increases, up-extending and leaning back when the gradient decreases.

## CLASS 1

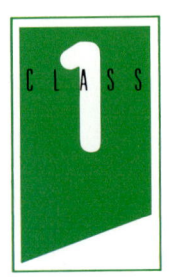

# SIDE-SLIPPING

Side-slipping – where the skis move at an angle to their axis – is a very important skiing technique. It is affected by the grip of your skis, the degree of gradient, type of snow and extent of edging, together with the force of gravity, effect of pivoting and centrifugal force, either combined or separately. Since side-slipping is an essential part of skiing technique, it should be practised at all stages during your skiing tuition. You will feel yourself slipping sideways very early on in your skiing days, in particular when you come to learn the elementary turn, and control of this movement should be studied from that moment on. Side-slips can be linked together (simply, with stem movements, or with counter-rotations) to help you improve the first part of your turns. Another use for the side-slipping technique is in braking, and it is thus invaluable for skiers of all standards, whether beginners, advanced, or even Olympic champions. The underlying principle of side-slipping is very simple: you use the joints of the lower body to enable you to vary the degree of edging of your skis and, if you 'release' the edges, your skis will start to slide down the slope, while, if you push them into the slope, this movement will stop.

Now for the difference between rounded, diagonal and linked side-slipping...

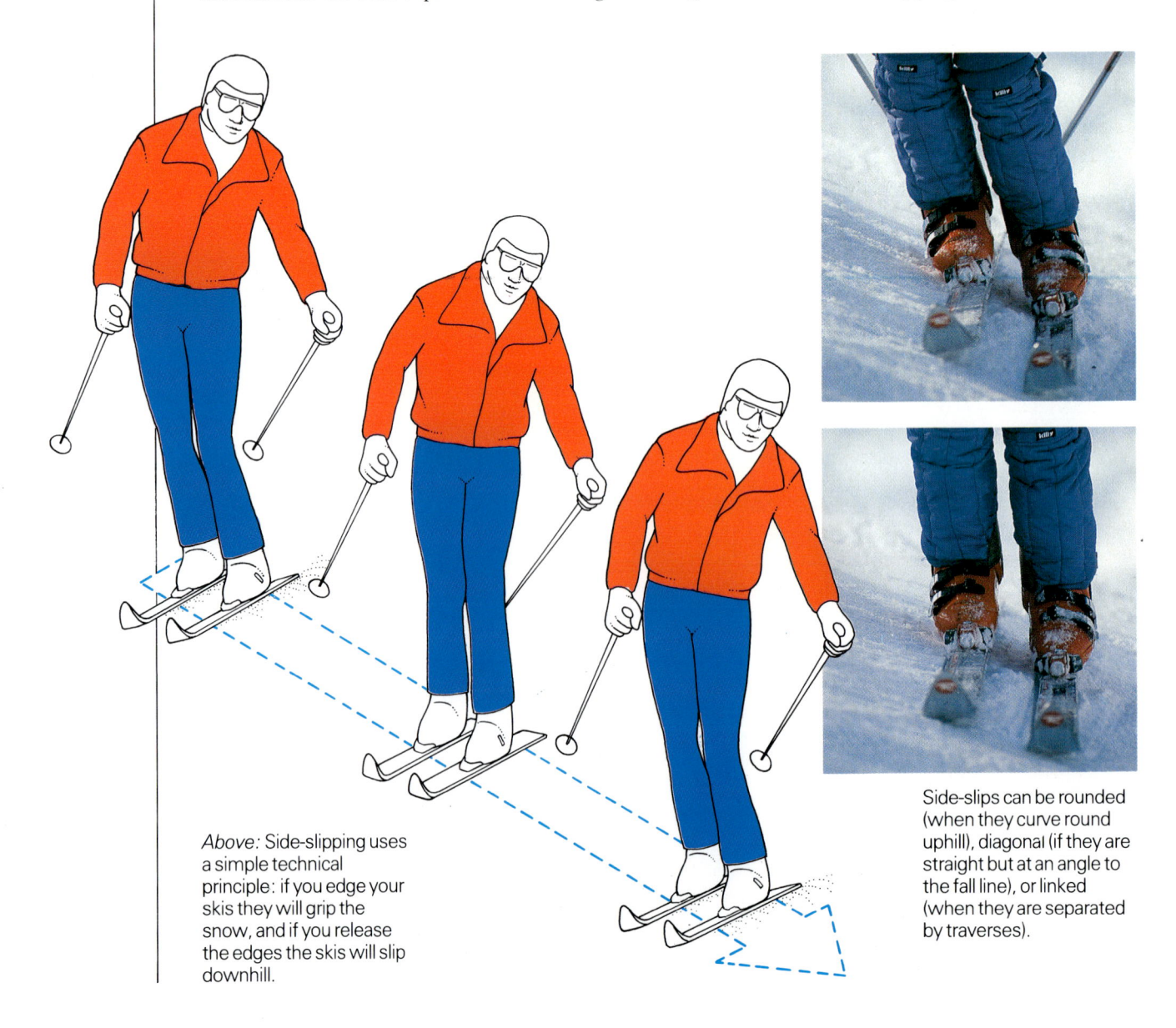

*Above:* Side-slipping uses a simple technical principle: if you edge your skis they will grip the snow, and if you release the edges the skis will slip downhill.

Side-slips can be rounded (when they curve round uphill), diagonal (if they are straight but at an angle to the fall line), or linked (when they are separated by traverses).

*Below:* The rounded side-slip is ideal for beginners on gentle slopes. Your steering will consist less and less of skidding as you progress. Starting with a wide stance and skis parallel; pivoting and releasing the edges; controlling the edging; turning uphill.

A rounded side-slip takes the shape of an uphill curve. When you first try this, the steering phase will be largely skidded, and this is known as an 'elementary rounded side-slip'. Later on, your steering will be more skill than skid, and this side-slip is described as 'advanced', or 'refined'.

To return to the elementary version: you start with a traverse movement across a gentle slope, with your body in a slightly flexed position. You then bend down further as you release the edges. This 'releasing' of the edges has to be controlled, since the flatter your skis the faster they will slide. Steering is effected with your body in a balanced position, slightly flexed, weight on your heels, body facing the way you intend to go, and your skis describing a wide curve.

As you improve, look for increasingly steep slopes where your side-slips will be, hopefully, less skidding and better steered. On a steep slope, start with a traverse close to the fall line and at a fair speed. While balancing your weight over the outside ski, gradually flex down and push your knees sideways and forward into the curve to increase the edging: this should get you turning. Sustain the turn by controlling the edging and pivoting of the skis. During long curves, the body is virtually upright but in tight turns it is angulated.

*Below:* To steer a side-slip, your weight should be on the downhill ski, your body facing in the direction of the side-slip and the edging adjusted to control your speed.

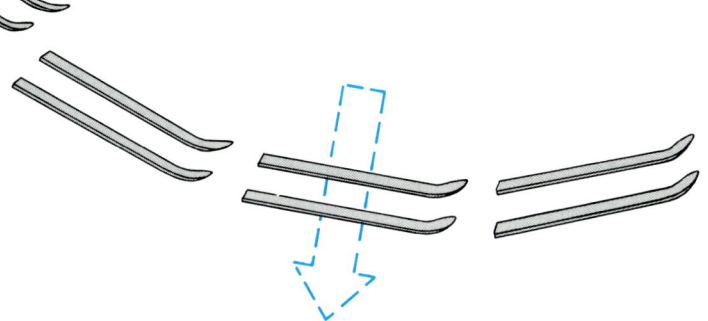

## CLASS 1

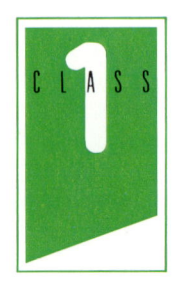

# SIDE-SLIPPING DIAGONAL AND LINKED

You will quickly come to terms with rounded side-slips, but you also need to master the diagonal side-slip (a Class 2 topic) if you are to execute linked side-slips. During this progression you will refine many side-slipping and turning techniques, as they have elements of stem, GT and performance turns, as well as rounded side-slips in certain cases.

Compared to the rounded side-slip, the diagonal version is a straight side-slip executed at an angle to the fall line. The simple link is a series of diagonal side-slips joined by traverses. Starting on a gentle slope, in the traverse position, begin a diagonal side-slip by releasing your edges, then go back to a traverse by edging your skis again for a few metres before doing another side-slip. The speed with which you change from traverse to side-slip is, of course, up to you. A series of quick changes makes an excellent edge-control exercise.

Initially, you will consciously have to flex down as you release the edges and up-extend when you edge the skis in order to keep a good balance, but, as you improve, you will find that this comes naturally. Once you have mastered this technique of simple links, you will find that the flexing-extending movements will disappear and that the continuous working of your legs will show only as a sideways movement of your knees. You will then need to learn and practise stemmed linked side-slips (snowplough-turn starts linked to rounded side-slips) and side-slips linked by counter-rotations (side-slips separated by edge-checks and pivoting releases). Remember: rhythm is the key to success.

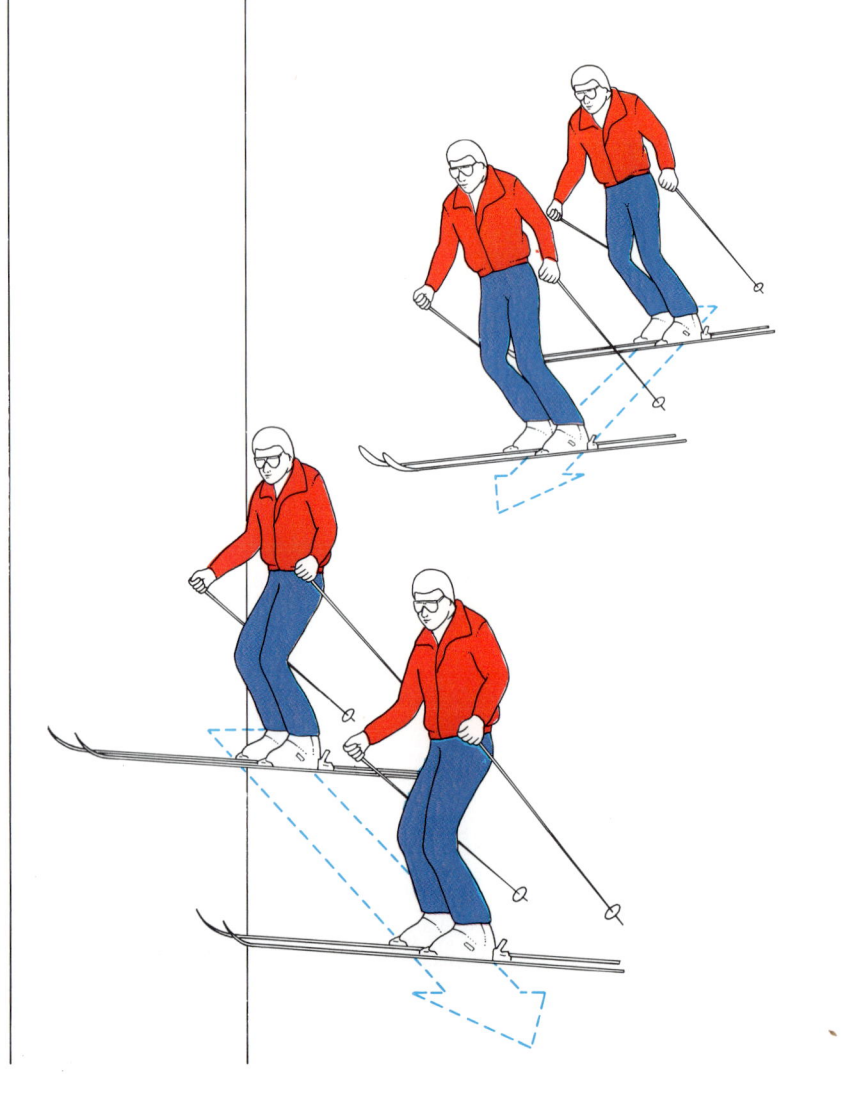

The diagonal side-slip
Start in a traverse position
Weight on the downhill ski
Body facing in the direction of the side-slip
Controlled edging...
...initiated by a slight flexing down.

1. Diagonal side-slip
This is a straight side-slip at an angle to the fall line.

2. Simple linked side-slip
A series of diagonal side-slips linked by traverses. The rhythm will depend on the snow, terrain, and your technical expertise.

3. Simple linked side-slip
The principle is easier to grasp in theory than in practice, since the technique is affected by factors such as snow conditions, the degree of slope, how comfortable your boots are, and the condition of your edges.
Traverse
Diagonal side-slip
Traverse
Rhythm

Instructor's tip: one of the most important applications of the side-slip for skiers of all levels is in braking. Consequently, whatever your class, concentrate on perfecting your side-slips. We shall return to this topic later on.

**Simple linked side-slips**
Start with a diagonal side-slip by progressively releasing the edges...
...then edge into the slope and go into a traverse, followed by releasing the edges, and so on.

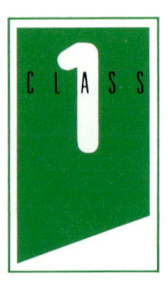

# THE ELEMENTARY TURN

These will form your test at the end of Class 1: perfectly performed elementary turns. The elementary turn is a complete downhill turn, initiated by a snowplough or a stem, and finished with a wide-radius side-slip. It will not take you long to learn this movement, which constitutes an extremely important part in your progress.

Begin in a traverse, skis apart, then adopt the snowplough position. Carry on with a snowplough turn until the outside ski crosses the fall line. At this stage, pivot your inside foot to bring that ski parallel and in a wide arc. All that remains is to steer the turn by some finely judged edging and pivoting with both feet. Above all, remember to keep a flexed position throughout the turn.

The aim of this movement is, of course, to turn; but it does bring other results. For example, you will have your first experience of side-slipping which will lead you naturally into the study of side-slips, whether straight, rounded, braking, or sliding. Also, this turn, executed in different conditions, will enable you to perform the stem and basic parallel turns without any problems. Take care not to force your skis to converge, since this will happen of its own accord, but will be less visible with shorter skis.

Finally, a few pieces of advice to speed up your training: choose a gentle slope to begin with, and try for a long steering phase, without forgetting to increase your speed gradually. Then slowly build up a rhythm by making your turns closer to the fall line. This way you will have your first – albeit premature – taste of wedeling, a technique which is based on good rhythm. Another advantage of mastering the elementary turn early on in your skiing career is that it enables you to accelerate and to learn stem turns easily. Stemming being a move in which one ski is placed at an angle to the other, with the tip converging and the tail out, while the other ski points in the direction of movement – the stemming ski can be either the uphill or the downhill one, hence the terms 'uphill stem turn' and 'downhill stem turn'.

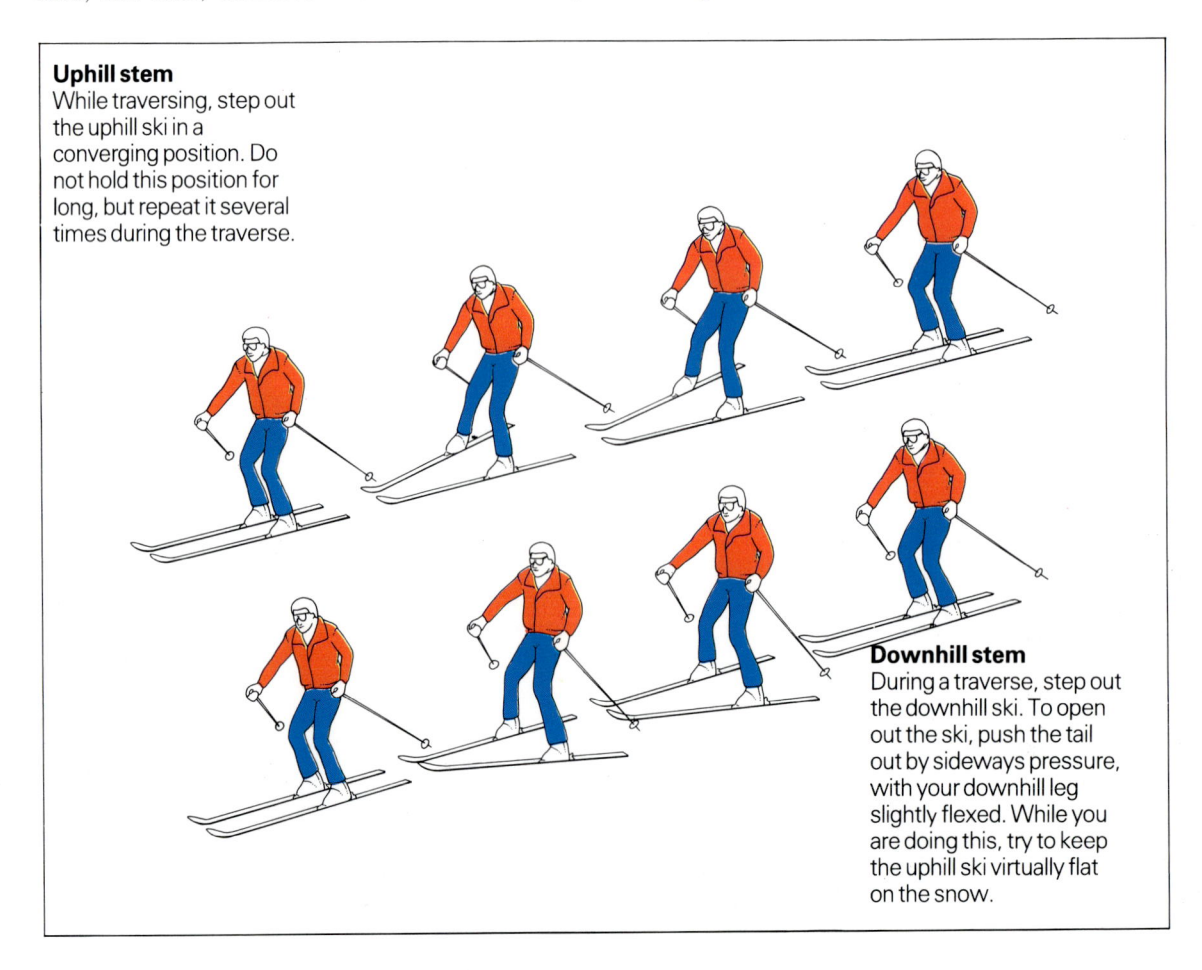

**Uphill stem**
While traversing, step out the uphill ski in a converging position. Do not hold this position for long, but repeat it several times during the traverse.

**Downhill stem**
During a traverse, step out the downhill ski. To open out the ski, push the tail out by sideways pressure, with your downhill leg slightly flexed. While you are doing this, try to keep the uphill ski virtually flat on the snow.

The elementary turn starts out as a snowplough turn, but your skis will move back into a parallel position as they cross the fall line. The remainder of the turn is steered in a considerable side-slip.

Do not force your skis into a converging position. This will happen of its own accord, but will be less noticeable with short skis and if you are skiing on a good slope.

Thanks to the elementary turn, you will soon experience your first sensation of side-slipping. This is also a very important stage in your progress towards parallel turns.

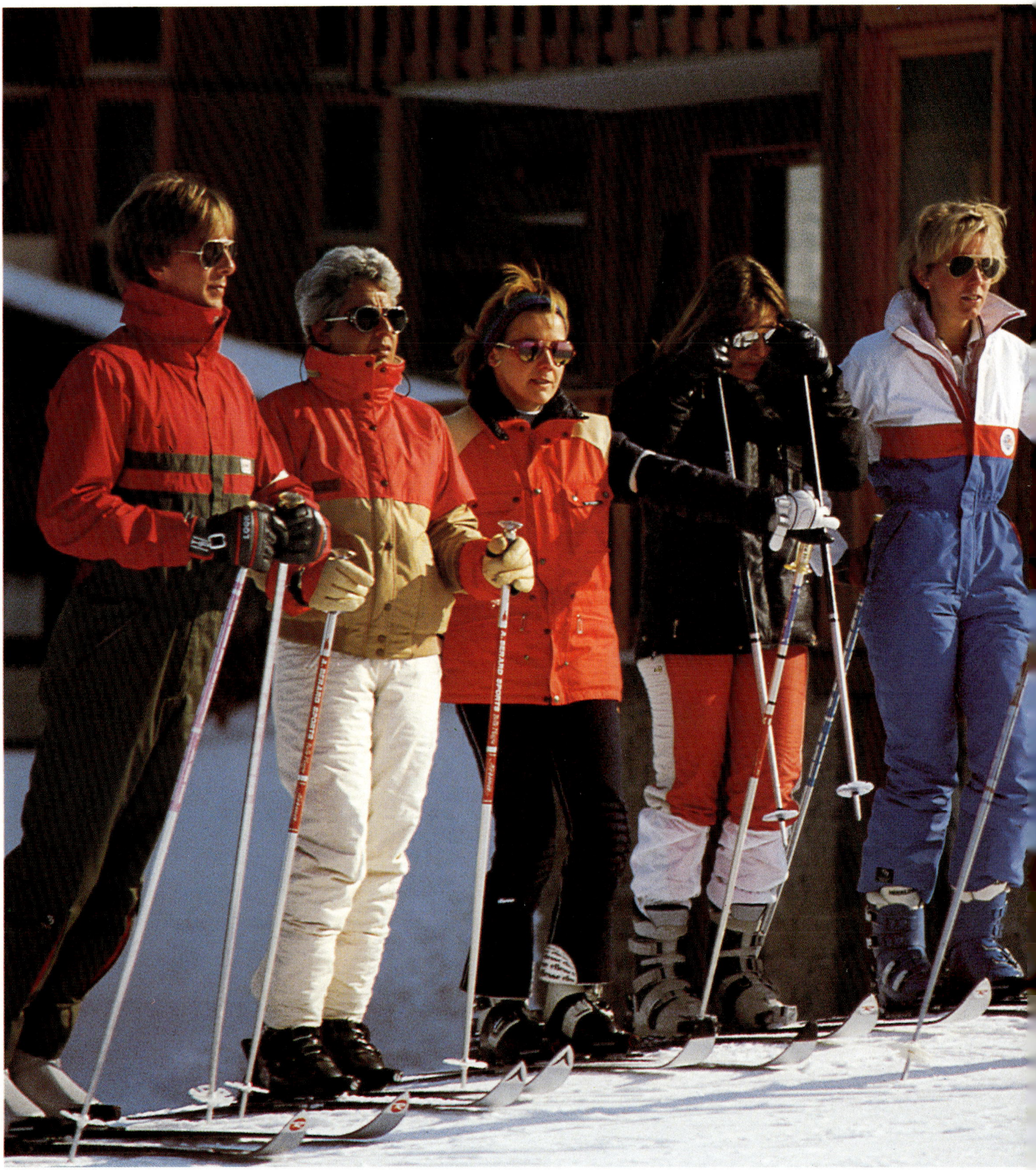

# INTERMEDIATE SKIERS

Having learned about elementary turns, straight running and the principles of side-slipping and stemming, you are at the international first-degree level, and can now move on to Class 2, taking your intermediate-length skis with you – skis some 10 cm taller than you are. The syllabus for this class includes:

PERFECTING BALANCE AND GLIDING: working on the skating step, third-degree straight running, and your first small jumps.

SIDE-SLIPPING: perfecting the rounded, diagonal and linked side-slips.

TURNS: plenty of practice to improve your step-turns and stem turns, plus tuition in the basic parallel turn and wedel.

# DIAGONAL SIDE-SLIPPING

The time has come for perfecting your diagonal side-slips. As an effective way of controlling your skis and speed on moderate and steep slopes, they allow you to brake, lose altitude and ski at low speed with great safety.

How do you execute a perfect diagonal side-slip? Start in a traverse and, to begin the side-slip, balance yourself over your downhill ski, then release the edges by allowing your ankles to relax so that your feet are almost flat on the slope. To steer the side-slip maintain a balanced position on the downhill ski, staying in the basic position, keeping your joints flexed and your body facing in the direction of the side-slip. Control your speed by edging slightly. All you have to do to stop is to increase your edging by gradually pushing your knees into the slope, so that your upper body is markedly angled. To counter the imbalance caused by the edging, flex down and steady yourself with the downhill pole.

If your traverse is at a very sharp angle to the fall line, the change in angle of the skis to the slope will be that much greater, and you should start the side-slip by flexing down and then up-extending. The closer the initial traverse to the fall line, the more your tails will have to be brought round, and consequently you will have to adopt a more extreme position.

The skidded stop and braking side-slip are two more examples of diagonal side-slipping, since they both entail a quick sideways movement of the skis.

The skidded stop (a simultaneous movement of both feet in a flexed position, used to edge the skis by ankle muscle power alone) is used at low speeds, and the braking side-slip when you are travelling faster. This, therefore, has an element of steering included.

The detail in the left hand illustration shows the correct method for side-slipping with the ski edge cutting into the slope. The position adopted in the illustration on the right will result in the ski sliding down the slope.

77

## THE BASIC PARALLEL TURN

The basic parallel turn is the key to good skiing. It makes use of a number of basic turning elements: for example, to unweight your skis – thus allowing them to turn – you can flex down then up-extend, or simply use a bump; to pivot, you use an edge-change combined with an extension and pivoting. This basic parallel turn will gradually lead you to the goal of all novice skiers – keeping your skis parallel during a downhill turn.

As its name suggests, the basic parallel is a rudimentary turn, executed with parallel skis, and it is brought about mainly by a transfer of weight. It is also the key to further progress, since all the other parallel turns use it as a base.

PREPARATION: starting in a straight line movement, be it traversing or side-slipping, step out the uphill ski, keeping it parallel to the downhill ski, while turning your upper body slightly downhill and getting ready for the pole-plant. Flex down slightly, keeping most of your weight on the downhill ski.

INITIATION: once in this flexed position, plant the pole, then up-extend quickly and pivot, transferring all your weight to the uphill ski.

All that remains is to *steer* the turn. Flex down again while still edging your skis and pressing mainly on the outside ski. If you want to execute another parallel turn, start again from the preparation phase.

NOTE: you already know the basics of the stem turn. Here, all that is needed is to replace the stem movement with the sideways step, keeping the skis parallel, first of all without unweighting, over a small bump or level section on the slope, then with a flexion/extension on an even slope.

If you want to perfect your basic parallel turn, you first have to try to tighten the curve and, above all, to vary your methods of pivoting by gradually eliminating the edge-check and refining steering techniques which favour using the counter-turn: this means that you have to become very proficient at transferring your weight, and it is also a good idea to have some experience of the basic wedel.

Initiating the turn: straighten slightly and pivot as you bring the skis together, remembering to transfer your weight on to the uphill ski.

Steering the turn: hold on to your balance position, and keep the skis together. Return to a straight traverse or side-slip before linking another turn.

## THE BASIC WEDEL

As a rule, most novice skiers think that wedeling is a stylish, fiendishly complex activity which only advanced skiers can contemplate. Nothing is further from the truth. You, too, can start practising wedeling, if you have not already tried some with the snowplough or stem – although the less your instructor knows about that the better!

A wedel is nothing more than a series of linked downhill turns, with no traverses in between, and often such short steering phases that the actual turn sequence is all that remains, the completion of each initiation phase acting as a link to the next initiation phase. The first wedel we shall look at is the basic wedel, in which the skis are kept parallel. Start with a traverse or facing down the slope, skis slightly apart, and go into a rounded side-slip. Once you have flexed, with most of your weight on the downhill ski, plant the pole that is on the inside of the turn. Immediately up-extend – with an edge-change or counter-rotation in some cases, but usually with a weight transfer – keeping a balanced position with your skis 10 to 15 cm apart. Then link a turn in the other direction. You will soon find that rhythm is the key to good wedeling.

The turning technique used (weight transfer, edge-change or counter-rotation) depends on your technical ability and/or the skiing conditions (powder snow or ice, and the slope gradient). However, the basic wedel should be used only on gentle and moderate slopes, in a long, flowing sequence. Its main use is as training prior to the GT and performance wedeln.

Do not lose heart if you find that, when you try to push off the outside ski, the tail drifts out to produce a stem wedel. This is not disastrous, and practice will make perfect.

Making turns close together on a prescribed course – marked with slalom poles – is a useful training aid on the path to a good wedel. The important element in both cases is maintaining flow and rhythm.

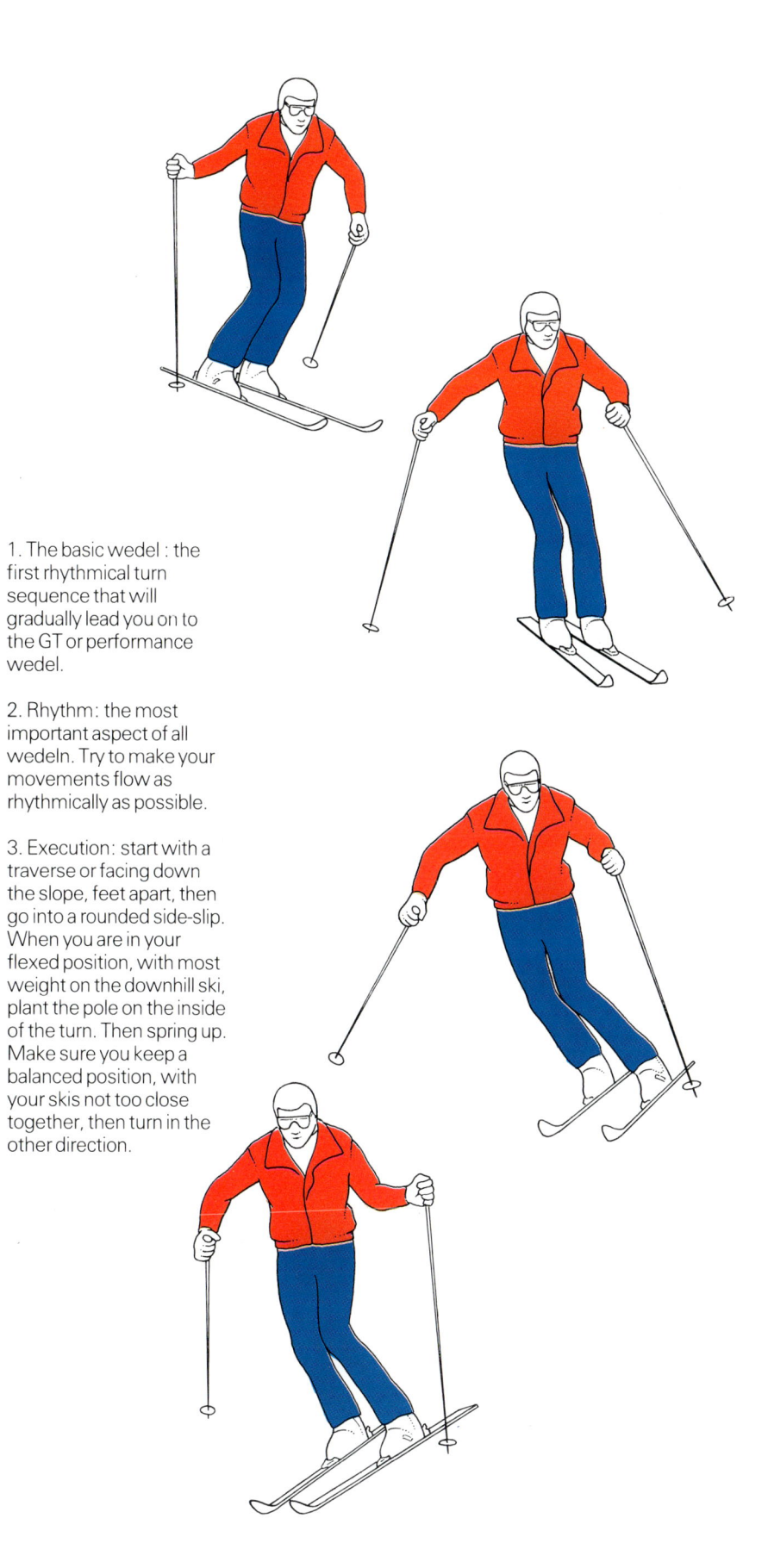

1. The basic wedel: the first rhythmical turn sequence that will gradually lead you on to the GT or performance wedel.

2. Rhythm: the most important aspect of all wedeln. Try to make your movements flow as rhythmically as possible.

3. Execution: start with a traverse or facing down the slope, feet apart, then go into a rounded side-slip. When you are in your flexed position, with most weight on the downhill ski, plant the pole on the inside of the turn. Then spring up. Make sure you keep a balanced position, with your skis not too close together, then turn in the other direction.

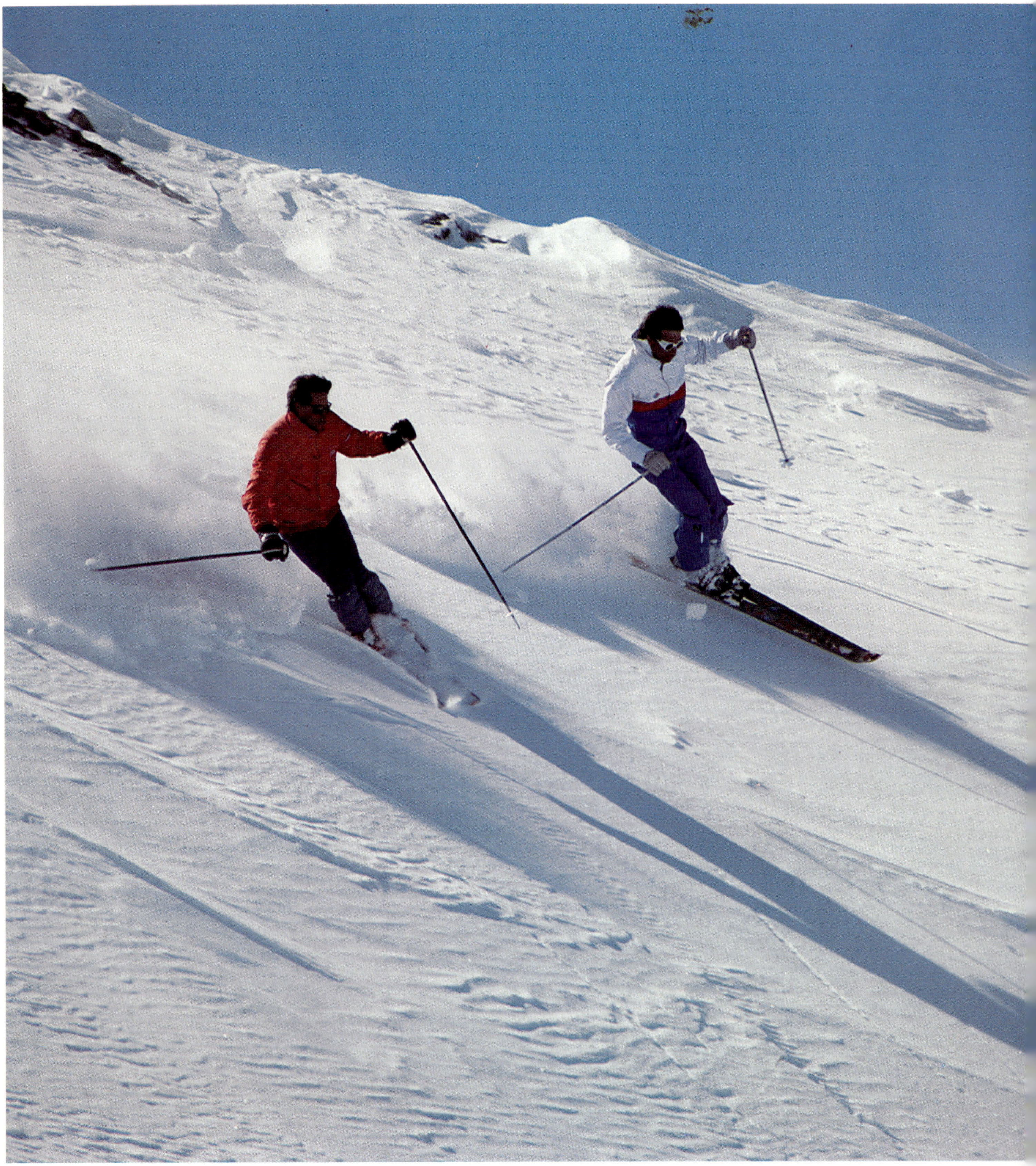

# CLASS 3

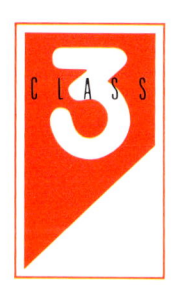

# ADVANCED SKIERS

Once you have mastered the basic parallel turn, leave Class 2 and join Class 3, in which you will perfect all the techniques you have been acquiring, learn the joys of skiing on different terrains and types of snow, and be introduced to new techniques.

BALANCE AND GLIDING: you will try your first jumps off ramps, schussing over all terrains, pistes with different snow conditions. The mountain is virtually your oyster!

SIDE-SLIPS: while perfecting your side-slipping technique, you will also learn the flying step turn and, probably most useful of all, the braking side-slip. (It is all very well to ski like an express train... provided you know how to stop!)

TURNS: the ultimate in turns – the evasion, GT and performance turns, together with, of course, the associated GT and performance wedeln.

A DIFFERENT SORT OF SKIING: A different sort of skiing: Class 3 is, above all, about discovering a new world of skiing; deep snow, all terrains, steep slopes, mogul fields and an introduction to slalom.

## SIMPLE JUMPS

Knowing how to jump bumps and ramps is vital for any skier, particularly in straight running (it is, in any case, much harder to jump during a high-speed turn or a side-slip). Use the natural features of the terrain for practising – bumps or small ridges – or build yourself a small ramp. Do not try to emulate those acrobatic skiers yet. You will find that a 'pedalling' jump will be much more fun for your friends than for you, especially when you land, if you have not learned how to approach the take-off.

Jumps are of varying lengths and are taken at different speeds, depending on the obstacle to be crossed. Starting from a straight run down the slope, or a traverse, get ready as though you were about to perform a standing jump off both feet. When you reach the point where the slope changes, stretch upwards and forwards from your crouched position. At the same time, you can give yourself a push up with your poles. If the terrain calls for it, or you would like to do a longer jump, bring your knees up towards your chest, keeping your skis parallel to the slope. Landing on your tips invariably gives you a sore nose, while landing on your rear is hardly elegant and can damage your spine or your pride. So, with your skis parallel to the ground, absorb the impact as you land by bending your knees and supporting yourself on your poles (do not do the latter if you are travelling fast).

If you are using a small training ramp, you can jump normally, with or without your poles, at full stretch, crouched, with a pedalling action, skis spread wide, in a streamlined position, depending on whether you are after distance or effect. Whatever the case, your body should be at right angles to the slope, your skis parallel and, above all, remember to flex as you land to absorb the shock. At this stage in your tuition you should always plump for safety rather than spectacle. Currently, the best jumpers can perform a backward triple somersault with triple twist. However, they have made thousands of practice jumps over water to reach this standard.

Prepare yourself as if for a standing long-jump. At the point where the slope changes, straighten your body.

*Far left:*
An artificial ramp on a parallel slalom.

Your body should be in a crouching position...
...skis parallel to the slope.

Always be ready to absorb the impact of landing.
*Left:*
Badly positioned skis: the fall is likely to hurt his back...and his pride.

## SKIING MOGULS

When practising straight running, you will have discovered how important your legs are for 'swallowing' bumps – rather like a car's shock absorbers. When there is only one bump you can absorb it with your whole body in an 'avalement' (literally, 'swallowing') movement, but if there are many, one after the other, you will use only your lower body. At this stage you will begin learning to use bumps in the slope for braking or for helping with turns, rather than looking on them as problems. For the moment, we shall concentrate on skiing bumps during straight running and touch on turns with *avalement*.

The normal consequence of skiing over a bump is that you take off into the air, and this needs controlling. The effect of this 'flying' and subsequent landing can be to put you off balance, and remedying this will decrease your speed on landing – due to the impact – increase air resistance – you will have lost your streamlined body position – and, above all, will affect your flexibility. Let us refresh our memories concerning the profile of a bump. You can break it down into three parts: the last few metres before the bump itself (slope, flat section, incline), the point where the slope changes, and the slope at the other side. In straight running there are three possible ways of taking a bump: by flexing down, by bringing your legs up, or by jumping off the top.

FLEXING DOWN (rounded bumps): your skis remain in contact with the snow. Gradually bend ankles, knees and hips (anticipate the bump if travelling fast), holding your arms apart and in front of you. Your speed will determine when you flex, although, at the latest, this should be when your ski-tips reach the slope change.

BRINGING YOUR LEGS UP (short bumps): lift your skis off the snow just before the slope changes by bringing your legs up towards your chest in one quick movement, and stretch them down again as soon as possible after the bump. This move is sometimes known as pre-jumping. This way a controlled, voluntary jump replaces an unexpected, uncontrolled leap which is liable to put you completely off balance.

BUMPS TO JUMP OFF: make sure that you are perfectly balanced over both skis. Your take-off should be controlled, and you can even flex down as you leave the ground to reduce the length of the jump. While in the air, do your best to maintain a crouching position (this is the most effective position for cutting down wind resistance), then stretch your legs to soften the landing.

To round off this section on bumps, it is worth mentioning that the *avalement* technique (see the section covering 'competition turns') is one of the quickest ways of skiing down a mogul field, although it is also the most demanding on your thigh muscles. It is a satisfying method for the good skier and one which all aspiring skiers should try.

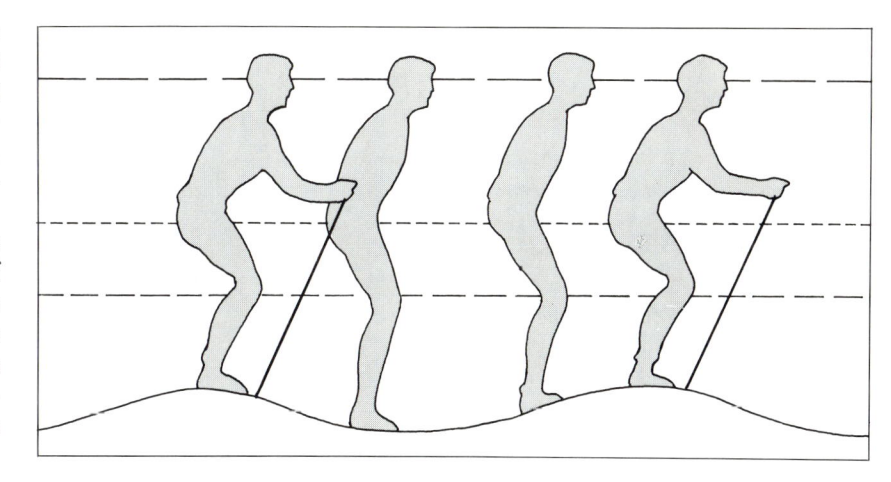

Your legs are your shock absorbers: arms held in front of and away from the body. The top of the bump should seem to go through the skier's body.
Flexing down: your skis should stay in contact with the snow.
Bringing your legs up: lift your skis off the snow just before the slope changes.
*Below:*
If the change of slope is abrupt, you can take a short jump. Otherwise, flex down and lean forward slightly to compensate for the acceleration and unbalancing effects.

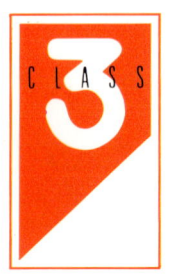

## THE EVASION TURN

Now you have mastered the basic parallel turn, it is time to explore its possibilities by working on certain turning techniques so that you can adapt your basic turn to cope with different circumstances. This exercise will produce the evasion, GT and performance turns.

The evasion turn is a downhill turn produced by a pivoted extension, which has already been used in the basic parallel and is defined as a pivoting mechanism comprising an upward movement of the body – causing unweighting – combined with another movement of the body towards the inside of the turn which is intended to counteract the centrifugal force and so permit an edge-change. This movement is combined with a pole-plant. The evasion turn is fairly simple to execute:

PREPARATION: balance yourself evenly over your skis, then anticipate the pole-plant as you flex down.

INITIATION: once you are in a flexed position, plant your pole, and simultaneously up-extend and pivot with most of your weight on your outside ski, and upper body leaning into the turn.

TO STEER YOUR TURN: quickly flex again while still pivoting your skis. Make sure that your weight is mainly on the outside ski, and keep a well-balanced position with your shoulders at right angles to your skis and your arms held slightly away from your body.

It goes without saying that to link on another evasion turn you merely start again with the preparation phase.

This turn is particularly useful for wide turns on gentle and moderate slopes, but it also comes into its own in powder snow. Intensive training on gentle slopes will help you to perfect the technique. Begin this training with the basic parallel turn and progressively reduce the stepping-out of the uphill ski. Use the terrain wherever possible (changes of slope, moguls) to make the turns easier, and remember to lean into the turn for easier edge-changing.

One exercise in particular will help you to make fast progress. Go back to rounded side-slipping, getting closer and closer to the fall line. You will soon find yourself crossing it, and you will then be close to mastering the evasion turn.

**The key points**
Weight evenly distributed over both skis, get ready for the pole-plant.

Shoulders should be at right-angles to the skis, arms slightly away from the body.

Plant the pole when in a fully flexed position.

Weight the outside ski as you return to the flexed position.

To execute the turn, merely plant the pole when you are flexed, then up-extend and pivot, weighting the outside ski. Remember to keep your upper body leaning into the turn.

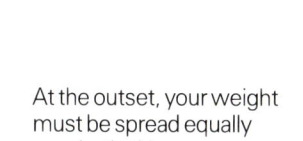

The evasion turn, unlike the basic parallel, follows a fairly tight line.

Three important points before starting a turn: a balanced position on both skis; anticipating the pole-plant (level with ski-tip and 20 cm outside); and flexing down.

At the outset, your weight must be spread equally over both skis.

The evasion turn is steered with your body in a balanced position, shoulders at right-angles to the skis, and arms held slightly away from the body.

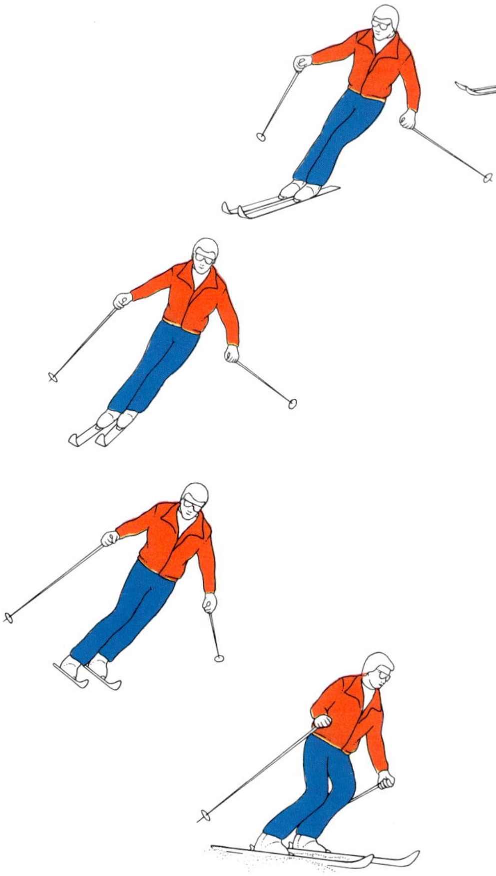

# THE GT TURN

This, too, is a progression from the basic parallel turn, in which the initiation consists of a counter-turn with rebound (this is a two-stage procedure: firstly a counter-rotation with the lower body and skis pivoting uphill while the upper body stays facing downhill, and second an unwinding, where unweighting releases ski pressure on the snow and allows the legs to resume their natural position, thereby turning the skis downhill).

Preparation for the GT turn is a gradual flexing and angulation to produce sliding pressure, and anticipation of the pole-plant.

To initiate the turn, once flexed you merely have to plant the pole. This will help you to up-extend with your weight on the outside ski, while your body leans into the turn.

To steer the turn, flex down again, then weight and pivot the outside ski. Always keep your upper body facing the direction of the turn. If you want to do another GT turn, you can skip the counter-turn stage, since your body position at the end of a GT turn enables you to go into another one with no preliminaries.

Points to watch for: avoid steep, icy slopes and adapt your speed and movement to changes in the terrain. If the counter-turn, which aims to give good edge control and to act as a brake if needed, is long, the accompanying flexion will be gradual and the edge-ckeck only slight. If, on the other hand, the counter-turn is short, flexing will be quicker, angulation greater and the edge-check sharper. It is this edge-check produced by the counter-turn which transforms itself into anticipation.

Note that on steep slopes you will have to make much tighter turns. To achieve this, you will need to initiate them with force and decisively, and there are several techniques you can use: end the counter-turn more abruptly; flex down much more decisively; increase the anticipation. The tighter your turns, the steeper the slope, and the faster you are travelling, then the further from the downhill ski your pole should be planted, keeping your arm well away from your body. Lastly, you will have to increase the flexing of your knees and the amount of sideways movement. Remember to increase your opposition as the turn tightens and your speed.

A distinguishing feature of the GT turn, intended for on-piste skiing, is the edge-check, which enables you to pivot the skis slightly during the turn through leg action alone, while the upper body maintains its position.
The key points
Angulated position, upper body anticipating the turn. A good pole-plant for a better up-extension. Your body should still lean inward during the turn. Gradual pressure while pivoting on the outside ski.

Like any other turn, the GT can be split up into phases:
Preparation: counter-turn with sliding edge-pressure during angulation. Remember to anticipate your pole-plant.
Initiation: when you are in a flexed position, plant your pole and apply increasing pressure on the outside ski, while pivoting it.

The turn is steered by the shape of the skis, controlled edging, pushing your knees inwards, and by pressure on the snow.

Steering: in a balanced position on the outside ski, flex down again. You will then be ready to enter the preparation phase of your next GT turn.

# THE PERFORMANCE TURN

The performance turn is really the province of advanced skiers and is derived from those used in competition skiing, although intended for on-piste use. It is a downhill turn involving weight transfer (as in the basic parallel), rebound and the flexing down/up-extending of the evasion turn. This is the turn used by the great slalom skiers.

PREPARATION: you must begin from a stable position, with your weight on the downhill ski. Flex down to get a sliding pressure on this ski and push the downhill knee in towards the slope, co-ordinating this movement with a sideways step of the uphill ski. Remember to position your body facing into the turn and to anticipate the pole-plant, which is optional.

INITIATION: when you are flexed plant your pole and up-extend as you replace the uphill ski and transfer your weight on to it, then, finally, bring the inner ski back.

STEERING THE TURN: begin to flex again, mainly on to the outside ski, as you guide it round the curve. To steer this ski, use edging control and angulation by pushing your knees inwards.

There are two important points to note about this turn, which is similar to those used in competitions. First the uphill ski can be placed flat, or on its inside or outside edge, and, second, the up-extension is slight and relatively slow. Your skis should stroke the snow, not pound it.

These turns taught by the ESF have to be adapted later to different snow conditions, skiing styles and terrains. Ski-touring, for example, where you may be far from the lifts at high altitude, with a rucksack on your back, needs a radical alteration to the techniques you learned on the pistes. In particular, you will have to look for better stability through wider-radius turns, increase the efficiency of your pivoting through the use of your edges, or even by stemming, and, most importantly, you will need to control your speed with downhill stems or side-slips. On very steep slopes or crusty snow, you will lose your balance if you go too fast. To control your speed you can lean on both your poles; or you can extend an unweighting movement by bringing your legs up towards your body so that your ski-tails lift as they cross the fall line.

At the outset, you must be balanced over the downhill ski, before you can increase the weighting on it by flexing down. This movement is followed by an up-extension with a sideways step and weight transfer.
The key points
Keep your arms away from and in front of your body for better balance. Adjusting angulation and the amount you push your knees inwards gives edge control.
During initiation, keep an eye on your up-extension and weight transfer.

The performance turn is another three-phase downhill turn: begin by balancing over the downhill ski, weighting it by flexing down and pushing that knee inwards. Next, up-extend with a sideways step and weight transfer on to the outside ski. Then steer the turn by bringing your inside ski closer, and guiding your trajectory with the outside ski.

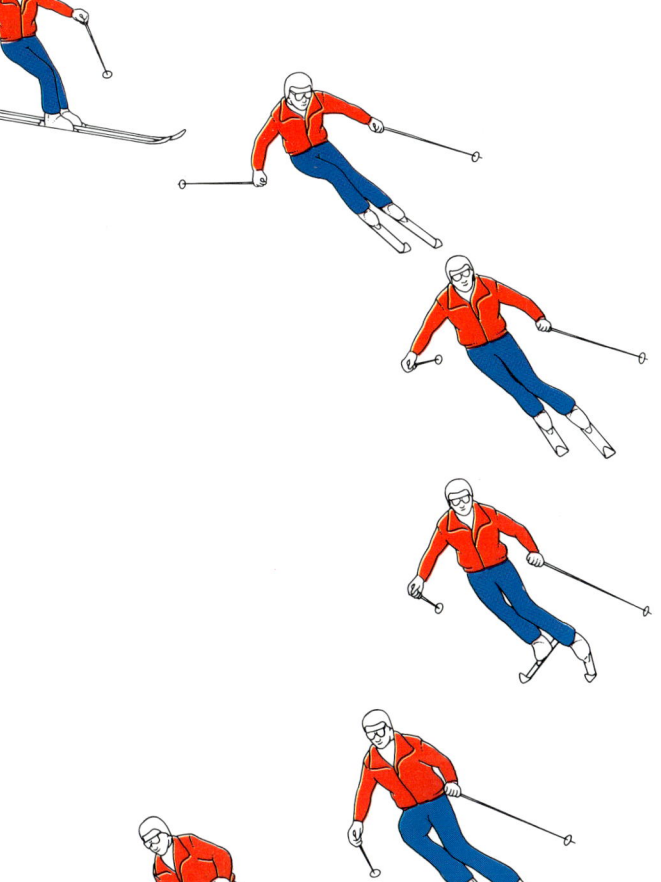

# GT AND PERFORMANCE WEDELING

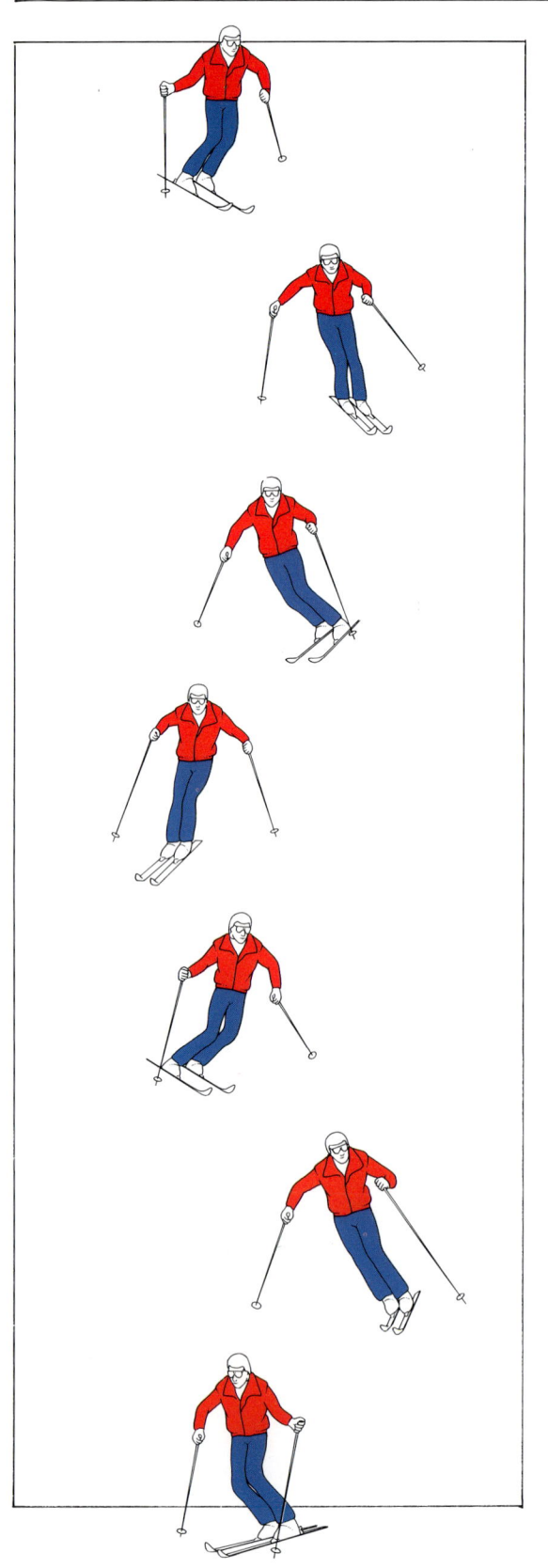

Wedeln are consecutive series of linked turns with no traverses between and greatly reduced steering phases. As with the basic wedel, you will have to link your GT and performance turns rhythmically to produce the corresponding wedeln.

THE GT WEDEL: begin with a traverse or by facing down the slope. Flex down or pivot your feet to go into a counter-turn, then push your knees further into the slope while turning your upper body to face downhill. Remember to plant the inside pole (arm well away from the body) while up-extending slightly or on the rebound from the twisting movement. Your weight is usually evenly distributed over both skis in this wedel, but in some cases you may find it useful to use weight transfer to make the execution easier. Always aim for that balanced position, keeping your hips as relaxed as possible, so that angulation and opposition are easier and you have good control on pivoting. Lastly, using a flow-

In the GT wedel with weight transfer the inside ski comes right off the snow if the skier is in the basic position, but only the tip leaves the surface if the skier leans back.

ing wedel on gentle slopes will avoid the need for braking, while on steep slopes you can control your speed by more exaggerated pivoting and the use of the rebound.

For a PERFORMANCE WEDEL, you should always start, facing down the slope, by performing a rounded side-slip controlled by weighting the outside ski. Then link your turns without pausing: flex down on the outside ski while shifting the inside ski, make a slight up-extension as you transfer your weight, and pivot the outside ski a little. You then control the curve by a slight down-flexing on the outside ski. You will find that the uphill ski tends to drift off at the beginning of the movement, but do not let this worry you. Another peculiarity is that you may find yourself leaning back in the intermediate stage between pivoting phases as you try for maximum slide.

It should also be noted that the performance wedel requires a longer steering phase than the classic wedel, despite the greater weight transfer and energy involved, although this should not give you cause for concern.

The performance wedel has two characteristic features: the extent and aggression of the weight transfer, and a longer steering phase than in the classic wedel.

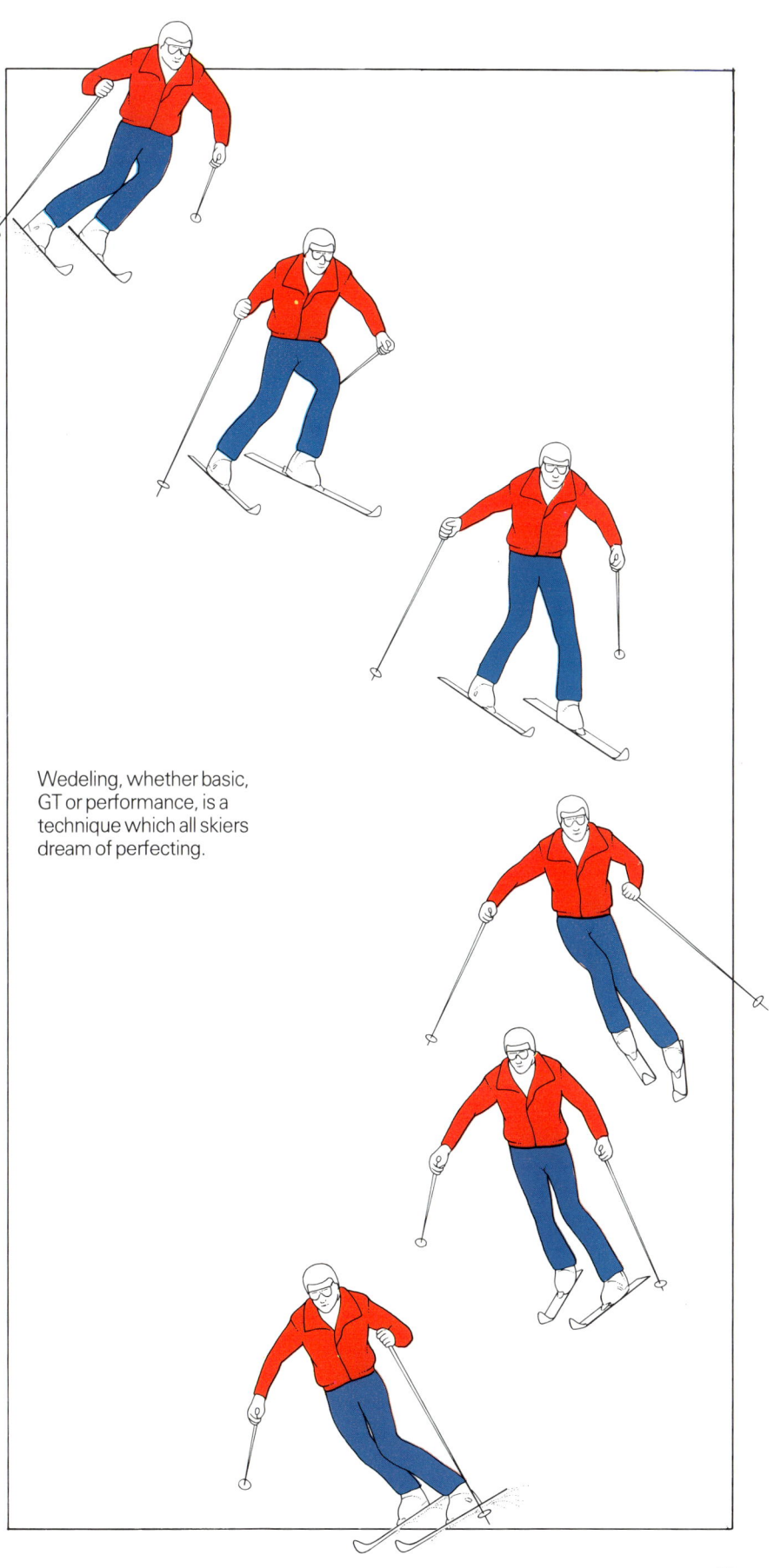

Wedeling, whether basic, GT or performance, is a technique which all skiers dream of perfecting.

# POWDER SKIING

Knowing how to perform GT, evasion or performance turns at varying speeds on perfectly groomed pistes is very satisfying; it is even the final goal of Class 3 students. However, you will soon start to feel that even the most difficult pistes are lacking in excitement. Right from the first day, you were probably tempted by visions of yourself whooshing through powder snow, while your friends took some spectacular photographs to show to the folks back home. Sadly, you cannot just zoom off the piste into the powder without adapting the techniques you have learned to these new conditions.

The problem with making turns in powder snow is mainly the difficulty of applying pressure effectively. If your weight is not spread evenly over your skis, one will go deeper than the other, and you will lose your balance. Then again, if you do not up-extend sufficiently (the consistency of powder makes this very tricky), your skis will not clear the snow and it will be difficult, if not impossible, to go into the turn. Also, on a prepared piste, the firm surface exerts an even pressure under the whole ski, whereas in powder the tips are subject to most resistance, which means you have to resort to a slightly different method of pivoting your skis. Lean back so that the tips clear the snow.

Speed is another important factor when you are turning in powder snow. At slow speeds you will have to lean back considerably, whereas, if you are travelling faster, you must lift your tips above the snow at the outset, then they will stay clear due to the increased pressure from below them which comes with increased speed. Once your ski-tips are safely clear, you can go back to the basic position.

Starting from the basic position, you therefore have a choice of several techniques to produce unweighting when initiating turns, notably:

FLEXING DOWN, UP-EXTENDING: this is the most common method. If performed with sufficient verve, it will lift the skis clear of the snow. Take care, because the increased pressure caused by the preparatory flexing down can put you off balance if the movement is not performed smoothly.

AVALEMENT: in this case there is no preparatory pressure increase, so it is a more reliable method and one to use in snow that will not take vertical pressure.

*Below:* At low speed, lean back considerably. At high speed, return to the basic position as soon as your ski-tips clear the snow.

*Left:* Is there anything in the world more exciting than carving long parallel tracks through virgin snow? Surely not!

*Below:* The evasion turn is ideal for deep snow. Make sure that you are balanced over both skis during preparation, and that you are in a stable position as you steer the turn.

Deep snow is tremendous fun, but it is difficult to find a firm base when initiating turns.

# SLALOM RACING

Your Class 3 days are almost over. Your instructor has taught you to use the appropriate turn for varying snow conditions, to control your weighting in powder, to keep your balance whatever nasty surprises the snow might have in store. All that remains is the introduction to competition skiing. Here you will try your hand at slalom gates, with their alternating red and blue posts marking out a twisting route down the fall line. There is no more choosing where to make your turns, and the only criterion for judging your technique will be the stopwatch.

The main problem of slalom is that you have to steer your curves through the gates while keeping up your speed. You will therefore have to learn how to minimize braking factors and some methods of accelerating.

This is the purpose of the competition class, as outlined in the diagram.

There are two ways of passing the poles in slalom gates. The traditional method, with orthodox poles: feet go through first, hip pushes pole out of the way, allowing the rest of the body to follow.

The second, ultra-modern method: the inside ski deflects the pole at its base. It is a very quick... and illegal manoeuvre, but almost impossible for the judges to spot.

The special slalom: the racers adopt high profiles, which sometimes make them look like cats, ready to pounce on each gate. A carved turn with sideways step, turn with *avalement*, down flexing, up-extending, rebound, edge-changing and, sometimes, step turns are all used to reduce braking elements or to pick up speed.

A slalom is a race in which the competitors have to follow a course marked out by alternate blue and red gates (between 35 and 70 for a special slalom).

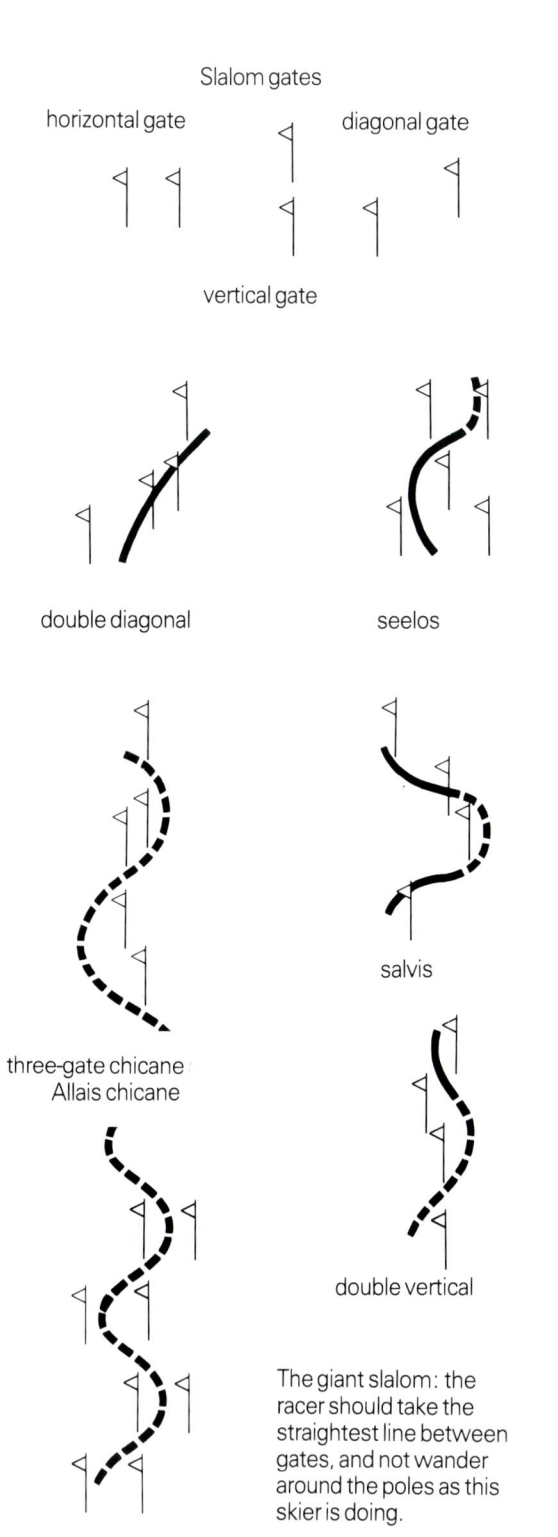

### Slalom gates

horizontal gate

diagonal gate

vertical gate

double diagonal

seelos

salvis

three-gate chicane
Allais chicane

double vertical

The giant slalom: the racer should take the straightest line between gates, and not wander around the poles as this skier is doing.

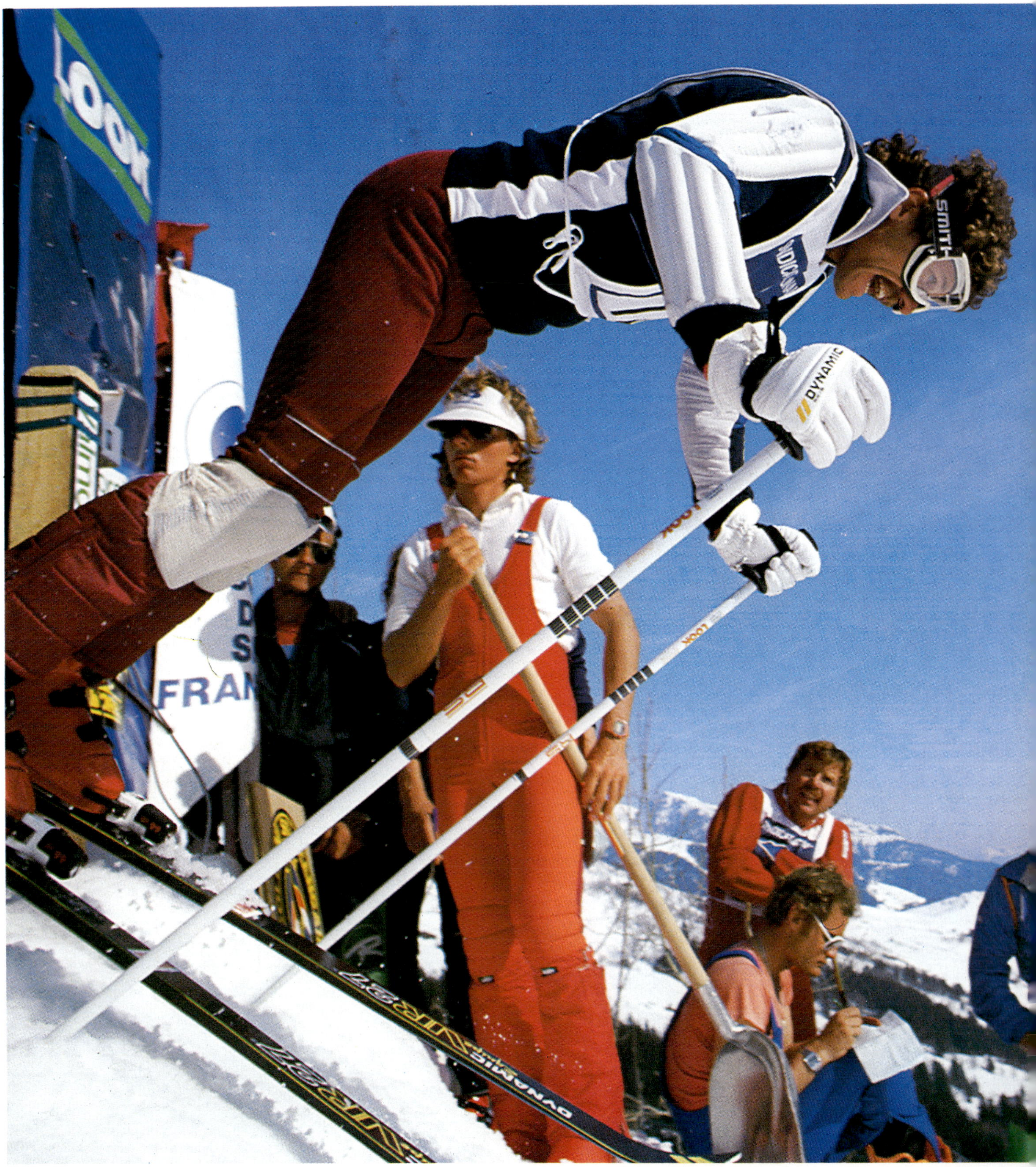
LOOK
SMITH
DYNAMIC
FRAN

# COMPETITION SKIING

You are about to be rewarded for all your hard work. Three or four weeks of training have enabled you to master the fundamental techniques of Alpine skiing, to try out all types of snow and slopes, so that you can 'get by' anywhere. All that is left is to perfect your technique, and to make the choice between relaxed skiing on all kinds of terrain and snow, going as and where you please, or competition skiing, involving training for slalom, downhill, speed and so on. This choice will govern your ski selection, physical preparation for skiing... and the nature of your après-ski activities! The one offers work on perfecting your technique, with plenty of free skiing, while the other entails training runs and practising turns through a seemingly endless succession of gates. The choice is yours, although it is worth remembering that you can always change from recreational skiing to competition, and vice versa.

**COMPETITION**

# REDUCING SOURCES OF BRAKING

If you are going to be able to keep up your speed as you turn, or schuss down the fall line, you will have to learn some new positions and adapt traditional skiing techniques. To some extent, the advice we are going to give you comes from the racers' creed. Here are just some of the things you must learn to do:

- Master the simultaneous action of both feet by perfecting your ability to control each leg independently.
- Establish a skiing position that enables you to keep your balance by subtle adjustments in your angulation.
- Keep your upper-body movement separate from that of your legs to obtain better balance and extension.
- Be able to judge precisely the degree of edging needed depending on the curve, snow, and your line.
- Avoid any sudden, unintentional side-slipping.
- Ski as close as possible to the fall line.
- Race according to your technical ability.
- Even out the pressure in turns and on moguls; this requires a mastery of vertical movements (flexing down, up-extending and *avalement*), longitudinal techniques (*avalement*, heel pressure), and lateral control (independence of your legs, angulation, knee turning).

Finally, you should always be prepared to adjust your movements to the terrain.

However, reducing braking effects is not, in itself, enough to gain those precious extra seconds; you will also need to learn ways of increasing your speed. There are many possibilities here: effective use of your poles; stepping forward from one foot to the other (the skating step, or half-skating step as you come out of a turn); as well as exploiting the flexibility of the skis as they bend under pressure either from your weight or from the terrain. At the same time, one must admit that trying for a faster glide by a change in body position (the schuss or 'egg' position, for example), looking for the ideal line, finely judged edging and, in general, trying to avoid braking, are of much greater value than specific methods of accelerating.

There are no standard racing turns. Competition skiers use a range of basic techniques and combine them depending on their own personalities and the specific problems each turn poses.

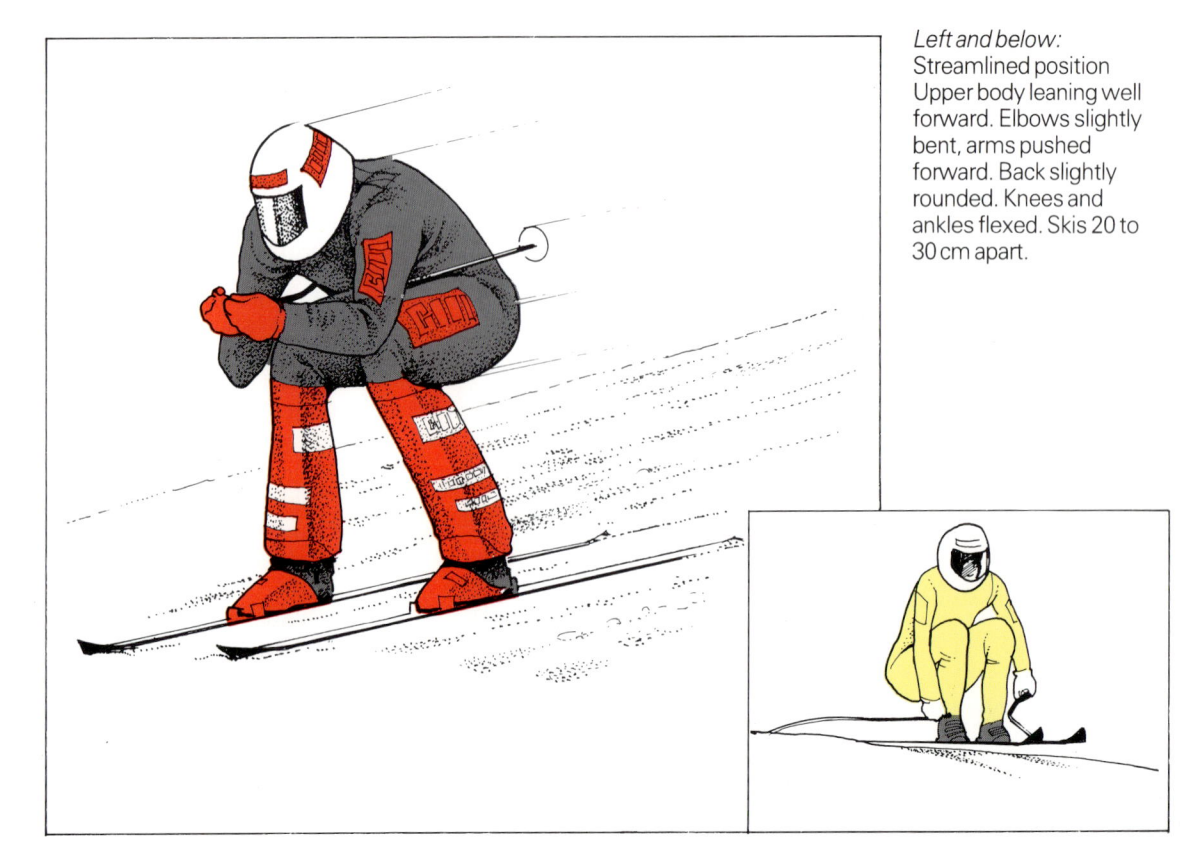

*Left and below:*
Streamlined position Upper body leaning well forward. Elbows slightly bent, arms pushed forward. Back slightly rounded. Knees and ankles flexed. Skis 20 to 30 cm apart.

*Above:* This is the typical 'aerodynamic' position assumed for the flying kilometre. There are no turns, no obstacles, and the piste is perfectly smooth. At a pinch, a good stuntman who 'slides' rather than skis could clock up a respectable time.

*Left:* Frenchman Michel Canac in a slalom. The three aims of a slalom skier are to find the ideal line through the gates, brake as little as possible on turns, and to accelerate between, and going through, the gates.

## COMPETITION

# SKID TURN: AVALEMENT

These are downhill turns initiated by a combination of unweighting by *avalement* (raising of the legs in front of the skier due to the terrain or muscular effort) and one or more pivoting movements, the turn being steered with minimum edging. So, how do you do it? As you are coming up to a bump following a counter-turn, push your feet slightly forward to avoid braking, let your legs come up while anticipating with your upper body, balance yourself with your downhill pole, arms apart, and pivot your skis with most of your weight on the outside ski. Then resume the basic position. It is important that you set your edges correctly when steering the outside ski; the inside ski should remain more or less flat on the snow.

When and where should you use this competition turn? The steering phase should be used whenever you meet soft snow, often at the start of a turn, sometimes through slalom gates, with your weight on both skis, or straight downhill – in which case you need a sufficiently flexed basic position to enable you to control sideways movement of your knees. As for the *avalement*, it can be either passive or active, and can be combined with a weight transfer. The *avalement* is particularly effective in deep snow and on moguls, and should be used to even out the pressures when you are skiing moguls, rutted slalom courses or in a counter-turn.

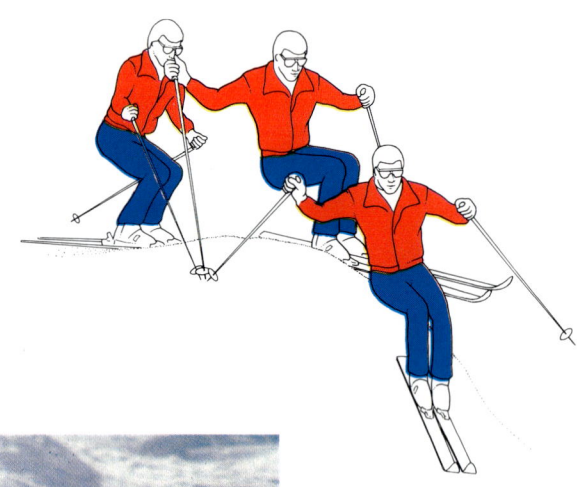

*Above:* Your upper body should be flexed in anticipation.
Lean on the downhill pole, arms spread.
Keep most weight on the outside ski.
Let your legs come up.
Push your feet forward slightly.

# CARVED TURN WITH SIDEWAYS STEP

This downhill turn is initiated by an energetic weight transfer combined with one or more pivoting and unweighting techniques. Steering is effected by establishing and maintaining the carving effect. This time, then, you have to balance over your outside ski, and gradually adopt a flexed position with heel pressure. Then, by pressing your knee inwards, you will set the edge firmly, while positioning the upper body in anticipation, arms apart. At this point, simultaneously rebound on to the downhill ski, step the uphill ski out sideways, and transfer your weight with an energetic movement. You can then pivot the outside ski, trying all the time to create and maintain the carving effect of the outside ski for steering. The inside ski can be either lifted completely off the snow or left more or less flat.

Carved steering is very effective on hard snow or ice, often as you are coming out of a turn, and on steep and very steep slopes. This sideways step involves a hefty weight transfer. You need good pressure on the downhill ski and a reasonable amount of strength. It can be combined with an *avalement* and counter-rotation, with an up-extension, or rebound with counter-rotation. It should also be noted that the uphill ski can be at a slight angle to the downhill one (forward thrust), parallel (pivoting of the outside ski by steering), or in a converging position (towards the next curve).

*Right:* The carving effect is produced by the outside ski (note the reverse camber), while the inside ski is lifted.

*Right:* The uphill ski can be placed in a diverging position. In this case you have a combination of sideways movement with forward thrust.

## COMPETITION

# SLALOM SKIING

Slalom was introduced in the 1920s by Arnold Lunn, with official rules from 1923. The idea behind it was to help winter sports enthusiasts to discover the joys of skiing without having to plod to the top of the downhill pistes (ski-lifts were not invented until some 15 years later). Twisting and turning round poles soon became a favourite skiing activity: slalom was born. The giant slalom followed – much later – but since then it has developed an enthusiastic following.

Slalom gates are not very wide and are positioned according to different permutations laid down by the Fédération International de Ski which are designed to test skiers' skills. The vertical drop must be between 180 and 220 m for men, and 130 to 180 m for women in Olympic or World Cup events. In other international events, the drop should be 140 to 220 m for men and 120 to 180 m for women. Men have to cope with between 55 and 75 gates, whereas women have between 45 and 60, set out on a piste at least 40 m wide with an incline of 20 to 27°. The gate width lies between 4 and 6 m, and the distance between the pivot poles should never be less than 75 cm or greater than 15 m. A slalom course consists

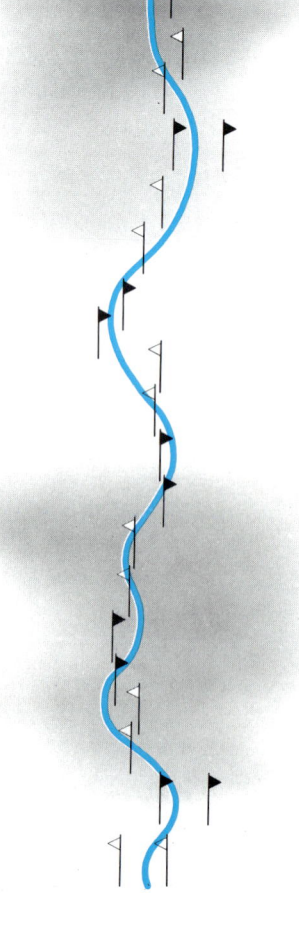

*Left:* A slalom course. Between the two photographs on the left there are at least 60 gates, a drop of 180 m, and the need to be as lithe as a cat if you are going to avoid the poles and keep on the right line.

of horizontal (open) and vertical (closed) gates, and where possible there should be two or three chicanes consisting of between three and five gates, together with at least four double verticals. A slalom race is contested over two runs, down two courses laid out alongside one another.

For many years, wooden poles were used for the gates, but a recent development has been the introduction of hinged poles (rapid gates), especially in major international events. These new poles have presented some problems for skiers such as Ingemar Stenmark, who had to change his technique. If you hit the pole with your arm, shin or foot, you stand a fair chance of being hit on the head by the top of the pole, as a result of which you could well lose your goggles, if not your balance!

*Right and below:* You must have lightning reflexes, precision and self-control in the slalom. Time is all-important, although few skiers exceed 40 km/h, and the race is won or lost on the turns. Angulation, anticipation, acceleration – everything is grist to the mill in the attempt to save precious hundredths of a second.

**COMPETITION**

# GIANT SLALOM

Giant slalom is a fairly recent arrival on the competition scene, 1952 saw its first inclusion in the winter Olympic Games. Technically this event comes between the special slalom and the downhill, combining the turns of one with the speed of the other, although, surprisingly, the greatest slalom exponent of all time – Ingemar Stenmark – equally brilliant in special and giant slalom, has never won a downhill. However, the giant slalom is considered the most physically, technically and athletically demanding event by the specialists, and the Swede fears no one as these are his strengths.

The first noticeable differences between the two slaloms are that the giant has wider gates, placed further apart, producing a faster race, and the course drop and length are greater. Compared to the downhill, the giant slalom obviously needs more care on the high-speed turns.

As with the special, rules for the giant slalom are laid down by the FIS. The drop must be between 250 and 400 m for men, 250 and 350 for women, and the piste should be at least 30 m wide. The gates are different from the special slalom design in that they consist not of two single poles each with its own flag, but of a pair of poles (which can be jointed) linked by a rectangular red or blue flag 75 cm wide and 50 cm deep. The gates are between 4 and 8 m wide, and the minimum distance between the nearest poles of any two gates is 10 m. Giant slalom is also run over two legs (on the same day, where possible), although both legs can be run down the same piste, provided the gates are repositioned. Electronic timing is used; the clock is triggered by the competitor as he leaves the starting gate.

As far as technique is concerned, you will notice that a giant slalom skier always keeps low to give himself better control of turns and steering, while in the special slalom he would be more erect to allow faster turns through the tighter, narrower gates.

Obviously, when you enter your first giant slalom as part of an ESF test, the course is likely to be shorter than a World Cup one, but you can still enjoy the same sensations of speed and control.

Giant slalom courses: gates must be between 4 and 8 m wide, and the two flags forming a gate should be placed vertically to the piste. For closed gates, the flags should be 30 cm wide and about 50 cm high.

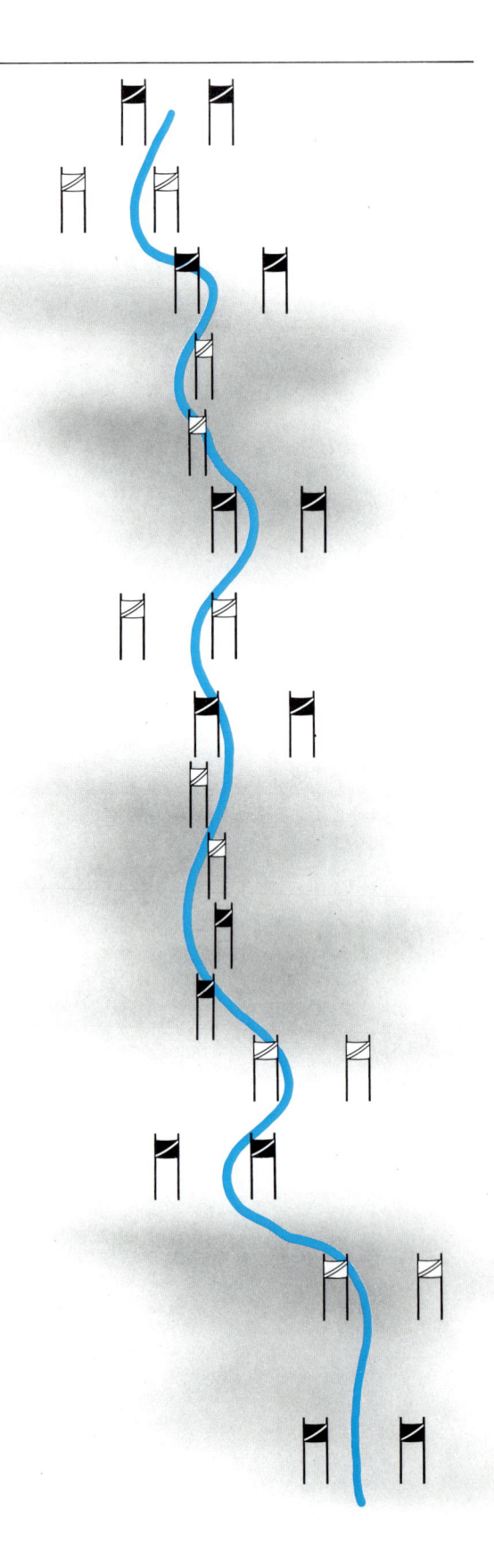

How do you tell the difference between a special and a giant slalom? By the length of the course and the width of the gates, by the ski techniques used and, most easily, by the shape of the poles: a single pole with a triangular flag for the special, and two poles joined at the top by a strip of material for the giant slalom.

The giant slalom skier: a specialist in rounded, flowing turns, usually executed in a crouched position. Above all, he must be a brilliant athlete – physically, psychologically and technically.

**COMPETITION**

# DOWNHILL TECHNIQUES

It is a very long time since downhill races consisted simply of a start and finish line, with the competitors being able to choose which route to use between the two; time was the only consideration. Nowadays, major downhill events have strict rules, and the competitors are top-level athletes with mini-computers for brains; witness Jean-Claude Killy, one of the greatest skiers of all time, talking after a victory on the Lauberhorn – the most technically difficult of all downhills: 'By the end of my training runs, I had photographed every inch of the piste inside my head: I knew it by heart. A non-stop run reinforced this visual memory and all I had to do in the race was to re-run the mental film... always looking 100 metres ahead. It was that easy.'

This is the formula adopted by all the best downhill skiers, and it enables them to gain those extra hundredths of a second needed for victory.

The downhill has always been the showpiece of the Alpine events and, both for the racers and the men who prepare the courses, it has become a highly sophisticated affair. To get some idea of the complexity of a modern downhill you need only read the FIS booklet of international rules. Among other specified conditions, you will find: It should be possible to glide down the course, from start to finish, without needing poles... excessive speeds which increase the risk of accidents and endanger competitors should be limited by appropriate measures to reduce speed by placing an adequate number of gates at certain points on the piste.'

Other specifications for officially approved FIS courses are that, for men, the drop should be between 500 and 1,000 metres, the piste width should be at least 30 metres where it is bordered by trees, gates should be a minimum of 8 metres wide, and that a competitor should not be able to complete an Olympic downhill course in less than two minutes. For women, the drop has to be between 500 and 800 metres, and the minimum time one minute and forty seconds. Another notable difference between slaloms and downhills is that the downhill practice runs take place over the actual race course and in the same conditions.

If, for example, due to bad weather, the competitors have not been able to make three practice runs down the course in the days immediately preceding the race, then the whole event is cancelled. The rules also state that, 'a competitor should cover the course on two skis, but may finish on only one ski'.

Even though he would be travelling at something like 140 km/h during the final schuss.

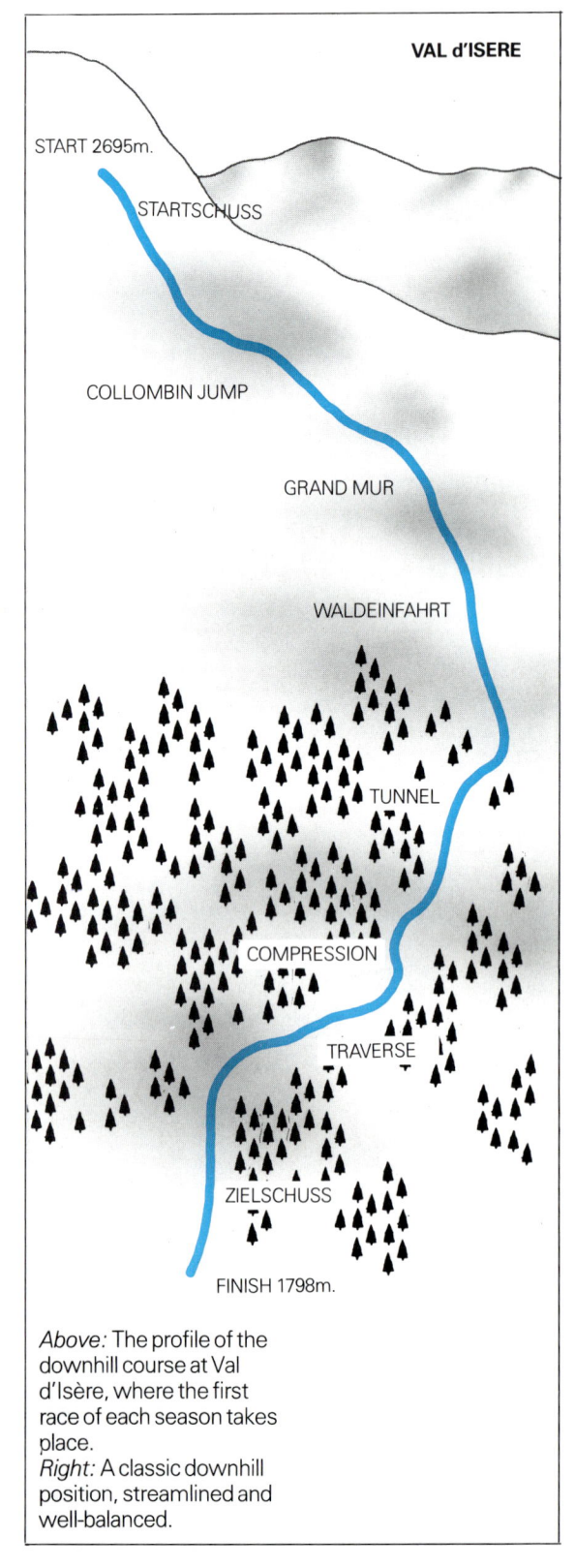

*Above:* The profile of the downhill course at Val d'Isère, where the first race of each season takes place.
*Right:* A classic downhill position, streamlined and well-balanced.

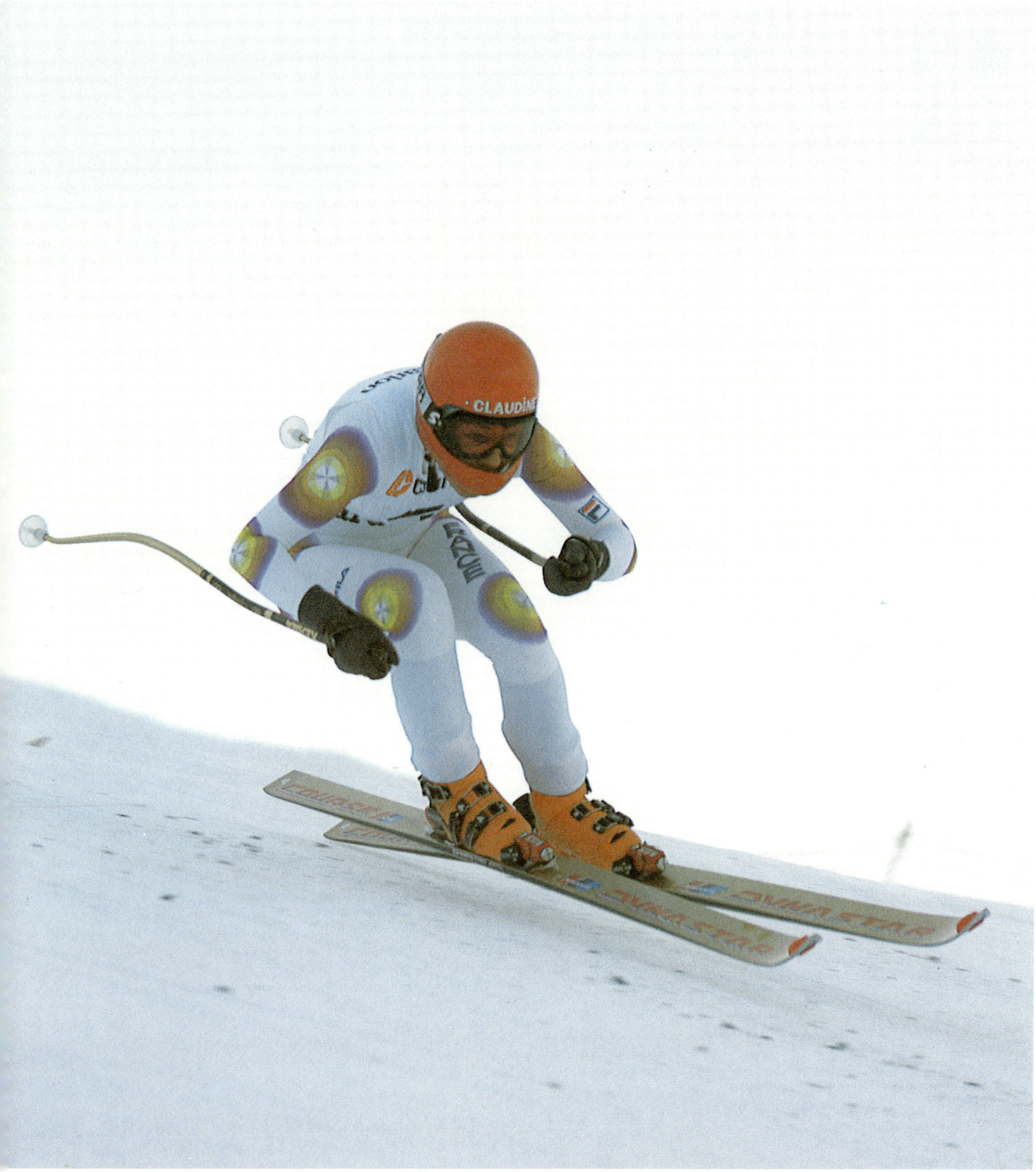
CLAUDINE

**COMPETITION**

# SUPER GIANT SLALOM

Dreamed up by the organizers of major international competitions – definitely not by slalom or downhill racers – the super giant comes halfway between the traditional giant slalom and the downhill. Its creators saw the super giant not so much as a new type of Alpine competition, but more as a way of preventing modern racers from over-specializing. The days when a skier could shine in all three of the traditional Alpine events are long gone. Jean-Claude Killy was the last of that extinct breed of racer equally capable of winning either a slalom or a downhill, as he proved at the 1968 Grenoble Olympics, when he won three gold medals (the only other man ever to complete this grand slam was the Austrian Toni Sailer at Cortina in 1956). Today's downhillers rarely compete in slaloms, or vice versa, unless they are looking for points for the combined competition; but they have no real hopes of victory in their second-string event. Admittedly, this seemingly inevitable specialization, mainly due to the large number of meetings held each winter on all the world's mountains, is not so prevalent in women's competition. Some, like Anne-Marie Moser-Pröll from Austria, and the German Rosi Mittermaier, won all three Alpine events only seven or eight years ago.

In any case, in an attempt to stop the rot, the World Cup organizers in particular (this series comprises about 30 races in each discipline annually) wanted to introduce the super giant. The competitors showed a marked lack of enthusiasm and, during 1983/4 – its first season as a World Cup event – even the top skiers steered clear of the super giant. Consequently, it is hard to predict the future of the super giant slalom in international competition. It would be a shame if the event disappeared from the slopes, since this single-leg race combines the risks of a downhill (racers wear helmets in the super giant) with the need for suppleness of a slalom and a great deal of stamina!

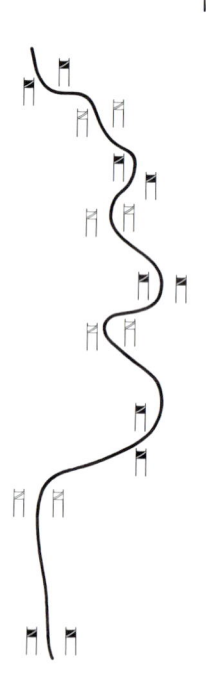

*Right:* A super-giant slalom competitor wears the same clothing as a downhill racer: body-hugging suit for low air-resistance, and protective helmet.

# PARALLEL SLALOM

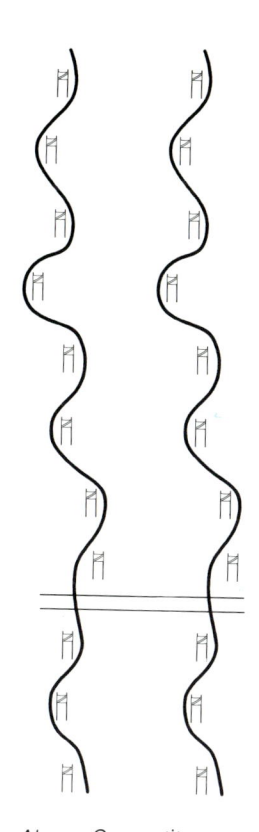

*Above:* Competitors are racing not against the clock here, but against each other. It is a demanding discipline, since the winner may have to compete up to ten times in less than two hours to eliminate his rivals.

Some purists still think, 20 years after its introduction by Honoré Bonnet (former trainer of the French national team), that the parallel slalom is a spectator sport rather than a test of skill. This is true to a certain extent, but there can be no harm in enjoying the sight of two racers battling to be first across the finish line. The event has been given competition room in the World Cup, but with inconclusive results. Nevertheless, today, parallel slaloms and even parallel downhills are being staged on pistes all over the world and, precisely because they are spectacular and capture the imaginations of millions of skiers, both amateur and professional, they gain plenty of television coverage (mostly in the United States, where the majority of the World Professional Championship events – always in the parallel version – are staged).

As for the salient points of parallel events (which take place every week in all the French resorts under the auspices of the Ecole du Ski Français or Club des Sports), they are races in which two or more competitors ski simultaneously, side by side, down two or more pistes, all of which have as nearly as possible identical tracks, terrain and snow preparation. The drop in a parallel slalom is between 80 and 100 m, with 20 to 30 gates, corresponding to a race duration of about 20 to 25 seconds. The race is started by the lifting of automatic barriers: this is often the vital part of the race, since the skier who is first away is frequently first to finish. Each two-competitor race is staged over two legs, with the skiers changing pistes for the second leg. So is it just a spectator sport? Maybe, but we shall end this chapter with the opinion of a true expert – Jean-Claude Killy – who, after an amazing amateur career became, only four years later, Professional World Champion. Soon after this victory he admitted, 'To take the starting line ten times consecutively is much more tiring than in a traditional slalom, however difficult that may be. I don't think I've ever had to work as hard in my life as I did for this title!'

The maximum number of competitors in the final of a parallel event is 32, split up into two groups of 16. If both competitors in any one race fall, then the first to pass the finishing line with both skis on goes through to the next round, and, if both fail to finish, the one who has skied further wins. If a competitor fails to drag himself and his skis across the line on the first leg, he cannot compete in the second.

This is a fun event for amateurs so, if you ever have the chance of taking part in a parallel race, go ahead – you will not regret it!

# ESF SLALOM TEST

Ski tuition in France is a serious business, as is shown by the training received by all the instructors in French ski schools (see page 40). After their training and passing their exams, however, French instructors keep up their practice sessions, some with a view to making a name for themselves at the instructors' national championships, held annually as part of a week of demonstrations and festivities to mark the end of the winter season.

The following competitions are organized during this week: special slaloms for women, veterans and seniors who, after regional qualifying events, have reached this 'open' final, with its prestigious team prize: the Instructors' Championship; a national cross-country event organized along the same lines; a giant slalom restricted to women who hold a certificate for children's skiing instruction.

These events are organized by the national union of instructors and enable thousands of instructors to meet each year, to compare their skiing skills, and also to exchange technical and teaching notes, thereby standardizing the teaching methods in the different schools.

The instructors benefit by getting to know each other better, finishing the season in style, and comparing their technique and skills against the best in the world. For, although racers who are members of national teams are not allowed to compete, they are invited to 'open' the different events. This means that, rather as in the ESF performance tests, the instructors can compare their own times with those of world-class skiers, and thereby have some idea of their relative ability.

The recently built resort of Valmorel had the honour of staging the 1984 Instructors' Championships. Even at World Cup events, it is rare for so many competitors and interested spectators to be seen.

115

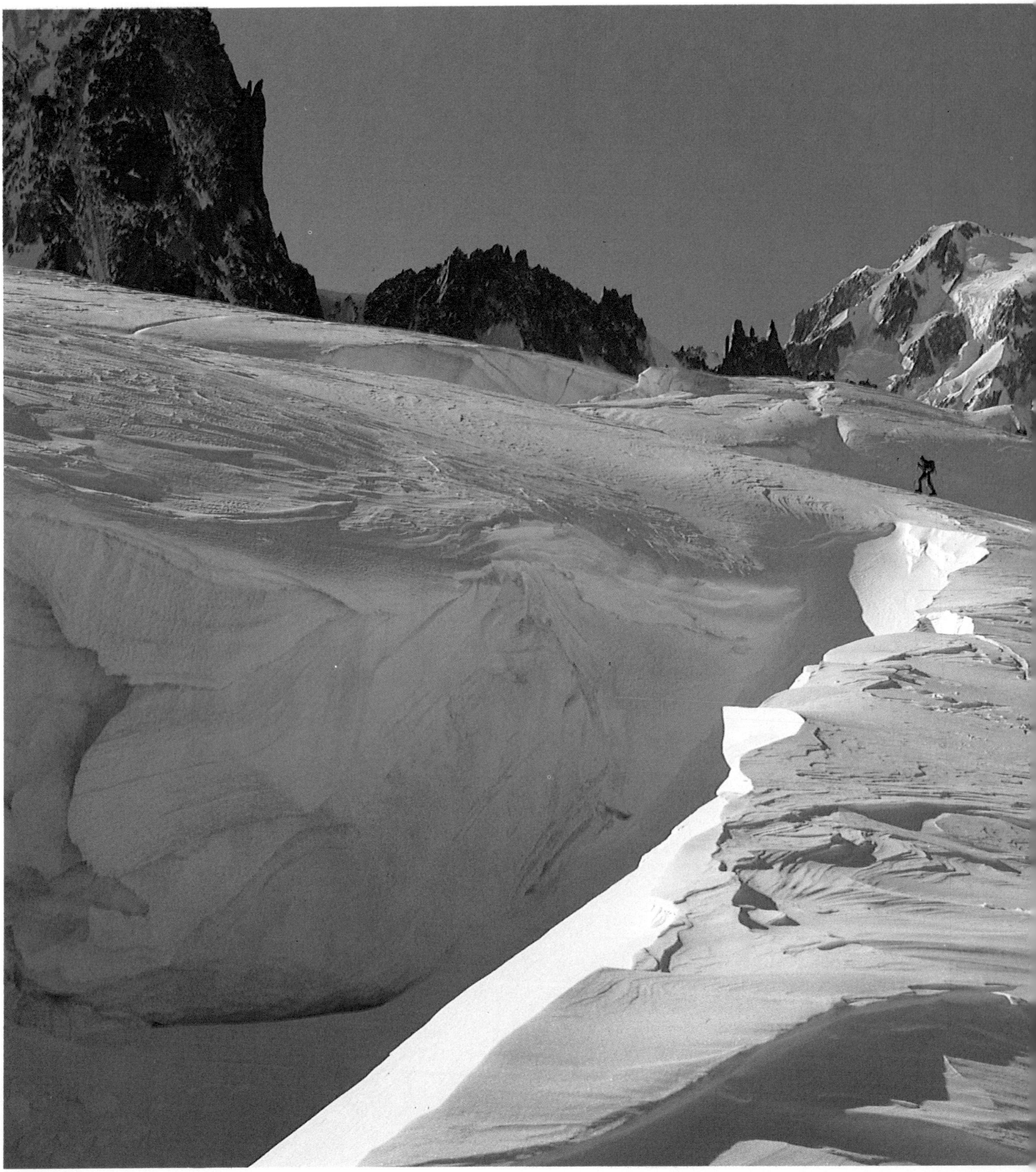

# LE GRAND SKI

After Class 3, you may have chosen to concentrate on competition skiing, or you may have opted instead for learning more about ski touring. Both are excellent choices, and open up the infinite realm of 'le grand ski'. However, a little caution would not go amiss here, since you are going to be dealing with unpredictable nature, not with carefully manicured pistes where there are no hidden rocks, no danger of avalanches, no crevasses lurking beneath an inviting expanse of virgin snow. Henceforth your instructor will be concentrating not so much on improving your technique as on telling you about your environment. He will teach you about snow in all its manifestations, the weather and how it can change suddenly, the sun, and how to choose the best routes. Your instructor will repeat time and time again that you should always remember to ask about snow conditions before setting out, that you should never ski off on your own... in fact, all the safety rules which will make it possible for you to enjoy one of the most satisfying of all Alpine activities.

# FREE SKIING IN TREES

Free skiing will be your long-awaited introduction to off-piste skiing, which is the goal of any reasonably ambitious student. But before you set off for the great virgin expanse of the mountains, the ungroomed areas of your resort will be perfectly adequate for your first, and even later, forays. Accompanied by your instructor, you can perfect your skiing technique in all kinds of snow and, above all, start to let your hair down in that vast area which lies between the pistes, in the trees, setting your sights on your first steep-sided, narrow gullies, and experiencing your first spectacular, but relatively harmless, tumbles due to unforeseen increases in gradient, or the odd branch that you cannot avoid.

From all these possibilities, we shall begin with skiing through forests, which is perhaps the most enjoyable form of off-piste skiing and the only one you can contemplate attempting in mist or a snowstorm. It is also an excellent training ground, since you can treat the trunks of the fir trees rather like slalom poles – with the exception that you should avoid hitting them, since they will not bend! This difference between trees and slalom poles means that you will have to master your turns and speed control in all snow conditions. Forests are also the places where the snow changes suddenly, due to shaded corners, melting snow and wet pine needles dropping from the trees, and where there are mischievous branches which are barely visible under their snowy mantle and seemingly eager to catch you out. Within a few hundred metres you may find fluffy powder, crust, ice, wet snow, or just plain rotten snow. So you will be able to ski to your heart's content for days on end through the trees, without having any technical problems – just aching legs!

As for skiing between the pistes, this is even easier. All you need do is to adapt your technique to the snow conditions. The only major precaution you must take is to ensure that there is no risk of an avalanche, and you should also steer clear of following other skiers' tracks unless you know where they lead. Consequently, you would be well advised to ask the advice of the piste preparers, even if you are planning to ski only 100 metres or so off the pistes, just to be sure that there is no risk.

To come to the last of the free-skiing options: harebrained skiing down impossible gullies. You should try this only if you are aware of the great danger involved and your skiing is ultra-expert. There have always been skiers eager to risk life and limb, but it was not until 1970 that Sylvain Saudan put 'impossible' skiing on the map. Many others, such as Vallancourt, Anselme-Baud and Boivin, have tried since and coped with equally precipitous gullies. However, it does seem that the maximum gradient (more than 65°) is the limit.

Free skiing is all about venturing into – what is for you – the unknown. It is a fascinating sport...

...but not without its falls which, although spectacular, are rarely dangerous. Nevertheless, you should never ski off on your own, since an awkward tumble when you are alone could prove very nasty.

# CRUST AND ICE

With the coming of spring, the powder snow on the downhills begins to disappear. Subjected to the increasingly warm sun and cold nights, the snow gradually alters its character. The piste surfaces become more like glass, and if you venture on to the virgin slopes, the surface is often not strong enough to take your weight, and you find your feet held in a vice-like grip by the frozen crust. It goes without saying that this sort of terrain is not going to give you those unforgettable downhill runs you read of in the holiday brochures. Nevertheless, any skier worthy of the name should be able to cope with any situation.

To begin with, ice: your main concern is to get as good a grip on the surface as possible. Consequently, if you are going to have any success in this area, you will need top-quality skis. You should therefore choose top-of-the-range skis which will have been researched and developed to give optimum performance. You can make do with almost any old skis in deep snow, but here, in contrast, your control has to be so finely tuned that nothing must be left to chance. For example, making sure that your running surfaces and edges are well prepared is of vital importance. If you are a dab hand at do-it-yourself, you can learn how to sharpen your own edges. Your instructor can give you some useful tips to ensure that you do not make matters worse rather than better! However, if you are no handyman, entrust the job to a sports shop, since they are very well equipped to handle such tasks these days. At the same time, it is worth remembering that, even if a racer's skis are in tip-top condition, he will probably still spend an hour or two fiddling with the running surfaces or sharpening the edges, which just shows how much attention you should pay to your equipment if you want the best results.

Even if you are properly equipped, it will still be your technique which will get you out of tight corners. The first point to remember for skiing on ice is to dispense with any superfluous actions and to make all your moves very precisely. Unweighting and pivoting are hardly ever used in ice skiing, and flexion-extension is needed only for absorbing any irregularities in the snow surface. Changing direction is mostly achieved by a gentle edging of the outside ski by pushing your knee slightly inwards. Since your grip on the snow will be very weak, the equally weak centrifugal force means that you should only lean slightly inwards during the curve. It is rather like walking a tight-rope, with the outside ski edge being the rope.

Using brute strength, although this is the complete opposite of what we have just recommended, is equally effective. Instead of evening out the pressure which is extremely useful on long curves, you can opt for wedeling. You will find this technique adapts best to ice skiing if you set your edges very firmly. You are looking for maximum impact on the snow, combined with a knee-shift to set your edges. If it feels as though you are giving the snow a good kick, then you are getting the idea.

Crust also, depending on the situation, needs either gentleness or aggression. Sometimes you will be skiing along without a care in the world, and then suddenly the snow gives beneath you. This is the time to bring those stem turns into play, but link all the actions together smoothly and try to keep your speed constant. On the other hand, if, every time you put pressure on the snow, your feet sink into the depths, you will need strength and aggression to take you down safely to the bottom of the slope: clearing the skis rapidly, followed by pivoting during the unweighted phase and a balanced landing on both skis is a simple, if tiring, solution.

A more physically demanding option is to keep your skis close together beneath the surface crust. When you have reached this stage, you will have mastered a technique which combines the practical with the aesthetic. Finally, take heart: the sun and frost will change the snow into that magic carpet on which, before you know where you are, you will be skiing like a champion!

Skiing on crusty snow, as opposed to ice, rules out repeated weight transfers. Spreading your weight evenly over both skis is the best recipe for avoiding preventing your ski-tips from being buried in the snow.

Also, when the crust is really brittle, you should not feel embarrassed if you have to do a few kick-turns to negotiate a difficult passage.

# MOGULS

Moguls, or bumps, probably gave you nightmares in the beginners' class but, with a little practice, they can become your allies. Instead of avoiding them like the plague, one day you will find yourself seeking them out.

The problems which need tackling are both technical and tactical. Once you have discovered the right line to take through moguls, you will find this type of skiing surprisingly easy. The first vital factor is to start the initiation of your turn at the exact moment when the centre of your skis are on the top of the bump. At the beginning, you will judge this visually, but to gain speed and ski more efficiently, you must learn to 'feel' the terrain.

Initiating your turn at the right moment is not necessarily a guarantee of success since, according to your ability, you must choose between a braking curve and one which gives a maximum slide. The solution to the first is simple: use the banking of the mogul to side-slip, thereby slowing yourself down. The second is trickier, but also very enjoyable since it demands so little effort on your part: once you are into the curve, keep your skis along the axis of the hollow behind the mogul, and you can even use the reverse slope of the next one.

Even in this case you can check your speed, although it needs a high degree of precision: braking follows a quick pivoting of the skis as you come out of the dip, combined with edging produced by pushing your knees uphill.

The purely technical problems can be put in a nutshell: how to absorb the irregularities in the terrain, since this task in itself affects both your sideways and front/back balance. The first exercises you can practise consist of straight runs through mogul fields, trying to combine two apparently contradictory goals: to keep your skis in contact with the snow at all times, and to prevent your head moving up and down, rather as though you were balancing a book on top of it as an exercise in deportment!

The most important part of this little game is to push your feet down into each dip and, gradually, to become used to the sequence of stretch/bend/stretch/bend which varies in speed depending on the distance between moguls and your own rate of travel. Marrying this exercise with down-flexing/up-extending as you initiate your turns, in this particular case, will bring to light another difficulty. Until now, you have been used to initiating your turns as you up-extend; unfortunately, you will have to unlearn this habit for mogul skiing!

122

*Above:* A position of anticipation: the former downhill pole (skier's right hand) is lifted as a counter-turn is executed just before the bump. The left-hand pole is brought forward in preparation.

*Left:* Four stages in the execution of a turn on a bump. Firstly, the counter-turn with edge-check for control just before the bump. Secondly, the initiation of the turn on the summit of the bump, the pole is planted and pivoting starts as the minimum area of the skis is in contact with the snow. Finally, the steering of the turn.

*Left:* Two examples of classic positions for absorbing bumps. The knees are well flexed, the arms apart, the upper body upright – ready for the next bump and the next turn. The lower picture shows more than masterful control of balance, avalement and pivoting. To cope with bumps with this style requires a good deal of practice…

# ULTIMATE OFF-PISTE

The ultimate goal for most skiers must be off-piste skiing in complete freedom, far from any trace of man's interference with nature. There are no words to express the feelings of an off-piste skier when the weather is fine and he has prepared himself adequately – both physically and psychologically – for the experience. You do not set out for off-piste skiing in the same way as you would approach a black, or even an Olympic-standard downhill course, or would go off to ski among the trees close to the resort. This section will, therefore, contain more advice than instruction.

To begin with, you do not need a competition-level technique to hoist your rucksack on to your back and enjoy your first off-piste outing. If the snow conditions are very good (spring snow, or a thin layer of powder on top of hard, stable snow, etc), and if your planned descent is not too steep, there is no reason why you should not sample these delights; provided you are with an instructor, as it is vital that you should be with someone who knows and can teach you about the mountain and snow. At this point, take note to steer clear of unqualified skiers who claim to know the region, since off-piste skiing inevitably brings with it the risk of avalanches and, at high altitude, of crevasses, or the possibility of losing your way if the mist suddenly descends. You are also going to be skiing on a different surface: no more snow that has been pounded a thousand times; no more ice that has been thoughtfully broken up by the 'ratracs'; no more pistes to indicate the route to take. Your instructor will know where to find terrains to suit your level, or even some that are slightly above it as, whatever the sport, it is always satisfying to feel that you are stretching yourself. Never go skiing off-piste with friends, even though they may be very advanced skiers, if they have not watched you ski – your relative lack of expertise would be an unpleasant surprise for them (and embarrassing for you) if they always had to wait for you to catch up.

Lastly, there is ski-mountaineering. You can reach your starting point by helicopter (although only outside France, since landing skiers on the mountains is banned in the French Alps – you can always cross the border with your ESF instructor to a country where it is allowed) or wearing 'skins' (synthetic skins which you attach to your skis to prevent them from sliding backwards). Do not attempt ski-mountaineering until you are a good skier in all snow conditions and on all gradients, are fit and know how to do a kick turn.

*Above and right:* This series of photographs show various off-piste skiing (not to be confused with free skiing in a resort. Or high-altitude ski touring in which skiers climb under their own steam wearing skins under their skis and pushing on their poles). This skiing opens up new horizons, but not without certain dangers: crevasses, avalanches and alarming physical symptoms due to the high altitude. You should never, therefore, embark on off-piste skiing without an instructor to guide you.

125

# FRINGE SKIING

*Above:* Winterstick or snowsurfing: fantastic downhills through deep snow and, even better, through the trees in a sport which combines the off-shore with the off-piste!

Skiing has, of course, been the most common 'sliding' sport in the mountains for a very long time, but this book would not be complete without a look at two new fringe sports which, over the last two or three years, have brought pleasure to many who were looking for different ways of enjoying the snow: monoskiing and snowsurfing. Both originated in California, but they did not take off until they arrived in the French Alps.

Monoskiing hit Chamonix in the early 1970s, courtesy of Pierre Poncet, a ski-mad photographer. As with many prototypes, Poncet's monoski was far from perfect: it did not work on piste snow, was unstable above a certain speed, and so on. Following on from Poncet, the French ski manufacturer Duret, then Rossignol, TUA from Italy, and Monoski and Co developed new materials which performed much better. Thanks to their efforts, this winter virtually all skiers, whatever their abilities, will be able to try the monoski under the watchful eye of the ESF instructors.

You are probably wondering why this idea of skiing on just one board has proved so popular: after all, two do the job perfectly well. More than likely it is because monoskiing, like snowsurfing, enables its practitioners to let themselves go, to enjoy free skiing, wide curves through the powder, elegant jumps from corniches, and hard physical exercise in crossing changes in the slope by turning with their poles.

As for snowsurfing, this is an even more recent development in that it was 'invented' by Pacific surfers only three or four years ago. The first boards were manufactured in Australia and the United States, and were marketed under the name 'Winterstick'. The first Winterstick championships were organized soon after in California and Australia, while a few boards found their way across the Atlantic to Les Arcs. Almost overnight, snowsurfing became the 'in' sport. Two seasons later, several hundred surfers regularly glide over the virgin snow of the French resorts.

*Above:* The Winterstick is a sophisticated surfboard, with straps to secure your après-ski boots.

*Above:* The monoski allows you to let your hair down and go, but keep away from the crowded slopes with their more conventional skiers.

*Left:* A single ski is fantastic for moguls, wide curves and for jumping corniches (no risk of crossing your tips!), but watch out for the slope levelling out, for you will need to push hard on your poles.

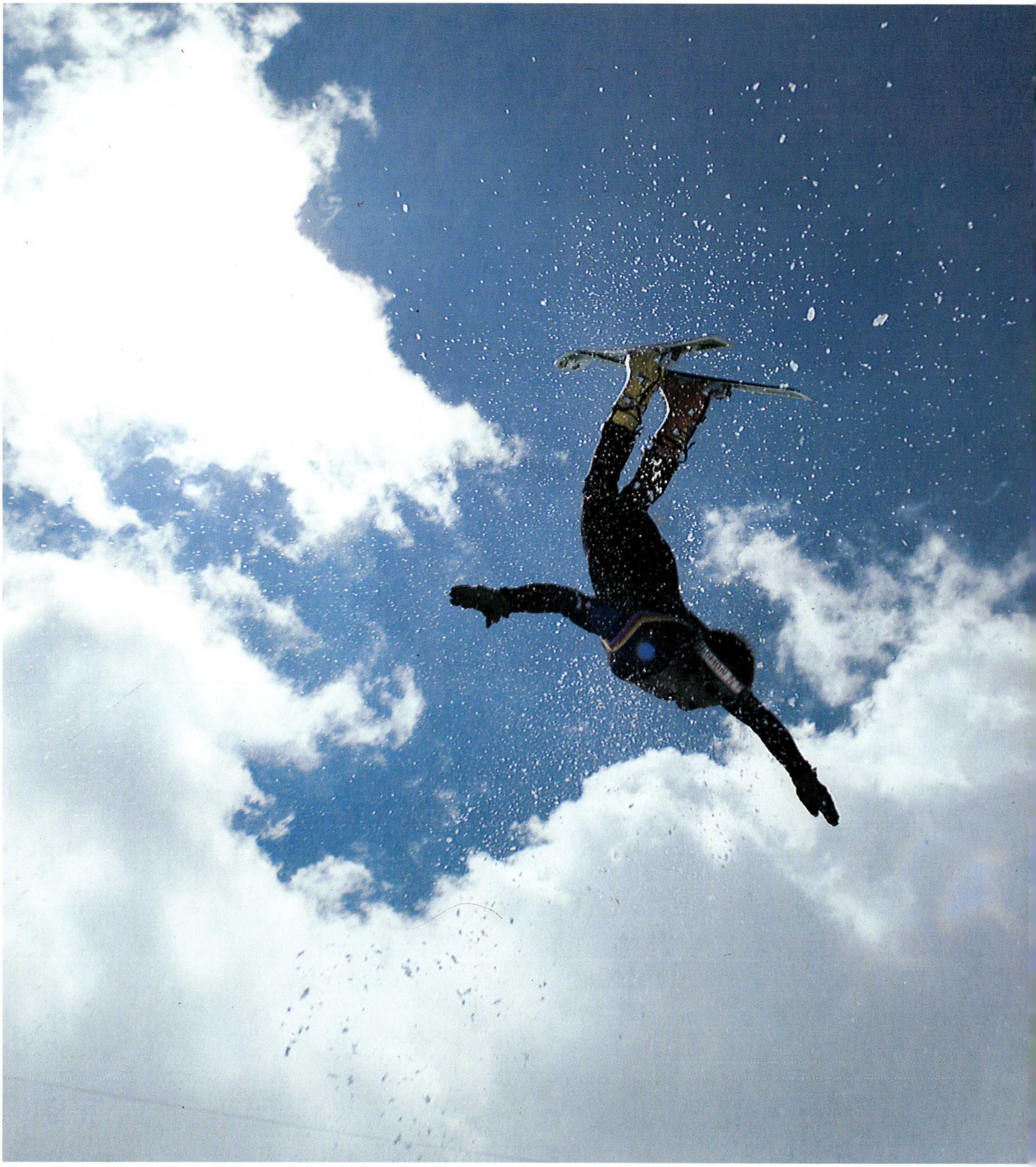

# FREESTYLE SKIING

This, the youngest of the Alpine disciplines, will feature in the Olympic Games for the first time in 1988 at Calgary (Canada). It is also the most original type of on-piste skiing and competition as, in each of the three events – ballet, moguls and jumps – skiers are virtually free from restrictions and time is of little importance. The only judging criteria are effectiveness, risk factors and aesthetic merit.

Skiers all over the world have always been attracted by the idea of performing spectacular jumps, but true free-style skiing was not born until the 1970s, in the American east coast.

BALLET: as its name suggests, ballet comprises a sequence of linked figures which, as in figure skating, aims to please the eye. The most impressive movements are the waltz, the crossed waltz, the helicopter, and a crossing/uncrossing figure. The sequence is performed to music on a sloping perfectly prepared piste. This is the least dangerous of the free-style events, and any athletic skier who would like a change from downhills could try his hand.

HOT-DOGGING: this is the principal free-style event, and one which seems to suit French skiers, since three of them have already become world champions since the championship was inaugurated: Henri Authier, Nano Pourtier and Philippe Bron. You have to be a world-class athlete to excel at hot-dogging – skiing down a mogul field as fast as possible, while making use of the bumps to perform jumps, twists, or any other insane aerobatic movement you can think of.

JUMPS: this is a true spectator sport and is, without doubt, the event which has seen the most progress over the last 15 years. Starting from simple forward, reverse, and sideways jumps, the best have managed to perform a triple forward somersault with triple twist before touching down. The event is not as dangerous as it used to be, surprisingly, since competitors undertake rigorous gymnastic training, especially on trampolines.

*Above:* Moguls the principal free-skiing event. Nano Pourtier, twice world champion: 'To start with you need nerves of iron and an exceptional sense of balance.'

*Left:* Jumps are the supreme spectator sport with ever more complicated jumps being devised. Henri Authier caught in mid-air at Tignes. He is one of the leading exponents of this art.

Ballet is essentially aesthetic gymnastics.

# SUMMER SKIING

Summer skiing areas consist mostly of glaciers, but it is obvious that not all French resorts can offer all-the-year-round snow. Your choice is, in fact, limited to the six resorts blessed with glaciers: Alpe d'Huez and Les Deux Alpes in the Dauphiné, and Tignes, Val d'Isère, La Plagne and Val Thorens in the northern Alps.

Since, even here, the snow cover is very limited during the summer, there is no question of off-piste skiing; rather you will have to concentrate on intensive training, which will be of enormous help in improving your technique. Summer-season instructors are adamant that one week's training at this time of year is worth a month's during the winter. This is due to several factors. To begin with, the snow conditions are very different. In summer you will ski between 8.00 am and 1.00 pm only, but during these five hours you will have to cope with ice, soft snow and 'sugar', and, at the end of the morning, slush. You may not encounter such varied snow conditions during an entire week's winter skiing. The location, also, counts: you will be skiing at almost 4,000 m, close to crevasses, in glorious scenery, and far above the tree line. Then again, although the sun is strong (keep those goggles on!) it is not that hot (except in sheltered spots, such as the restaurant terrace), so you will have to work hard to keep warm, rather than glide lazily down the pistes. Finally, summer skiing is primarily for the serious skier who wants to put in some hard training. Although there are no pine-trees on the summer slopes, some of the glaciers are transformed into forests of slalom poles, so that you will have plenty of opportunities for practising your slalom technique under the watchful eye of your ESF instructor.

Then, when you return to the resort centre after a morning on the mountain, you will find tennis courts, riding stables, a swimming pool and other facilities which you can use to continue your physical training. Summer skiing is, in short, like being at an open-air health farm with a curious extreme of two totally opposite climates.!

Summer skiing: the location is high-altitude glaciers. Skiing in swimming costumes is sometimes practicable, but be very careful, for the temperature can drop by as much as 20° within a few minutes and, more importantly, a fall can be very uncomfortable, since summer snow is particularly abrasive.

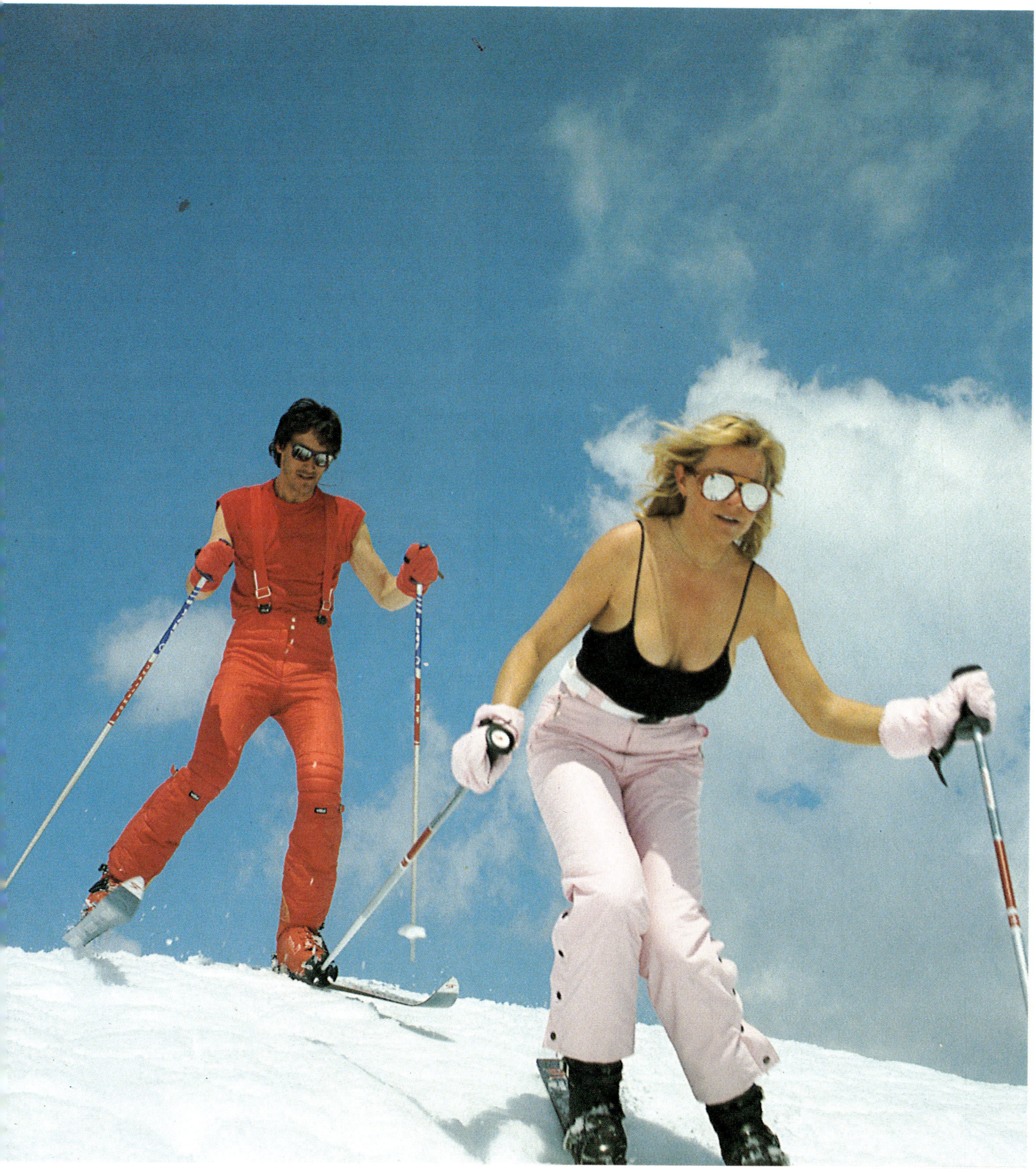

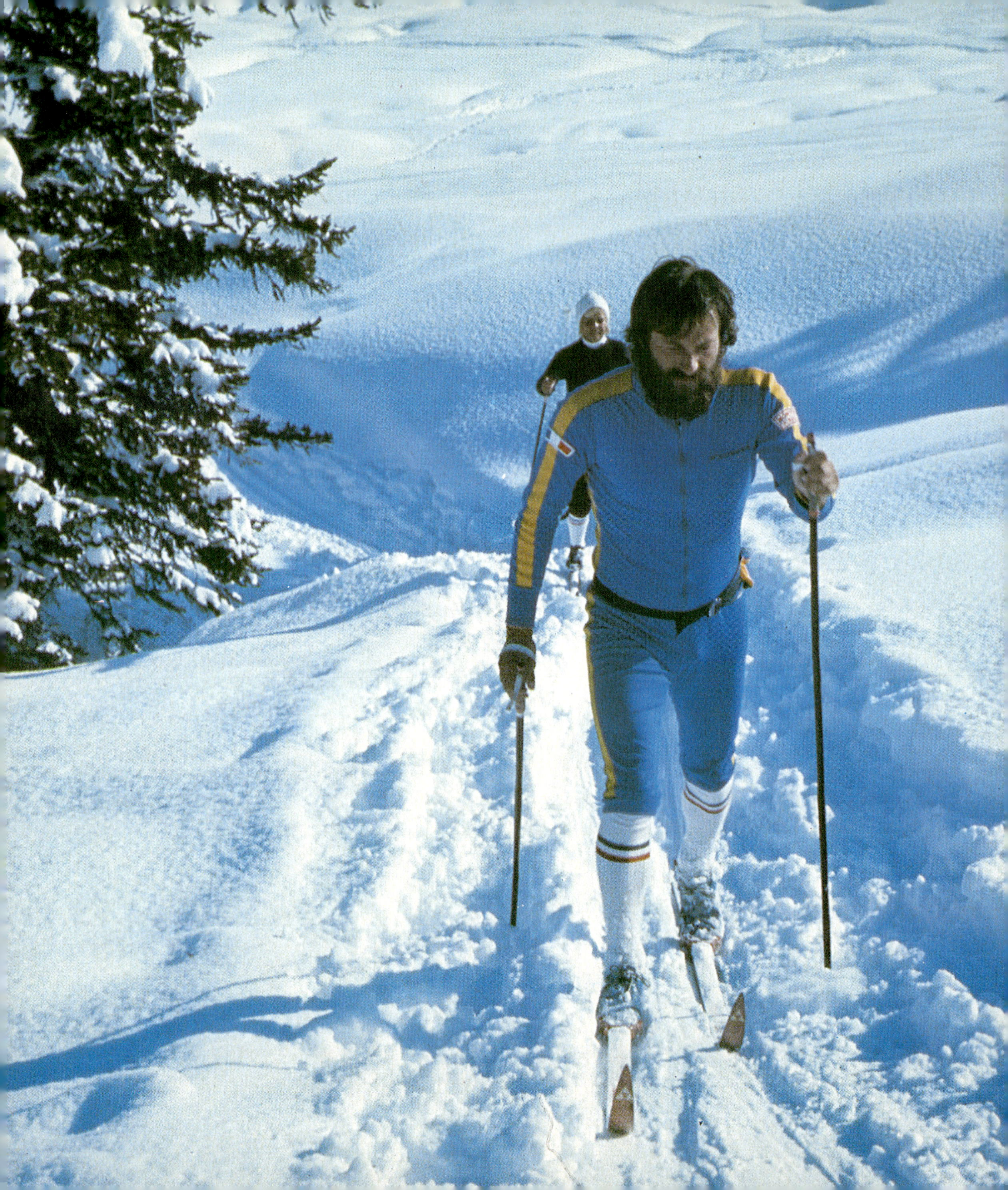

# CROSS COUNTRY

Skiing only became a recreational activity at the end of the last century, but it was not long before these new skiers formed two factions. The Scandinavians preferred skiing on the flat while Alpine skiers opted for slopes. Although Alpine skiing is still thought of as somewhat of a minority sport in Scandinavia (an attitude that Ingemar Stenmark's victories have helped to change), the converse does not now hold true, particularly in France. There were only handfuls of skiers weaving their way round the French mountains in 1965, but now the numbers can be counted in seven figures. The Ecole du Ski Français realized what was happening, and now every ski school offers tuition along similar lines to that for Alpine skiing.

At first glance, this sport may look simple, but do not be misled, for the three or four basic movements need plenty of practice if you are going to execute them skilfully. Your first tasks during your introductory lessons, which will be held on the flat, will be: learning natural walking, sliding steps, keeping your skis parallel, and lateral stability.

# SKIS, BOOTS AND ACCESSORIES

For many years cross-country skis were made of wood and were very fragile, especially the tips. Gradually, manufacturers adapted the technology of Alpine skis to cross-country skis, and recently glass fibre, carbon fibre, polyurethane, metal, and other more resilient materials have been used. Despite this, cross-country skis still retain their unique profile (narrower, longer, with higher tips and greater camber than their Alpine equivalents), and light weight, which is a vital consideration.

One other important difference lies in the running surfaces. Cross-country skiing is mostly over the flat, and so it is up to the skier to provide the impetus for forward movement. This can, of course, be achieved by pole-pushing or, more significantly, by pushing his skis forward with his legs. In the latter case, a skier does not want his skis to slide back when he takes off the pressure, so the soles have to be waxed, or he has to use skis with a mechanical non-reversing system. The latter are preferable for newcomers to cross-country skiing, or for more advanced skiers who will be skiing through ever-changing snow conditions. Of course, dedicated cross-country skiers and purists will prefer lengthy waxing sessions, since those who have acquired a high degree of skill in this difficult art can gain a few precious hundredths of a second over a course of several kilometres.

Cross country skis: longer, narrower and, essentially, much lighter than Alpine skis.

The silhouettes of downhill and cross-country skiers are entirely different, not just because of the difference in technique, but above all because of the difference in equipment. In Alpine skiing, the sole of your boot stays rigidly attached to the ski, and all the equipment is heavy. The cross-country skier, on the other hand, wants to keep weight down and, also, his heels are free to move and his arm movements are much more expansive, etc.

*Poles:* longer and lighter, with curved points.
*Straps:* always adjusted to exactly the right length.
*Boots:* ultra-lightweight (some weigh only a few hundred grams) and give the heel freedom of movement.
*Skis:* very light, narrow, longer and with higher tips than Alpine skis. Some soles can need waxing and others have special structured surfaces to prevent the skis sliding back.
*Bindings:* are simple toe-pieces which leave the heel free.

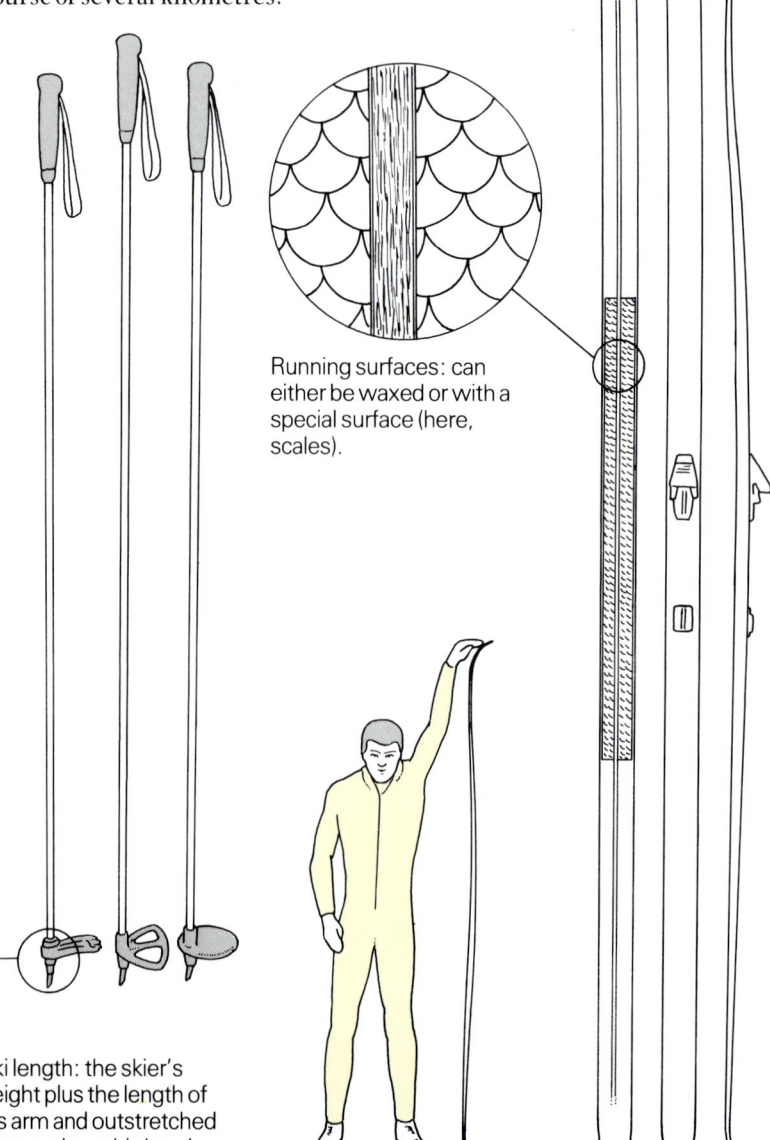

Running surfaces: can either be waxed or with a special surface (here, scales).

Poles for cross-country are longer than those for Alpine skiing, and the tips are slightly curved.

Ski length: the skier's height plus the length of his arm and outstretched fingers above his head.

BOOTS
While Alpine ski boots are heavy and rigid, cross-country boots should be light and allow your heels to move upwards and forwards since, whatever the type of binding chosen, only the toe is attached to the ski. (Be careful when you are buying or hiring your skis separately from your boots, since your choice should be governed by the binding system used.)

BINDINGS
These are just simple devices for securing the front of your boot sole to the ski. Several different systems are available internationally which is why you should never buy, or hire, your boots separately from your skis.

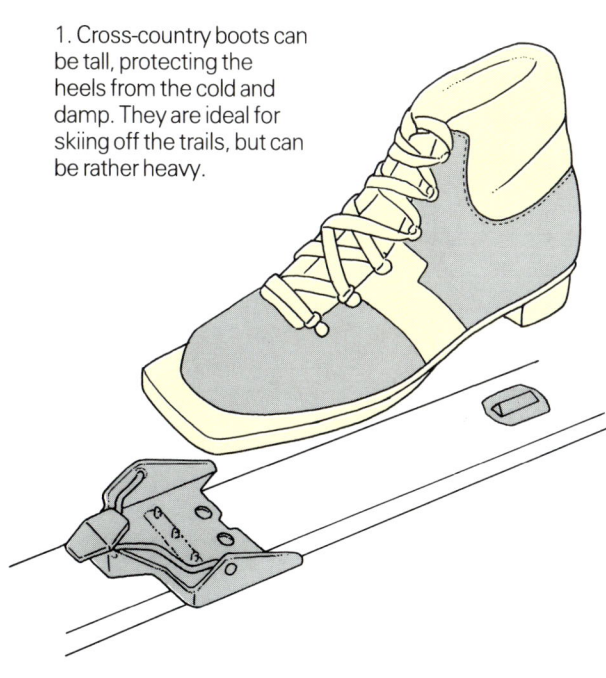

1. Cross-country boots can be tall, protecting the heels from the cold and damp. They are ideal for skiing off the trails, but can be rather heavy.

2. They can also be short, in which case you should ensure that the heel is supported; best for well-prepared tracks and competition skiing.

# FINDING YOUR LEVEL

Cross-country tuition is now organized along the same lines as that for Alpine skiing, and French ski schools provide lessons (either individual or group) for adults and children from the beginners' to the competition class. To find your level, so that you know which class to join, simply refer to the table below. Again, as with Alpine skiing, the ESFs hold one or more performance test sessions each week.

## ADULTS

**Beginners' class**
Introduction to the equipment
Introduction to the trails
Moving:
　on the flat
　uphill on gentle slopes
　downhill on gentle slopes

**Class 1**
Gliding walk
1st degree straight running
Double pole-plant
Changing direction
Sliding snowplough
Sidestepping
(Goal: short rambles)
Bronze level

**Class 2**
Sliding step
Double pole-plant
2nd degree straight running
Traversing
Changing direction:
　step turn
　snowplough turn
Herringbone
(Goal: touring)
Silver level and hare

**Class 3**
Alternating step on the flat
Alternating step uphill
Double pole-plant with intermediate step
Crossing bumps and dips
3rd degree downhill

Sliding step turns
Side-slipping
Elementary turn
(Goal: long-distance touring)
Gold level and hare

**Competition class**
Adapting your technique to the terrain
Parallel turn
Training
(Preparation for competition)
Hare

## CHILDREN

**Beginners' class and kindergarten**
Walking, changing direction on the flat over set routes and double pole-plant
1st degree straight running
Sliding snowplough
Cross-country 'snowflake'

**Class 1**
Sliding walk
Changing direction between posts on a gentle slope, without poles
2nd degree straight running and crossing bumps and dips
(Goal: short rambles)
Cross country 1 *étoile*

**Class 2**
Short circuit with linked sliding step, double pole-plant, double pole-plant with intermediate step, and changing direction
Four snowplough turns, linked by two changes of direction with snowplough turns
Downhill run and traverse
(Goal: short rambles)
Cross-country 2 *étoiles*

**Class 3**
Short circuit, linking techniques, alternating step, crossing bumps and dips, changing direction
Using elementary turn on

4/6-gated set course
Set course using step turns, with acceleration and 'take off' (4 gates)
(Goal: touring)
Cross-country 3 *étoiles* and hare

**Competition class**
Adapting techniques to the terrain
Parallel turn
Training
(Preparation for competition)
Hare

# ON THE FLAT AND UPHILL

The alternating step consists of an alternating movement of the arms and legs, in which the diagonally opposite arm and leg work together (hence its other name – the diagonal step). It is therefore rather similar to ordinary walking or running, but the rhythm is unique as the final aim is to slide along the snow. The alternating step is the most widely used technique in cross-country skiing. You will need to use it when your speed (which depends on your ability level and strength, the terrain, snow, waxing, etc) is such that frequent pushes are required to maintain it. Leg movement can be divided into two phases – preparation and push – while arm movement falls into three – traction, push and recovery. For the leg preparation phase, bring the leg you are about to push with level with the leg which is sliding, on which you have your weight. This should be a relaxed flowing movement, accelerating towards the end when the other leg will flex slightly. For the push phase, your legs will be together for a fleeting moment, skis parallel and 20cm apart. At this stage, straighten the sliding leg (the one which has been bearing your weight), extending it behind you, simultaneously transferring your weight to the other ski, which then becomes the weighted, sliding ski. The weight transfer should be total. Gradually, the push phases will become stronger, with good rear extension of the non-load-bearing leg and will be considerably aided by strong arm movements. In the traction phase, you should plant your pole slightly in front of, and on the opposite side to, the sliding leg; you should pull on the pole until your elbow is level with your hip. The pushing phase follows.

The skiers weight is on the right ski, allow the other to be brought forward at the same time as the right pole for the next step.

In the alternating step, the extension of the pushing leg makes possible the sliding step of the other, while the sliding leg is the one on which the skier's weight rests.

This movement is divided into two phases of leg work – the preparation and the push – with three phases for the arms – traction, pushing and recovery.

Your weight should always be vertically above the sliding ski. Take great care not to swing your hips or to angle your upper body too far to the front. If your weight transfer is efficient, your alternating step will be technically effective.

**The uphill alternating step**
The movement is the same as on the flat, but the sliding distance will shorten as the slope gets steeper, to the point where, if the angle of inclination is too great, you will be walking rather than sliding. The push should therefore be as powerful as possible, the arm movement energetic, although, overall, the movement will not be so expansive. Your rhythm will change, too. As the sliding phase disappears, opposing arms and legs will work simultaneously.

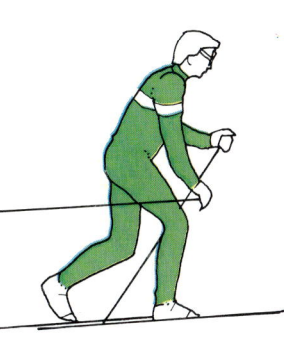

137

# THE DOUBLE POLE PUSH

After the alternating step, you can then learn two other basic cross-country moves: the double pole-plant, and the double pole-plant with one or two intermediate steps. Although you can start learning the first early on in your training, the second needs considerable skill if it is to be performed properly, and a finely tuned sense of balance.

THE DOUBLE POLE-PLANT: the sliding of both skis obtained by the simultaneous action of both arms. It is frequently used for gentle downhill slopes to maintain or increase your speed. One of the main purposes of this technique is to give your legs a rest, as only the arms and upper body do any work. The simultaneous pole-plant can be divided into four phases: the pole-plant, just in front of your boots; an energetic pull on the poles; a hefty thrust backwards; and the return of the poles.

DOUBLE POLE-PLANT WITH ONE (LATER TWO) INTERMEDIATE STEP(S): this is a combination of one or two alternating steps without using the poles, followed by a double pole-plant. You can use it when synchronizing the alternating steps is too difficult because you are travelling too fast, or when a double pole-plant would not be effective.

*Below:* Double pole-plant with intermediate step (stawug): can be divided into a push with one leg, sliding on the other ski, double pole-plant and sliding on both skis. When inserting two intermediate steps, you must add a second slide on one ski and another pole-plant.

*Right:* Double pole-plant (stakning): can be divided into a simultaneous planting of both poles, energetic pull followed by maximum thrust backwards ending with the arms free, then a return of the arms to the planting position.

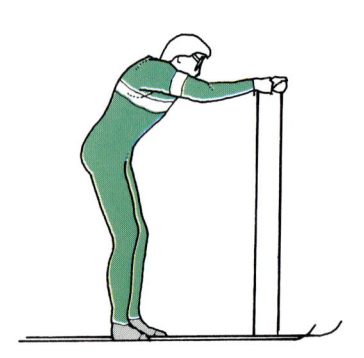

*Left:* The double pole-plant is useful when your momentum is great enough (down a gentle slope, for example) for it to be maintained by arm action only.

*Right:* Double pole-plant with intermediate step: used when synchronizing alternating steps is impossible due to too great a speed, or when a simple double pole-plant is insufficient.

# STEPPING TURNS

As its name suggests, this is a way of turning, defined as 'a change of direction obtained by successive angular movements of the skis'. It can be used on all terrains, and for turning, avoiding an obstacle, or stopping.

Begin with your skis parallel, then quickly put all your weight on the outside ski, while increasing the flexing of your knee and ankle. This should be followed by a vigorous push off the outside ski and weight transfer on to the inside ski, which is placed to point slightly away from the line of the outside ski. You then bring the outside ski parallel to the sliding ski. Repeat this operation as many times as necessary. Success in executing this movement depends on a good push off the outside ski and a well-balanced weight transfer.

The leg action can be accompanied by a double pole-plant: on level ground, at the same time as the push off; in gentle descents, before and after the step turn. At high speed, step turns should be executed very rapidly; they can even be replaced by skidded turns on prepared pistes.

In this chapter on cross-country skiing we have not discussed specific training for this discipline, since it is similar to that for Alpine skiing. However, it is worth noting that a sport with similar movements – roller skating, or even better, roller skiing – can be useful training.

*Left:* The step turn is a change of direction produced by a series of angular movements of the skis.

*Below:* The skating step is used to accelerate on hard snow with no tracks. From a quick push off the left leg, move your body forwards and to the right, moving your right ski forwards to form a V. Then transfer your weight to the right ski. After sliding a few metres, repeat the movement with your other leg.

# AT THE RESORT

You will probably have been dreaming of your winter holidays for months and now, after a long car or train journey, or a couple of hours in flight, you have at last arrived at your resort. You are weary and may feel like a fish out of water, wondering where you are supposed to go. Keep calm! Just take things one at a time. Take a look at our check list which should make sure that you remember to do everything, even though the order might not be quite right.

The first priority when you arrive is to go to your hotel/guest house/apartment. If you are self-catering, you may have to collect linen and buy a few basic food items. As soon as you are settled in, start thinking about your skiing kit: hiring or buying, getting your bindings adjusted, etc. Make sure you have all the smaller items such as goggles, gloves and sun cream. Then, off to the Ecole du Ski Français. This is where you book your lessons (if you have not previously done so by letter), and remember to tell the staff what level you have reached (see the relevant table). If the children are with you, remember to book them in at the same time, either into the nursery if they are tiny tots, or the kindergarten if they already want to start skiing. Another vital piece of business which needs taking care of (if you did not deal with it before you left home) is to take out third-party ski insurance for the whole family. This can be done either at the ESF or at the sports club.

Using the map (*right*) as a basis, you can now sit down and plan your long-awaited skiing holiday. Marked on this map you will find:
a) the pistes, in different colours: green for Class 1, blue for Class 2, red for Class 3 and black for the competition class;
b) areas which are out-of-bounds, rocky terrain, avalanche zones;
c) all the lifts; ski-tows, chair-lifts, gondolas, etc;
d) the pistes which lead down to the resort;
e) all the assembly points for lessons.

Before putting on your skis and charging off to the nearest slope, check:
a) which pistes are open and which closed;
b) the weather forecast for the day;
c) snow surface conditions (if you are skiing off-piste);
d) whether the yellow and black flag (a danger signal) is flying at the bottom of the pistes;
e) that you have remembered everything you need (lift pass, goggles, sun cream).

Finally, never go off skiing on your own, especially if you are planning to stray from the pistes.

143

# A SELECTION OF ALPINE RESORTS

Here is a selection of ski resorts representing the different regions, and the tremendous scope and variety of skiing available in France.

## LES ARCS

Located in the Tarentaise region of the Alps, the resort of Les Arcs consists of three villages, at altitudes of 1,600, 1,800, and 2,000 m, in a valley above the Isère. It is a centre for advances skiers, providing a wide range of off-piste and 'fringe' skiing (monoski, skisurfing, etc) as well as lessons for beginners (Les Arcs was one of the first resorts to introduce the *évolutif* method). There are facilities for children in each of the three villages. Since Les Arcs was a purpose-built resort, the lifts and the piste finishes have been sited right within the centre, and these link with those of La Plagne and Peisey Nancroix to further increase the possible range of skiing.

Les Arcs has a total of 18,000 beds for visitors, of which more than 14,000 are in furnished apartments. Five night clubs and 4 cinemas provide entertainment in the evenings, although those hardy skiers who have attempted a run on the Aiguille Rouge, which has the world's largest vertical drop (2,100 m), might prefer to rest instead!

**Altitude:** 1,500-3,226 m.
**Location:** Savoie, 220 km from Lyons.
**Lifts:** 50.
**Length of pistes:** 150 km.
**Instructors:** 150.
**Open:** 15 December to 14 April.
**Address:**
ESF Les Arcs,
F-73700 Barg St Maurice.

## AVORIAZ

A resort built in 1966-67 above the village of Morzine, Avoriaz has traditional-looking buildings covered in wood, and a traditional means of transport – horse-drawn sledges. Situated in the Northern Alps, on the edge of the 'Portes du Soleil' domain, which links 12 Swiss and French resorts with 600 km of pistes and 200 ski-lifts, Avoriaz provides a wide range of skiing, including cross-country. The resort is well suited to children, having a 'snow garden' at its centre, so allowing parents to make the most of their holiday.

Every January, Avoriaz hosts a festival of science-fiction films, so enabling film buffs to combine cinema and skiing – the proportions depending on how energetic they feel!

Although it has only three hotels providing accommodation for 400 persons, the resort has a total of 10,300 beds, almost all of which are in apartments. There are 2 cinemas and 3 night clubs, as well as a range of restaurants (of which 5 are located on the pistes).

**Altitude:** 1800 m (skiing from 1360 to 2340 m).
**Location:** 75 km from Geneva, in the Haute-Savoie.
**Lifts:** 39.
**Length of pistes:**
**Cross-country:** 70 km.
**Instructors:** 70.
**Open:** Christmas to Easter.
**Address:** ESF Avoriaz,
F-74110 Avoriaz.

## CHAMONIX

A first-generation ski resort, Chamonix was host to the 1924 Olympic Games. Slopes facing north and south are served by the lifts, ensuring that sunshine can be found in the early part of the season and good snow on the north side until late in the season. The altitude permits off-piste skiing over a vast area all through the season. The ski school has four offices, and 45 of the instructors speak English. Although the main attraction of Chamonix is the off-piste skiing, and, in particular, the 18 km descent of the Mer de Glace, the ESF offers the full range of classes for beginners, and Chamonix has 34 km of blue and green pistes. It is a cosmopolitan resort, attracting skiers from all over the world, and as a small town with a permanent population of about 9,000, offers a wide range of activities: ice-rink, indoor swimming-pool, sports hall, four cinemas, a casino and numerous shops. The town of Chamonix is surrounded by smaller villages, and in total offers 4,800 beds in hotels and 8,500 in apartments, all of which means that the resort can cater for a large number of visitors.

**Altitude:** 1,049-3,700 m.
**Location:** at the foot of Mont Blanc, Northern Alps.
**Lifts:** 12 cable-cars, 10 chairlifts, 19 ski-tows.
**Length of pistes:** 130 km.
**Cross-country:** 25 km.
**Instructors:** 143, 50 being mountain guides.
**Open:** December to April.
**Address:**
Maison de la Montagne,
Place de l'Eglise,
F-74400 Chamonix.

## LA CLUSAZ

A summer resort as long ago as 1880, it was only in 1924 that La Clusaz became a ski centre, and the Ski Club was formed in 1926. In 1955 the Beauregard cable-car was built and La Clusaz developed into an international resort. It now has four domains of pistes, tended by a team of 20, and the ski-lifts can carry up to 25,000 people per hour. There are pistes of all standards, of course, and also nine cross-country tracks including two blacks. Off-piste skiing and touring are also possible.

La Clusaz is a traditional village with many old chalets and farms, as well as newer buildings constructed in the same style to cater for visitors. There are about 2,000 beds available in hotels, and 12,000 in apartments, chalets and residences.

When you are not skiing, there are walks, an ice rink, an open-air heated swimming pool, a cinema, 5 night clubs and more than 100 shops, including 17 sports shops for buying or hiring equipment. Finally, weather permitting, you can always learn to hang-glide.

**Altitude:** 1,100-2,600 m.
**Location:** Haute-Savoie, 50 km from Geneva.
**Lifts:** 4 cable-cars, 8 chairlifts, 26 ski-tows.
**Length of pistes:** 180 km.
**Cross-country:** 48 km.
**Instructors:** 109.
**Open:** Christmas to Easter.
**Address:**
Ecole du Ski Français
F-74220 La Clusaz.

## LES CONTAMINES

Les Contamines is a traditional village in the Montjoie valley – one of the first inhabited valleys in the Alps. It consists of old farms and chalets nestling at the foot of the slopes and, thanks to its position, has exceptionally good snow throughout the season. The ski area can be divided into three parts, two of which are ideal for beginners, while the other offers a wide range of skiing served by 21 lifts. This area links up with the resort of Haute Luce.

With 18 hotels, 2 night clubs and a cinema, as well as plenty of apartments, Les Contamines can cater for up to 6,230 visitors ... who can enjoy the experience of travelling down the valley in horse-drawn sleighs to dine in one of the restaurants.

**Altitude:** 1,165-2,500 m.
**Location:** Haute-Savoie, near Mont Blanc, 80 km from Geneva.
**Lifts:** 25.
**Length of pistes:** 90 km.
**Cross-country:** 20 km.
**Instructors:** 55.
**Open:** December to April.
**Address:**
ESF Les Contamines-Montjoie,
F-74190 Les Contamines.

## FLAINE

A purpose-built resort in the northern Alps, Flaine was constructed in 1968. The pistes are close to all the hotels and apartments – you ski from your front door – and are linked to the resorts of Carroz, Samoens and Morillon by lifts. In total this gives access to 260 km of pistes, 71 ski-lifts and a wide range of skiable domain. The Ecole du Ski Français offers off-piste and ski-touring for more advanced skiers, while teaching beginners by the *évolutif* method. Many of the instructors speak English.

The modern complex set among the trees at the top of the valley contains more than 5,000 beds for visitors, of which 1,600 are in two- and three-star hotels and the rest in apartments. The resort has all the essential services, including more than 20 restaurants – from self-service to gastronomic – numerous shops, a cinema, a library, a sauna, an ice rink and a swimming pool.

The resort is well-suited to children, having a crèche, playground and games room specifically for them, as well as the ESF 'Jardin de neige'. It is very much a family resort while retaining a sporting atmosphere.

**Altitude:** 1,600-2,500 m.
**Location:** Haute-Savoie, 70 km from Geneva.
**Lifts:** 3 cable-cars, 1 lift, 8 chairlifts and 19 ski-tows.
**Length of pistes:** 150 km.
**Cross-country:** 10 km.
**Instructors:** 60.
**Open:** December to April.
**Address:**
ESF Flaine,
F-74300 Cluses.

## COURCHEVEL

The first of the new generation of ski resorts, Courchevel has become a very chic place for a skiing holiday during the last 30 years. It is laid out on four levels in one of the 'Trois Vallées' and has incorporated the charm of a traditional Alpine village into its modern architecture. As it is at the heart of the world's largest ski area and is linked with three other resorts, the skiing is virtually unlimited, and caters for all levels of expertise from beginners (there are 25 green pistes) to intermediates (35 red pistes) and advanced skiing (off-piste and touring). The quality of the snow is consistently good.

Courchevel provides its visitors (up to 30,000 at any one time) with 7 night clubs and more than 45 restaurants, many of which have Savoyard specialities on their menus. Accommodation is in one of the 61 hotels or 3,000 apartments.

**Altitude:** 1,300-2,700 m.
**Location:** 140 km from Geneva in the northern Alps.
**Lifts:** 64 (plus access to Trois Vallées).
**Length of pistes:** 130 km (plus access to Trois Vallées).
**Cross-country:** 36 km.
**Instructors:** 400.
**Open:** winter and summer.
**Address:**
ESF Courchevel,
F-73120 Courchevel.

## LES GETS

Lying along a north-south axis, the village of Les Gets is purpose-built for skiers – you can put your skis on at the door – but was designed in a traditional style; the church tower is still the tallest building in the area, in the Col des Gets. Its position makes for an exceptionally good snow cover on one hand, and there are links with Morzine on ski, on the other, opening up a total of 600 km of pistes. Within the resort there is a range of pistes to suit all levels – 8 blue and green, 11 red and 4 black – in the trees and in the open. The ESF was opened in 1950, and has its office in the centre of the village. It offers the full range of classes and guides for off-piste skiing.

Les Gets has a total of 12,000 beds, and is a typical Village resort, with 30 hotels and 800 furnished apartments and chalets. Apart from the skiing there is a motorbike circuit in the snow, 50 km of walks, a swimming pool, 2 cinemas, 3 discotheques, 20 sports shops, numerous other boutiques, two banks and all the necessary medical services. Also, there is an immense covered car-park to protect vehicles from the cold.

**Altitude:** 1,172-1,850 m.
**Location:** northern Alps, between Geneva and Mont Blanc.
**Lifts:** 2 cable-cars, 9 chairlifts and 20 ski-tows.
**Length of pistes:** 80 km.
**Cross-country:** 25 km.
**Instructors:** 80.
**Open:** Christmas to Easter.
**Address:**
ESF Les Gets
F-74260 Les Gets.

## MEGEVE

Situated close to Mont Blanc, Megève is a traditional village that has been a ski resort since the turn of the century and, although it has been developed and expanded since then, it still retains its original style. Megève has a wide range of pistes, and is linked to the other resorts around Mount Blanc so that it can offer a total of 500 km of pistes of all types. One of the first Ecoles du Ski Français was opened here and it provides the full range of classes for beginners up to those wanting to try their hand at artistic skiing.

Apart from its pistes, Megève has a vast sports centre with two indoor swimming pools, a skating rink, tennis courts, etc. It also boasts many shops, night clubs, bars, restaurants, and even a casino, all of which are very sophisticated, and where you might even meet some stars. The resort has more than 28,000 beds, including some 3,400 in hotels.

**Altitude:** 1,113–2,040 m.
**Location:** 70 km from Geneva, in the Haute-Savoie.
**Lifts:** 40.
**Length of pistes:** 150 km.
**Cross-country:** 55 km.
**Instructors:** 180.
**Open:** December to April.
**Address:**
ESF Megève,
F-74120 Megève.

## LES MENUIRES

A large resort recently constructed in the Belleville valley – which also contains the resort of Val Thorens – Les Ménuires was sited so that you can ski right from your door into the largest ski domain in the world: Les Trois Vallées. It is linked to the resorts of Méribel and Courchevel, and between them these three valleys have 175 lifts and 450 km of pistes. Les Ménuires itself has about a quarter of this number, and its ski area extends from 200 m below the resort to 1,000 m above it.

The large ESF has two offices, open seven days a week during the season, and offers classes of all levels in French, English, German, Italian and Spanish. There is enough room for 18,000 visitors, mainly in apartments; there are only 4 hotels. Children are well looked after: from 3 months to 2½ years old in the nursery; from 2½ upwards in the 'garderie'; and ski lessons are available to those over 4 years old.

**Altitude:** resort 1,850 m, skiing from 1,660-2,850 m.
**Location:** Massif de la Vanoise, 145 km from Geneva.
**Lifts:** 41 (plus access to Trois Vallées).
**Length of pistes:** 110 km (plus access to Trois Vallées).
**Cross-country:** 17 km.
**Instructors:** 130.
**Open:** 15 December-14 April.
**Address:**
Ecole du Ski Français
F-73440 Les Ménuires.

## MERIBEL

At the heart of the Trois Vallées, this resort consists of two centres: Méribel and Méribel-Mottaret, both built in traditional style following guidelines laid down in the late 1930s and so blending in with the impressive scenery all around. As part of the Trois Vallées complex, its 43 skilifts and 55 pistes link up with a total of 175 lifts and 450 km of pistes. Méribel has a downhill course reserved for training and competitions, and a slalom course, as well as offering a wide range of off-piste skiing. For beginners there are 23 blue and green pistes. Ski classes in English are available.

The resort has 21,000 beds divided between the 19 hotels and apartments and residences. To cater for these visitors' requirements there are 62 shops, 2 cinemas, a conference hall, night clubs, bars and restaurants, an indoor swimming pool, a school of driving on ice, an ice rink and even an indoor golf range.

**Altitude:** 1,600-2,850 m.
**Location:** Massif de la Vanoise, 200 km from Lyons.
**Lifts:** 13 cable-cars, 10 chairlifts, 20 ski-tows.
**Length of pistes:** 90 km (plus access to Trois Vallées).
**Cross-country:** 28 km.
**Instructors:** 130.
**Open:** from 15 December.
**Address:**
Ecole du Ski Français,
F-73550 Méribel.

## MORZINE

A ski resort for some 60 years, Morzine has learned a great deal about receiving visitors, and has an international reputation. Situated in the northern Alps, it has good quality snow, which has permitted international competitions to be staged here. Also, there are pistes that can be skied in all weathers due to their position, the regional climate and the snow conditions. The ski school at Morzine was founded in 1942, provides Alpine and cross-country classes for all levels and ages, and has 12 English-speaking instructors.

Morzine has approximately 25,000 beds, divided between more than 100 hotels and guest houses, and 1,500 chalets and apartments. It also has a wide range of high-quality restaurants, many of them specializing in Savoyard cuisine. A cosmopolitan resort, Morzine receives visitors from all over the world, all the year round. It has a large sports centre catering for all sports from ice-hockey to tennis.

**Altitude:** 1,000-2,460 m.
**Location:** Haute-Savoie, 60 km from Geneva.
**Lifts:** 60.
**Length of pistes:** 240 km.
**Cross-country:** 55 km.
**Instructors:** 90.
**Open:** December to April.
**Address:**
ESF Morzine,
F-74110 Morzine.

## TIGNES

Tignes boasts a vast ski domain of high quality, and offers skiing all the year round thanks to the Grande Motte glacier above it: it is one of the few ski resorts in the world to be open 12 months of the year. It is linked with Val d'Isère and so offers a total of 300 km of accessible pistes of all levels. For its half of these pistes, Tigne has high-performance lifts capable of carrying 55,000 skiers per hour, and in which the authorities have enough confidence to offer a free lift pass to anyone who has to wait more than 17 minutes. The skiing is suitable for all standards and ages of skier, and the Ecole du Ski Français provides classes for beginners and advanced skiers according to the ESF progression. There is also a wide range of off-piste skiing available.

Tignes, of course, has all the necessary services and shops, as well as plenty of après-ski activities – fondues, wine-tastings, restaurants, clubs – and its hotels have a family atmosphere.

**Altitude:** 1,550 m–3,600 m.
**Location:** Savoie, in the Tarentaise Alps.
**Lifts:** 8 cable-cars, 20 chairlifts, 26 ski-tows.
**Length of pistes:** 150 km (plus access to Val d'Isère).
**Cross-country:** 12 km.
**Instructors:** 120.
**Open:** all year.
**Address:**
ESF de Tignes,
F-73320 Tignes.

## LA PLAGNE

The idea of La Plagne saw the light of day in 1960, so making it the first of the third generation integrated resorts. It consists of ten interconnected villages, varying in style from the modern concrete of Aime 2000 to the chalet-type buildings of Belle Plagne, all set within a vast skiable domain of mainly north-facing slopes. Its position ensures good snow conditions all through the season, and summer skiing is possible on the Bellecote glacier, which is served by six lifts. All the lifts at La Plagne interconnect and have been designed to avoid bottlenecks. In such a large area, there are, of course, runs to suit every skier, from the novice to the advanced off-piste enthusiast. Each of the villages has its own ski school, and all provide the full range of ESF instruction, including monoskiing, cross-country and ski-touring.

Between the 10 centres, there are more than 50 restaurants, 6 cinemas, and all the shops you might need. Everything has been designed with the skier in mind; there are few cars, no walking to the pistes and the lifts start from within each village – the whole area is literally on your doorstep.

**Altitude:** 1,250-3,250 m.
**Location:** Tarentaise Alps, 147 km from Geneva.
**Lifts:** 86.
**Length of pistes:** 185 km.
**Cross-country:** pisted circuits.
**Instructors:** between 40 and 100 per ESF.
**Open:** December to end April, plus summer skiing.
**Addresses:**

ESF La Plagne
F-73210 La Plagne
ESF Belle Plagne
Lovatiere 24
La Plagne
F-73210 Aime

# CLUB PETER STUYVESANT INVITES YOU TO 'SKI THE FRENCH WAY'

## WELCOME TO CLUB PETER STUYVESANT AT LA PLAGNE

Following the success of Club Peter Stuyvesant holidays in Switzerland, Peter Stuyvesant Travel has further developed and refined the 'Club' idea, and has established what it believes to be the perfect holiday base for all skiers. It's Belle Plagne, in the Tarentaise region of the French Alps, the most picturesque of the high altitude villages that make up the resort of La Plagne.

'The most comprehensively equipped ski area in Europe', as it has been described, boasts 185 kilometres of magnificent runs, superb views of Mont Blanc, and a range of après-ski facilities, including discos, bars, specialist restaurants and bistros. There's even a heated outdoor swimming pool and at Belle Plagne, you literally ski from your own front door. Club Peter Stuyvesant gives you this choice and much, much more.

## A GREAT DEAL FOR SKIERS

When you book a Club Peter Stuyvesant holiday at Belle Plagne you immediately qualify for some remarkable bonuses.

- The Freedom of your own low-cost self-catering apartment.

- Discounts on Ski Tuition, Ski Pass and Ski Equipment hire.

- Special instructional courses with the ESF Ski School for Beginners, Intermediates and Advanced Skiers. Beginners can learn to ski in only 6 days with the brilliant Ski Evolutif method!

- FREE competition skiing for all levels of skill.

- FREE Honda snow-biking on a specially built course.

- Great Ski Clothing offers.

- Special Club evenings.

- The services of your own Club Representative and Ski Guide.

- Official Club Transport.

- .. and FREE Travel and Accommodation for one person if you book for a group of 12 and 50% off travel and accommodation for one person if you book for a group of 8. You will also receive FREE one copy of the 'Ski The French Way' video and book. You can see it all in the brilliant new 'Ski The French Way' video. See back flap of this book for details.

To book your **Club** Peter Stuyvesant ski holiday contact your local ABTA **Travel Agent** or phone 01 631 3278 Peter Stuyvesant Travel, 35 Alfred Place, London **WC1E 7DY**.

### PETER STUYVESANT TRAVEL

## VAL D'ISERE

Val d'Isère is a modern resort set in a traditional village. It has 1500 permanent inhabitants, many of whom live in the old stone chalets around the church. The skiing is spread over three areas, giving a total of 64 pistes, and there is access to a further 150 km at Tignes – the two resorts' lifts being included in the same lift pass. The pistes are skiable from the end of November to the middle of May, and summer skiing is also possible.

All types of skiing are offered, from the 47 blue and green pistes to the monoski and ski-surfing off-piste. Classes are provided by the oldest ski school in the Alps (founded in 1932). Every year Val d'Isère hosts the first two events of the competition season at the beginning of December.

With 15,500 beds, 48 hotels, 180 shops, 7 night clubs, 2 cinemas, 52 restaurants, an ice-rink and a swimming pool, Val d'Isère is well equipped to receive its visitors, although it is unlikely that any of them will equal the successes of the resort's most famous son – Jean-Claude Killy.

**Altitude:** 1,850-3,300 m.
**Location:** Haute Tarentaise Alps, 180 km from Geneva.
**Lifts:** 56.
**Length of pistes:** 120 km (plus access to Tignes).
**Cross-country:** 5 circuits of between 5 and 10 km.
**Instructors:** 183.
**Open:** beginning of December to end of April + summer skiing.
**Address:**
ESF Val d'Isère,
F-73150 Val d'Isère.

## VALMOREL

Although the modern, purpose-built resort of Valmorel provides all the advantages which go with a 'ski from your front door' location, its design was based on the traditional Alpine villages. The 62 pistes are fairly equally divided between the different levels of difficulty, and advanced skiers enjoy unlimited opportunities for off-piste skiing in the nine valleys of the Tarentaise Alps, while child and adult novices have their own special slopes. There is also a permanent slalom course, and in 1984 Valmorel hosted the French Ski Instructors' Championship.

There is room for 6,500 visitors in the Valmorel group of hamlets, and evening entertainment is provided in two cinemas and a night club. There are plenty of shops, of course, and as you wander through the narrow streets you may well come across performances by groups of musicians or actors.

The resort is ideal for children, with activities being organised for them from 18 months upwards – on skis or otherwise – since cars are banned within the village.

**Altitude:** 1,400 to 2,400 m.
**Location:** Savoie, 150 km from Geneva.
**Lifts:** 27.
**Length of pistes:**
**Instructors:** 75.
**Open:**
**Address:**
ESF Valmorel,
F-73260 Valmorel.

## VAL THORENS

The highest resort in Europe, and linked to the vast 'Trois Vallées' domain of interconnected pistes, lifts and resorts, Val Thorens offers a wide range of skiing nine months of the year. Surrounded by five glaciers – of which three are equipped for autumn and summer skiing – and facing south and south-west makes for a combination of excellent snow and good weather. Apart from giving access to the 450 km of pistes of the Trois Vallées, Val Thorens offers plenty of off-piste skiing, and the possibility of touring the whole Tarentaise region. The ESF was formed in 1972 – the year the resort was opened – and now provides classes for all levels, and guides for the off-piste skier.

Val Thorens currently has 10,000 beds divided between 8 hotels, 2,500 apartments and 9 other establishments. To cater for these visitors there are 41 shops, 21 restaurants in the resort (and 8 on the slopes), 2 night clubs, a cinema, six indoor tennis courts . . . and, for the summer, 15 open-air tennis courts and a football pitch.

**Altitude:** 2,300-3,200 m.
**Location:** Tarentaise Alps, 150 km from Geneva.
**Lifts:** 27 (plus access to the 180 of the Trois Vallées).
**Length of pistes:** 100 km (plus access to the Trois Vallées).
**Cross-country:** throughout the valley.
**Instructors:** 80.
**Open:** autumn – 20 Oct to 19 Dec; winter and spring – 20 Dec to 19 May; summer – 22 June to 31 Aug.
**Address:**
ESF de Val Thorens,
F-73440 Saint-Martin-de-Belleville.

## L'ALPE D'HUEZ

A classified resort, open in both winter and summer, the Alpe d'Huez is situated in the Isère, 63 km from Grenoble. The resort faces south, and has guaranteed snow cover until the beginning of May. Summer skiing takes place on the Sarenne glacier, and in winter the longest piste in Europe (16 km) starts from here. As well as apartments, the resort has 35 hotels and a youth hostel, and in winter the ski-lifts are capable of carrying 44,000 skiers per hour. The ski school provides classes for all levels and types of skiing, from cross-country to acrobatic and monoskiing. Skiing lessons in English are available. There is a slalom course and off-piste skiing for more advanced skiers, while beginners from the age of four upwards have 23 green pistes to choose from.

A wide range of other activities is available, including swimming in an open-air heated pool, skating or curling, and there are 5 night clubs, 23 restaurants (plus 5 at high altitude), a museum and a concert hall. In summer there is – apart from skiing – tennis, horse-riding, climbing, fishing... and grass-skiing.

The resort developers are currently building a further 500 apartments, and a new ski-lift on the Sarenne glacier.

**Altitude:** 1,450 m (Huez village), 1,860 m (Alpe d'Huez resort) to 3,350 m (top of the pistes).
**Location:** close to Gap and Briançon, in the Alps.
**Lifts:** 5 cable-cars, 14 chairlifts, 34 ski-tows.
**Length of pistes:** 165 km
**Cross-country:** 40 km
**Instructors:** 122, including 20 for children.
**Open:** winter and summer.
**Address:**
Ecole du Ski Français
B.P. 25
F-38750 – Alpe d'Huez.

## LES DEUX ALPES

Situated on a plateau between the impressive Pelvoux and Meije mountain ranges, on the border of the northern and southern Alps, Les Deux Alpes combines excellent snow conditions with Mediterranean sunshine. Skiing takes place both in summer and winter, thanks to the lifts on the glacier that go up to 3,568 m. There are 72 pistes, of which 19 are green, 28 blue, 15 red and 10 black, and the lifts have a capacity of 40,000 skiers per hour. One can also ski in 6 of the neighbouring resorts, and this is included in the lift passes of 6 days' duration or longer. Also, for more advanced skiers, there is a slalom course, and plenty of opportunities for off-piste skiing.

The resort has 40 hotels, and more than 15,000 beds in furnished apartments; there are 30 bars and restaurants, 3 night clubs and 2 cinemas, and for those who have more energy after a day's skiing (or instead of...) there is a heated swimming pool, an ice rink, squash courts, a gymnasium, etc. In summer, tennis, archery, volleyball, skating, swimming and grass-skiing are available, as well as skiing on the glacier.

**Altitude:** 1,650-3,568 m.
**Location:** In the Isère, 75 km from Grenoble.
**Length of pistes:** 160 km.
**Cross-country:** 20 km.
**Lifts:** 57.
**Instructors:** 150.
**Open:** 1 December-1 May, and 22 June-8 September.
**Address:**
ESF des Deux Alpes
F-38860 Les Deux Alpes.

## ISOLA 2000

Fifty kilometres from the Côte d'Azure, Isola 2000 is one of the main resorts of the southern Alps due to its position and ease of access from Nice. Its major attraction is the combination of sunshine and excellent snow conditions, which led to its construction on this site, and of which the resort is so certain that it guarantees them in contracts. One of the first purpose-built resorts, it provides pistes of all levels, the full range of ESF services, a Mini Ski Club and a children's 'village', and has five restaurants on the pistes to allow for the fullest possible day's skiing in the sun.

The resort is divided into two parts, the 'Front de Neige' centre, which contains most of the shops and services, and the 'Hameau' a few hundred metres away – a group of chalet-style buildings linked to the main resort by a free minibus service. The resort has eight restaurants, six sports shops, a supermarket, a cinema, two night clubs, a swimming pool, an ice rink and even free night skiing.

**Altitude:** 2,000-2,610 m.
**Location:** Close to Italian border, two hours' drive from Nice.
**Lifts:** 22.
**Length of pistes:** 115 km.
**Instructors:** 70.
**Address:**
Office du Tourisme,
F-06420 ISOLA 2000.

## PRA-LOUP

Situated in the southern Alps, amidst larches and pine trees, Pra-Loup is a purpose-built resort lying some 200 km from the Mediterranean. It is linked to the nearby La Foux d'Allos, thus offering a total of 120 km of easily accessible pistes, since those of Pra-Loup run right into the heart of the complex. Of the 29 pistes, 16 are blue or green, so beginners have a wide choice; 12 are red. Advanced skiers have the chance of ski-touring, or of learning free-style skiing at the ESF. Children from the age of six months can be cared for in the crèche, and those over three can have ski lessons.

Pra-Loup has more than 13,500 beds, of which almost 9,000 are in apartments. The centre has a large selection of shops, bars, restaurants, etc, in the arcade surrounding the ice rink, and for those who can never have enough of the slopes, there is a floodlit piste.

**Altitude:** 1,500 to 2,500 m.
**Location:** Alpes de Haute Provence, 180 km from Grenoble.
**Lifts:** 30.
**Length of pistes:** 60 km.
**Instructors:** 70.
**Open:**
**Address:**
ESF Pra-Loup
F-04400 Pra-Loup.

## SERRE CHEVALIER

A resort linking three centres (and three ESF's) in the Guisane valley above Briançon, Serre-Chevalier has a large skiable domain of inter-connected pistes of which 27 are blue or green and 40 red or black. There are also extensive off-piste and ski-touring areas around the resort. All three ESFs provide the full range of classes and offer the opportunity to take the ESF tests; in addition, that of Chantemerle offers monoskiing and ballet, while Villeneuve provides tours to neighbouring resorts. Cross-country lessons are available in all three centres on the five maintained circuits, and tours of one day and longer are organized.

Originally three traditional villages, Serre-Chevalier has been extended with many new buildings, and now has the capacity for 30,000 visitors at any one time, some in its 31 hotels, the others in apartments, chalets and in the winter caravan site. It has three ice rinks, a covered swimming pool, five cinemas, and four night clubs, along with all services and shops. The resort is well suited to families, while providing a wide range of skiing at all levels.

**Altitude:** 1,350-2,800 m.
**Location:** Hautes-Alpes, 100 km from Grenoble.
**Lifts:** 61, of which 43 are ski-tows.
**Length of pistes: 200 km.**
**Cross-country:** 80 km.
**Instructors:** 255 in three schools.
**Open:** Christmas to Easter.
**Addresses:**
ESF Serre-Chevalier, Chantemerle
F-05330 Saint Chaffrey.

Monetièr les Bains.
F-05220 Monetier Les Bains.

Villeneuve
F-05240 La Salle Des Alpes.

## LES ROUSSES

The main ski resort in the Jura, offering both Alpine and cross-country skiing, Les Rousses has a wide range of Alpine pistes – including 15 green and 4 black – and an unlimited variety of cross-country runs, both pisted and otherwise. The ESF provides all the classes and services usually undertaken by a ski school, and also offer cross-country courses and tours.

There are 14 hotels and numerous apartments, along with all the required shops and services. For après-ski, there are sledge rides, restaurants, three night clubs, two cinemas, an artificial ice rink and indoor tennis courts.

**Altitude:** 1,120-1,680 m.
**Location:** 40 km from Geneva, 2 km from the Swiss border.
**Lifts:** 36.
**Length of pistes:** 50 km.
**Cross-country:** 150 km of pistes and unlimited free skiing.
**Instructors:** 35 Alpine skiing, 15 cross-country.
**Open:** Christmas to Easter.
**Address:**
Ecole de Ski
F-39220 Les Rousses.

## BARÈGES

Barèges is a village resort combining a family and a sporting atmosphere. Being in the Pyrenees, it can guarantee a considerable amount of sunshine on its exposed pistes. There is also skiing in the forests surrounding the village. The lift-pass includes access to the 53 lifts and 90 km of pistes at La Mongie, as well as to the three areas linked by lifts around Barèges: L'Ayre, with plenty of skiing between the trees, competition pistes, and 850 m of descent; La Laquette, with pistes of all standards for the whole family; and Super-Barèges, with its wide open spaces and link with La Mongie. There are four high-altitude restaurants catering for skiers on the pistes. There is also an introductory course to hanggliding available. Access to Barèges is by train from Lourdes – which is easily reached by train or air from Paris.

**Altitude:** 1,250-2,350 m.
**Location:** in the central Pyrenees, 40 km from Lourdes.
**Lifts:** 24.
**Length of pistes:** 40 km.
**Cross-country:** a centre and maintained piste.
**Instructors:** 39.
**Open:** 15 December to end of April.
**Address:**
Ecole du Ski Français,
F-65120 Barèges.

## LE MONT DORE

One of the Massif Central resorts, Le Mont Dore became a ski resort at the end of the 1940s, and combines Alpine and cross-country skiing – to which the undulating terrain is well suited. The Alpine pistes are linked directly to those at Super Besse, giving access to 80 km of runs in all. The 18 pistes at Le Mont Dore include a slalom course, and for novices there are 12 green and blue runs. The cross-country tracks, few of which are prepared, take you through forests, round lakes, and across the plateaux of the Massif Central; their popularity is proved by the large numbers of skiers who enter the Massif du Sancy 'Equipée Blanche', a race which boasted more than 2000 participants in 1983.

There are more than 10,000 beds available for visitors, including nearly 4000 in the 70 hotels. Le Mont Dore also has 4 night clubs and 2 cinemas for evening entertainment. Children have the choice of the nursery (ages 3-10), or the ESF's 'jardin d'enfants'. The gentle slopes make this a good resort for families who wish to learn to ski together.

**Altitude:** 1,050-1,825 m.
**Location:** Massif Central, 50 km from Clermont-Ferrand.
**Lifts:** 22.
**Length of pistes:** 35 km.
**Cross-country:** includes 25 km of pistes.
**Instructors:** 40.
**Open:** December to April.
**Address:**
ESF Le Mont Dore,
F-63240 Le Mont Dore.

## VILLARD DE LANS

A traditional resort which has been a centre for snow and ice sports since 1906, Villard de Lans is easily accessible, being only 32 km south-west of Grenoble. Its slopes face mainly north, and the lower ones can be artificially maintained with the aid of 72 snow-cannons, thus ensuring a good snow cover throughout the season. These good snow conditions are complemented by the Mediterranean sunshine which is practically guaranteed.

Villard de Lans is a fairly large resort, with room for almost 20,000 visitors, who have the choice of 19 Alpine and 8 cross-country pistes, both disciplines having their own large ski school. There are also 15 instructors specifically for young children in the ESF's 'jardin d'enfants'.

**Altitude:** 1,050-2,170 m.
**Location:** Massif du Vercors, west of the Alps.
**Lifts:** 25.
**Length of pistes:** 100 km.
**Cross-country:** 80 km.
**Instructors:** 80.
**Open:** 15 December to Easter.
**Address:**
Ecole du Ski Français,
F-38250 Villard de Lans.

# A SKIING GLOSSARY

**Angulation:**
A body position in which, seen from the front, the skier's upper body is angled away from his lower body at the hips.

**Anticipation:**
A body position adopted before initiating a turn.

**Avalement:**
A compression of the skier's legs underneath him due to the shape of the terrain or muscular contraction, particularly used on bumps and in powder snow.

**Axis of the skis:**
An imaginary perpendicular line passing between the skis in the parallel position.

**Banking:**
Position in which the body, seen from the front, is angled to the perpendicular. Banking counteracts the effects of centrifugal force on the skier's centre of gravity when steering and initiating turns.

**Basic position:**
A position of preparedness in which the skier's lower body is half flexed, and the skier's centre of gravity is balanced evenly between the skis. The basic stance is a flexible position of readiness. It is also known as the intermediary position.

**Carving:**
The entire edge of the ski passes through a single groove in the snow.

**Counter-rotation (pivoting by):**
Turning the skis with a sharp movement of the lower body while simultaneously rotating the upper body in the opposite direction.

**Counter-turn:**
An uphill turn to provide push-off for initiating a further downhill turn.

**Cramponning:**
A severe edge-check with the inside edge to control side-slipping in a turn.

**Directional force:**
Changing or maintaining the direction of the skis by the friction created by snow resistance.

**Edging:**
General term for pressing the edges of the ski into the snow. When across a slope it prevents you from sliding downhill, similarly when traversing it can be increased to prevent forward movement – the edge-check – or reduced to allow a sideslip – edge-release.

**Edge change:**
Transfer of pressure from the edges on one side of the skis to the other side.

**Elementary turn:**
The first complete downhill turn. It combines a basic snowplough or stem movement with a controlled sideslip and is an important step on the path to parallel turning.

**Extension (up-unweighting):**
Straightening the legs by pushing downwards. The end of the extension movement reduces the pressure of the skis on the snow.

**Fall line:**
The most direct line down a slope, ie: that which a free falling object would take.

**Flexing down:**
Progressive weighting of skis by bending the knees to prepare for or to steer a turn.

**Forward stance:**
Position in which the skier's centre of gravity is slightly forward of his centre of balance.

**Heel weighting:**
A balanced stance in which the skier weights his skis by pressing down with his heel.

**Hip-turning (opposition):**
Position of a skier who has pivoted his skis while maintaining his shoulders parallel to the slope.

**Independent movement:**
Movement of the legs separately from each other, or of the upper body separately from the lower. An essential element of advanced skiing.

**Initiation:**
When the turn is set in motion.

**Low crouch:**
Position in which the skier's legs are tucked up beneath him, either actively or passively.

**Moguls:**
A series of natural or man-made bumps in the snow.

**Natural spread:**
Spread corresponding to the width of the hips: open parallel.

**Parallel turns:**
The ESF distinguishes different types of parallel turns, according to the movements involved and their conditions of use. The first is the *basic parallel*, the fundamental turn, which may be refined to give the *Evasion Turn*, a smooth, elegant turn, the *GT Turn*, a widely used dynamic turn, and the *Performance Turn*, a high-speed turn evolved from the racing turn.

**Pivoting:**
Where the skis are turned by pressure from the hips, knees and or feet.

**Pivoting force:**
Muscular contraction producing a controlled turn of the skis.

**Pivot with up-extension:**
A movement combining up-unweighting with pivoting the skis by rotating the entire body.

**Pre-jumping:**
A short, low, voluntary jump, simply to clear a slope edge or control take-off.

**Preparation:**
When the starting position of a turn is assumed.

**Rebound (unweighting by):**
Unweighting the skis by using the elastic qualities of muscles and skis following a rapid weighting.

**Rotation:**
Rotating the whole body into the direction of a turn in order to turn the skis.

**Schuss:**
A straight downhill run in a streamlined (eg. tuck or egg) position.

**Side-slipping:**
A sideways movement of the skis down the slope.

**Skidding:**
The ski is maintained at an angle to the direction in which it is moving.

**Ski evolutif:**
The "graduated length" method of learning in which the length of ski used increases with the proficiency of the skier.

**Snowplough:**
Gliding with ski tails angled outwards and most pressure on the inside edges.

**Spread:**
The distance between the feet in a parallel stance.

**Stemming:**
Movement in which the skier displaces one ski into a converging position to the other, which remains parallel to the skier's direction.
Stemming uphill: traversing with the uphill ski in converging position.
Stemming downhill: braking from a traverse with the downhill ski in converging position.

**Stepping:**
A sideways movement of a ski. A transfer of weight onto this ski will initiate a turn.

**Swivelling:**
Turning the body into the slope to initiate certain turns.

**Take-off:**
A controlled jump of limited length lifting the skis off the snow.

**Transitional (movement, etc):**
A basic movement containing one or more elements of a more complex movement and intended to facilitate the learning of the more advanced movement.

**Traverse:**
Skiing at an angle to the slope.

**Unweighting:**
The process by which a skier reduces the pressure exerted by their skis on the snow. It is one of the key elements in turning.

**Up-extension**
Straightening the legs in a "standing-up" movement.

**Wedeln:**
A rhythmic series of linked turns swinging to either side of the fall line and having a tightened steering phase.

**Weight-transfer:**
Shifting pressure from one foot to the other; sometimes used to initiate a turn. It may be active or passive, and associated to stepping against a ski or not.

**Weighting:**
The process by which a skier increases the pressure exerted by the skis on the snow.

# INDEX

## A
accessories 34
assess 20
accommodation 20
advice 20
alternating step 46, 134
altitude 18, 20
Alpine foothills 16
Alpine skiier 12
Alpine skiing 39
Alps 21
amateurs 113
ankles 13
Anne-Marie Moser-Pröll 112
après ski 100
Arlberg school, Austria 11
Arnold Lunn 10
avalanche 142
avalement 86, 96, 104
    in deep snow 104
    on moguls 104
    slalom 104

## B
balance and sliding 61
balancing 15
ballet 129
basic parallel turn 75, 88, 80
basic wedel 78
    counter-turn 78
    edge check 78
    steering 78
    weight transfer 78
basic wedel 80
    GT 80
    performance 80
    skiing conditions 80
    slope gradient 80
    weight transfer 80
beginners 43
bend 12
Bellecote 18
bindings 46
blue posts 98
body, the 13
box design 28
breaking effects 102
    body movement 102
    edging 102
    on moguls 102
    schuss 102
    skating turn 102
breaking 122
brown lenses 34
bumps 52, 86
    rounded 86
    short 86
    jumping 86
button lift 58

## C
cable cars 58
Calgary 129
California 11
camber 28
carbon fibre 28
carving 105
    in hard snow 105
    on ice 105
    strength 105
chair lift 58
Chamonix 11, 16
changing direction 61
children 24
children's legs 32
Chinese literature 10
climbing slopes 58
clothing 34
competition 100
competition skiing 98
competitor 12
Corsica 21
Cortina 112
crevasses 115, 140
cross-country skiing 12, 39, 132-8
    ENSA 132
    ENSFS 132
cross-country arm movement 134
cross-country bindings 135
cross-country leg movement 134
    phases 134
cross-country pole plant 136
    double 136
    skating 138
    with steps 135, 136
cross-country step turn 138
crust 118, 120
cycling 12

## D
downhill 110, 124
    finish line 110
    start line 110

## E
edges 28
elastic 32
elementary turn 72
electronic timing 108
Emile Allais 11
Ecole du Ski Français (ESF) 10, 24, 38, 39, 92, 114, 142
    instruction 39, 41
    tests 40, 108
evasion turn 88

## F
falling 32, 48
    backwards 33
    forwards 33, 48
    on a slope 48
    simple twist 33
fall line 54, 94
flexibility 28
flexing 15
Finland 10
fitness 13
foot 30, 31
forests 118
France 20
free skiing 118
freestyle 12, 129
French resorts 38
Fridtjof Nansen 11
frozen crust 120

## G
giant slalom 106, 108
    drop 108
    men 108
    women 108
    gates 108
    timing 108
    glass fibre 28
gliding movement 56
gloves 24, 34
goggles 24, 34
gradient 67
    changing 67
Grand Prix 13
Greenland 11
Grenoble 112
group lessons 39
GT turn 86, 94, 96
gyms 13

## H

hard snow 23
hats 34
heel-piece 32
Hautes Alpes 23
helicopter 124, 129
helmets 112
Honoré Bonnet 113
hot-dogging 129
'Hoting' ski 10

## I

ice 21, 90, 118, 120
ice skiing 120
icy snow 29
instruction 39
    children 24
Instructors' Championship 114

## J

Jean-Claude Killy, 110, 112
jogging 12
joints 13
jumping bumps 84
jumps 84, 129
    forward 129
    reverse 129
    sideways 129
Jura 23

## K

Kevlar 28
kick turns 64
    right turn 64
    left turn 64
    on a slope 64
knees 13

## L

Lapland 11
Lapp 16
layered construction 28
le grand ski 115
length 28
linked side-slipping 70
    rounded 70
    diagonal 70
    rhythm 70

## M

maintenance 18
Massif Central 23
Megève 17
mental stamina 12
Méribel 17
mist 118
moguls 122, 129
Mongol hunters 16
monoski 126
mountain villages 16
muscles 11

## N

Nevada 11
northern Alps 23
Nordheim 11
novices 45
Norway 10

## O

off-piste 115, 118, 124
organization 20
on-piste 92

## P

parallel slalom 113
    automatic barriers 113
pelvis 13, 15
performance turn 86, 92, 94, 95, 96
Pierre Poncet 126
piste 18, 20, 24, 92, 106
Plagne, la 18
plastic 28
poles 34
pole-push 46
powder 44, 96
press-ups 14
private lessons 39
problems 122
profile 28
purpose-built resorts 16
Pyrenees 21, 23

## R

recreational skier 12
    skiing 100
red posts 98
regional qualifying events 114
'ratracs' 124
rhythm 72
riding stables 140
rocking jumps 14
rounded side-slipping 69, 70, 86
    curve 69
    long curve 69
    skidding 69
    step slope 69
    tight turns 69
Rosi Mittermaier 112
rucksack 92, 124
Ruffier test 13

## S

safety bindings 32
sandwich construction 28
schuss 52, 102, 110
second-generation resorts 16
sensors 32
shoulders 13
skis 28, 32, 52, 54, 68
    bad 30
    care 29
    compact 28, 44, 45
    competition 28, 44
    cross-country 134
    design 62
    development 11
    edges 11
    giant slalom 44
    grand sport 28, 44
    high altitude 44
    invention 16
    length 44
    recreational 44
    short 62
    specialist 28, 44
    sports 28, 44
slalom gates 98
    chicane 99
    diagonal 99
    double diagonal 99
    double vertical 99
    horizontal 99
    race 99
    salvis 99
    seelos 99
slopes 15, 43, 46, 52
    virgin 120

# INDEX

ski boots 24, 30, 32, 46
    ankle 31
    clips 31
    competition 30
    cross-country 135
    fit 31
    front-opening 30
    foot 31
    lining 31
    plastic 30
    rear-entry 30
    reinforcement 31
    rigid 62
    sole 31
    spoiler 31
    support 31
ski clubs 11
    Switzerland 11
    Italy 11
    France 11
    USA 11
    Britain 11
ski évolutif 45
    length 45
ski resorts 16, 17, 20, 21, 126, 142
    with children 142
    with kindergarten 142
ski stations 18
ski tuition 114
ski-equipment shops 18
ski-lift 11, 16, 24, 50, 58
ski-mountaineering 124
ski-stopper 32
ski-tails 92
ski-tips 56, 96
ski-touring 92
ski-tow 11, 58

side-slipping 61, 68
    centrifugal force 68
    counter rotation 68
    effect of pivoting 68
    gravity 68
    linked 68
    stem movement 68
sit ups 14
skins 58, 124
snow 43, 118
    fluffy 118
    hard 66
    powder 120
    rotten 118
    soft 6
    Spring 120, 124
    surface 142
    virgin 126
    wet 118
snowplough 56, 72
snowplough turns 61
snowsurfing
southern Alps 23
special slalom 106
    course 106
    gates 106
    international events 106
    poles 106
speed 96
spine 84
'stakning' 132
stamina 112
stance 132
star turn 54

'stawug' 132
step turn 54
stiffness 52
stop watch 98
straight running 52, 84, 86
strength 13, 120
stress 13
summer skiing 140
    snow conditions 140
stretch 12, 15
suncream 142
sunglasses 24, 34
suppleness 13
Sweden 10
swimming pool 140
Sylvain Saudan 118

## T

T-bar 58
télécabines 58
telemark turn 11
tennis courts 140
terrain 100
thickness 28
thighs 13
toe-piece 32
Toni Sailer 112
torsion 28
training 39
travel 22
traversing 52, 66
    acceleration 66
    angulation 66
    breaking 66
    gentle slope 66
    speed 66
    wind resistance 66
tree line 140
trees 118
tuition fees 39
turns 62

## V

Valmorel 18
Vasaloppet 10
vibration 28
Vosges 21, 23

## W

walking uphill 50
    diagonal side stepping 50
    herringbone 50
    poles 50
    side-stepping 50
waltz 129
water 84
waxing 134
weather forecast 142
wedeln 72, 94
    linked turns 94
weight 28
winter holiday 12, 24
winterstick 126
World Professional Championship 113

## Y

yellow lenses 34

# ACKNOWLEDGEMENTS

Peter Stuyvesant Travel wish to thank the following
for their valuable contributions to the preparation of this book

For translating the
original French manuscript:
Nick Young
Sue Foster

**Editorial:**
Sue Foster
Nick Young
Fred Gill
Annie Blackburn

**Designers:**
Kevin Ryan
Hilary Sabine
Helen Jones
Colin Woodman
Steve Wilson
Sarah Collins
Maryse Worrallo

**Illustrators:**
Craig Austin
Malcolm Brown
Chris Forsey
Rick Blakely
Roger Coldwell

**Photographer:**
Kjell Langset

**Photographs:**
Sylvie Chappaz
François Leclaire
Del Mulkey
Musée National du Ski
Francis Lumley
John Price Studios

**Colour Separation:**
Tempus Litho